Also By Rebecca Massek

The Bell Tower Series

Truly & Deeply: A Bell Tower Novel

Slowly & Surely: A Bell Tower Novel

Utterly & Madly

A Bell Tower Novel

Rebecca Massek

ISBN 13: 979-8-9924498-2-2

Cover design by: Rebecca Massek
Printed in the United States of America

To all the "good time" girls. You deserve someone who sees you in your entirety – your messy, your sad, your real – and loves you because of it.

"You were never created to be hurt or scared or unloved. You were created for a life of joy, and fun, and love, where you can dream big dreams and have grand adventures." — Jade Miller

Content Warning

This book deals with some pretty heavy topics, and I want to make sure that my readers always prioritize their mental health above everything! Here is a list of topics that may be sensitive to some readers:

Mentions of and aftermath of Domestic Abuse/Intimate Partner Abuse
Mentions of child neglect
Mentions of Suicide
Mentions of Post Partum Depression
Mentions of Accidental Pregnancy
Death of a Parent
Violence
Stabbing
Stalking

Prologue

Raelynn

When someone says they're an open book, nine times out of ten they mean the censored version.

Not me.

I'd made it a point of pride to be one hundred percent myself. Unabashedly. Unashamedly. It was liberating. And polarizing. For me, life was just too short to waste energy hiding the parts of myself that other people might not like. I mean, I could've been hit by a bus at any time and what would people have said about me? She was kind? True, but there was more to me than that. She was full of life? Not anymore.

No. I wanted people to talk about me like a goddess of legend. She was a force to be reckoned with. She was vengeance and fireworks and the wind. Uncontrollable. Wild. Free.

She wasn't full of life, she *was* life. The only way people would say that about me was if I lived my life to the fullest. So that's what I did.

Which is how I found myself telling a ridiculously explicit story of the time I slept with a delivery man in New Orleans when I was twenty-two to some girls that I'd literally met an hour before. As I was finishing up the tale, my best friend Addy came up carrying our drinks. She set my Tequila Sunrise in front of me and gave me a wry smile.

"And what this one will never tell you is that the poor delivery guy, who nearly had a heart attack when she went out onto the balcony in the world's smallest hotel towel and invited him up for drinks, was in his seventies."

"What? Ew!" Emily, the bubbly blonde to my left exclaimed.

"Seriously, seventy?" her friend Joanna groaned, her lips twisting as she pictured it in her head.

"I'll try anything once," I said, winking at Joanna and sipping my drink.

It was good. Strong. It set off a familiar fire in my veins, making my muscles loosen and a soft sigh leave me.

Emily and Joanna were sharing their own ho stories, and I listened with glee. I loved going out and meeting new people. They'd invited us to share their table when there was nowhere else for us to sit. They were waiting on a few more friends, and I was more than willing to spend the night with their group. I knew Addy wasn't the most comfortable with strangers, and I watched her get more and more uncomfortable as the round robin made its way to her.

"Okay, Addy," Emily giggled. "We've shared our war stories. Your turn."

I took a sip as I watched my best friend go from uncomfortable to straight up nervous.

"I've never really done anything like that," she finally admitted.

I knew she hadn't. If I was someone who grabbed life by the balls and squeezed until I got whatever I wanted, Addy was the one who politely shook life's hand and avoided eye contact. We couldn't be more opposite. But that made us a pretty good balance. I got her to live, and she kept me out of jail.

"You're not still a - " Joanna left the question hanging.

I'd have to jump in here in a minute and save my poor best friend. But not quite yet.

"No!" Addy huffed, her cheeks turning pink. "I lost that to my high school boyfriend. All I'm saying is that the few guys I've been with haven't been…exciting."

Bullshit.

"Now, what she's too delicate to say," I interrupted, "is that all her guys have been too vanilla for her taste. Never willing to explore or experiment. Leaving her high and dry."

"Lynnie!" She lightly smacked my arm and I giggled. "That's not true! I never asked them to try anything new. They seemed to like what we were doing, so I just never bothered to tell them that I didn't."

That made absolutely no sense to me. I had never been shy, and sex was no exception. Why in the hell should guys be the only people that were allowed to have fun when they had sex? I'd done enough exploring by the time I lost my virginity that I got mine even then. It was a non-negotiable for me. To be fair, I'd lost it to a twenty-three year old from Portugal, and he very much knew what he was doing.

"But you've had an orgasm, right?" Emily was asking Addy.

"Not *with* anyone." Her cheeks were flaming and I subtly pushed her glass closer to her. Alcohol would help. "By myself I don't have any problems. I've just never got there with a guy."

I watched Addy carefully as I took a long drink. "You've never been into anyone enough to get close."

She blinked at me and then grabbed her glass and took a big gulp. Attagirl.

"You just need something meaningless and hot," Joanna said as if she were the Oracle of friggin' Delphi imparting wisdom. And if 'meaningless' came out '*meaninglesh*', we weren't going to point it out.

"Yeah!" Emily giggled. "The kind of sex that's purely animal. No real feelings, just…the moment you see them you want to rip their clothes off."

Was there any other kind of sex?

"Addy is way too careful to get into anything like that," I said playfully.

I watched Addy's hackles come up and cocked my head. I knew she was competitive. She loved to be the best at things and tended not to back down from challenges. It's why we'd been able to stay friends for so long. She may not have been as reckless as me, but she wasn't a coward.

"Fine," Addy finally huffed, her eyes flashing as she looked at me. "If you all think I'm so boring and vanilla, then tonight I won't be."

A wicked smirk unfolded across my face. "What exactly does that mean?"

Addy took a steadying breath and braced her shoulders back. "It means that tonight I end the driest dry spell in history. Tonight, I will have sex. And not just sex. Sex where I come first."

The other two girls broke down into cheers and giggles, and I let myself smile but was watching Addy carefully.

Addy was the closest thing I had to a sister. And I had two biological ones. She was my everything, and I knew that sometimes I could be pushy with her, trying to get her to live a little more, but I never wanted her to do something she'd regret just because of me and my need to see how far I could push people.

I watched her and swore I could hear her thoughts. She was already talking herself out of it.

4

I smiled softly and raised my glass. "To sex!" I cheered, clinking my glass with Addy's, and promising myself that I wasn't letting her go home with anyone tonight.

The conversation started flowing, and I let Addy sink into her head for a bit. It was her safe space, my adorable overthinker.

As I was about to launch into a testimony about what I would do if I was left alone in a room with a divorced Idris Elba, Emily's face suddenly lit up and she waved at the door.

"Hey, guys! Over here!" she giggled. "We made new friends!"

Three men approached our table. The one in the front beelined for Emily, swooping in to give her a flirty smile and kiss on the cheek in greeting. My spidey sense made me take a long look at the guy in the back of the group. His eyes were locked on Addy, and when I looked at her, I saw her cheeks going pink.

Shit. My job just got a little tougher tonight.

"Hey ladies, I'm Brett."

"And I'm Johnny," said the man I hadn't fully looked at yet.

The Australian accent caught my ear and pulled my focus. Johnny was giving an easy smile to everyone at the table, his dark eyes sparkling. He had a dimple in one cheek, curly brown hair, and the barest hint of a five o'clock shadow.

My practiced eyes skated down his body, appreciating the view, and when they came back to his face, he had a cocky grin as he shot me a wink. I rolled my eyes and downed the rest of my drink, letting a soft smile onto my face as I coyly flashed him a glance. He was still watching me from the corner of his eye. Good. Barring any other options, I'd be able to take Mr. Down Under home tonight. I was an excellent multitasker and keeping Addy safe while also making Australian Wonder Boy fall in love with me for an evening would be a breeze.

The third guy had introduced himself, Derek, and he was still staring at Addy. She seemed to be locked in his gaze, and there was something about it that was setting off alarms.

I leaned over and tapped Addy's hand. Her eyes shot to me, and I rested my hand on hers.

"Dude, that guy Derek is seriously eye-fucking you," I tried to say it lightly, but she could hear the concern in my voice.

"I know." A grin broke out on her face.

I blinked. Double shit.

Okay. Fine. I could be supportive. Addy *never* got excited about guys, and if she was attracted to Hannibal Lecter, then who was I to stop her from talking with him? She wasn't going home with him, but talking was fine.

I smiled at her and checked one more time. "Oh, so it's not a creepy vibe we're getting?"

"Definitely not," Addy blushed and ducked my gaze.

I took a breath and then gave a little clap. "Good!" I watched as Addy relaxed, her smile getting wider as her cheeks got pinker. "Wow, you need to make declarative statements more often."

"Meaning?"

"You literally just said you were going to break your dry streak, and then Derek over there walks up and starts undressing you with his eyes. It's like kismet or something," I said, keeping my tone light. I was still trying to figure out how she was feeling.

"Yeah, or something." Addy's eyes drifted back to Derek, who hadn't stopped looking at her.

I watched her for another long moment. I couldn't help but be protective of her. Addy had always been so careful, and I knew she hadn't learned all of the lessons I had. Maybe this was exactly what she needed? She could use a good fling. She seemed genuinely interested in him, and maybe I was just overthinking it.

I blew out a deep breath and gave her hand a squeeze.

"Well, if you're into it, then I'm going to go get a drink, conveniently leaving my seat open," I winked at her.

"What a good wingman you are," Addy winked back.

"Get some, love." I bumped her shoulder as I hopped down from the barstool.

I wasn't tall, by any means, so I landed and regained my balance in my heels before making my way over to the bar.

I felt someone in the group split away and follow me, and I had a sneaking suspicion it was a tall Australian with hair I wanted to sink my fingers into. Anticipation warmed my body.

Let the games begin.

I kept my eyes forward as I leaned against the bar. The bartender immediately came over with a grin for me.

"What can I get you, gorgeous?"

"Tequila Sunrise and a House Margarita," I said sweetly. "And you are?"

"Toby," he grinned. "Do you have a tab?"

"Mmm, nope," I popped the P and smiled softly at him. "Do I need one?"

He laughed out loud and shook his head, his eyes sparkling at my audacity. "Not yet," he laughed. "Sound good?"

"You're an angel!" I gushed, biting my lip and letting my hand touch his arm gently.

He wandered off to make the drinks looking a bit starstruck. I let out a soft sigh. Men were so easy. Never a challenge. They all worked the same. A smile here, a touch there, and they were putty in my hands. I felt someone come up behind me and had a strong feeling who it was. I leaned back and *accidentally* bumped into them.

"Oops, so sorry!"

"No worries, love."

"Aussie."

He moved around to my side and grinned down at me. "Johnny, actually."

"Right," I laughed. "Johnny."

"And you're Raelynn."

"I am. Nice to meet you."

"Very impressive work with the bartender, by the way," he said, lowering his voice as his easy grin turned mischievous.

I blinked up at him, giving him my best doe eyes. "I have no idea what you're talking about."

"I'm sure," he laughed, but seemed otherwise unaffected. I watched him curiously for a moment. He was going to be more of a challenge than I'd thought.

My drinks appeared on the counter, and I gave the bartender my full attention.

"Thank you, Toby," I sighed happily. "You're my hero."

"I do my best," he laughed before turning his attention to Johnny. "What can I get you, man?"

"Whiskey over ice, please. Whatever you've got handy is fine by me, mate."

"Sure thing," Toby turned and, with a practiced hand, plopped an ice sphere into a highball glass and poured two fingers of amber liquid over it. He slid it across the bar and looked expectantly at Johnny.

"Can I stick this on her tab?" Johnny asked, though I could tell he was mostly kidding.

Toby shot him a look and held his hand out, but was smiling the whole time. Johnny laughed loudly. It was a rich, warm laugh that sent tingles throughout my body.

His arm brushed my shoulder as he reached across to hand over a card, and I knew it was deliberate. Good move. The smell of his cologne wafted over me and made me bite my lip.

"How about this? Let's put whatever the lady gets for the rest of the night on my tab," Johnny offered.

Toby beamed at him like a proud momma hen before sending a playful wink my way. "Good call, man."

"You didn't have to do that," I said. "I wouldn't have paid for my drinks anyway."

"I don't doubt it, love," Johnny laughed again, and another thrill went through me. "But this way we know you and your friend are covered and no creeps will be buying your drinks."

"How do I know you're not a creep?" I asked, letting some playfulness into my tone.

"Just gotta trust the vibe, don't you?"

I took a step closer to him and studied his face intently.

Test number one. Most people got freaked out by intense scrutiny and invasion of their personal space. Admittedly, it was a weird thing to do. But I didn't want to bring home someone uncomfortable sharing themselves with a stranger. That made for boring, forgettable sex. That wasn't something I indulged in.

His eyes watched me, glittering with joy as an easy smile lit up his face. He had a nice smile. Soft, warm, and genuine. He even took a step closer to me, holding eye contact. Daring me to back off. When I didn't, heat flared in his eyes. We stayed like that for a long moment, drinking each other in. Testing each other. He wasn't like most of the men I played with. They knew the idea of the game, but not the intricacies of it. Johnny was different. He was probably at my level.

"I guess there's only one way to see if you pass the vibe check," I said softly.

9

"And what's that?" His breath fanned across my face.

His lips were so close to mine. All I'd have to do would be to press into him and he'd be mine for the night.

But this game was just getting started.

I leaned back and called Toby over. "Can I get a round of shots for our table? Tequila blanco, seven please. On Johnny Blue's tab, if you would."

Toby laughed, throwing a glance to Johnny to make sure that was okay. When he was met with a laugh and nod, he started lining up shot glasses on a tray.

Johnny was suddenly right behind me, his chest at my back and his lips at my ear.

"You're trouble, aren't you?"

I smirked and grabbed the tray from Toby.

"You have no idea."

***

Several rounds of shots later, Johnny and I were seated on a cushioned patio loveseat watching the rest of the group.

Emily was making out with Brett, Joanna was glaring daggers at Addy and Derek, who were leaned into each other and speaking in whispers. I didn't particularly care for where his hands were roaming, but Addy seemed enamored enough that I left it alone.

I was nestled into Johnny's side with his jacket draped around my shoulders. I was enjoying his arm around me, wrapping me in his delicious scent and warmth.

"So, you and Addy are close then?" he asked as he watched my eyes narrow when Derek's hand played with one of Addy's curls.

"She's as close as a sister to me," I said, pulling my gaze away from the scene in front of me to focus on Johnny.

10

"You're protective." It wasn't a question, though there was one dancing behind his eyes. He was smart enough not to voice it.

"I'm feral, darling," I smirked, hoping to lighten the mood.

It worked. His caramel laugh floated through my veins.

I flicked my gaze back to Addy and then turned to Johnny.

"What can you tell me about Derek?" I asked, letting my fingers play with the collar of Johnny's shirt.

He shrugged, his eyes watching Derek for a moment before finding me again.

"I wish I had more to tell, love, but I just met the guy. He works at the company that hired me to consult on a town project."

I hummed softly, my eyes finding Addy again as unease drifted through my chest.

I felt fingers on my chin, and when I turned, Johnny's face was inches from mine.

"What do you want most in this world, Raelynn?" His voice was soft, his accent creating music in my ears.

I stared at him for a long moment. Quite a change of topic, but he was looking at me intently. Something told me he was done playing and had decided to throw his own test my way. Intriguing.

Sometimes people will ask something and then say that there's no wrong answer. This wasn't one of those questions. There was a wrong answer. And the right answer was complex.

It needed to be vulnerable without oversharing. Something true but shallow.

That's what this was.

One night. Connection. Separation.

I let my lips curl into a smile that had a bit of an edge and leaned forward so that I whispered my answer against his mouth.

"Freedom."

Chapter One

Raelynn

It was midnight-thirty when we finally called it a night. We stumbled our way out onto the sidewalk where Johnny hailed a cab.

I glanced over my shoulder, where Addy had just been, and saw that Derek had pulled her away and was kissing her. His hand was tangled in her hair possessively.

They separated and Addy took a deep breath and just stared at him.

Nope. No way in Hell.

I ran over and grabbed her drunk ass around the waist, lifting and spinning her away from Derek before taking her arm and dragging her to the cab.

Johnny helped me pile her in, despite her weak protests, and we filed in after her.

I was small, but the way Addy was sprawled over the backseat of the cab meant that I was practically in Johnny's lap. Not that he minded.

He was pressing soft kisses to my neck, letting his nose run along the shell of my ear. Heat was snaking its way through my veins, and it got harder to keep my focus with each passing minute.

His fingers were tracing patterns along the hem of my skirt without seeking anything. He just wanted to touch my skin, feel it warming beneath his fingers. I hadn't kissed him in the bar. I hadn't kissed him yet at all. And he was still managing to build a fire in my core.

We finally pulled up to my little apartment that I rented just on the edge of town. It was on the ground floor, so we didn't have to get Addy up any stairs, thank God.

As soon as the cab stopped, Johnny hopped out and opened the door. He helped me get Addy out of the cab, paid the driver, and then lifted her in his arms and carried her into the living room without breaking a sweat.

I gathered some blankets for her and got her all tucked in with a glass of water and some aspirin next to the couch for when she woke up. She was out like a sack of bricks.

As soon as I was satisfied that Addy would be okay, I turned to Johnny with a grin. He'd been leaning casually against the kitchen counter, but when he saw my face his body changed. It tightened and seemed to snap with electricity.

In two strides he was lifting me over his shoulder and carrying me into my bedroom. He tossed me on the bed and climbed over me, boxing me in with his arms and legs.

My breath was shallow as I waited to see what he would do.

He nosed along my collarbone, up my neck. Inhaling. Breathing me in.

A shiver ran down my spine when his teeth nipped my ear.

"Raelynn." He drew my name out, tasting it.

I gripped his chin and drew his face back so that I could look at him.

"Time to see if you pass the vibe check, Johnny," I said, my voice low.

A low moan left his chest and vibrated through my own.

"I knew you were trouble."

"Feral," I reminded him.

"Promise?"

I threw my head back and laughed. His hand snaked up and grabbed my jaw. It was gentle but left no room for me to argue with his grip. He moved my face back to his and watched me intensely for a moment.

Then, his lips were on mine.

From that first kiss he possessed me.

He didn't kiss me like we were strangers. He kissed me like a long-lost lover. Like he'd been waiting his entire life to claim my lips.

My body arched into him as the fire he'd been building throughout the night exploded.

***

Usually, the morning after a one-night-stand, I felt like a new woman. Not this time.

Johnny had been perfect. He was attentive, demanding, giving, spontaneous. All. Night. Long. We went several rounds before finally tiring ourselves out enough to fall asleep on opposite sides of the bed.

That was normal for me. I wasn't a cuddler, at all. I liked my space. I liked my bed. Sharing it at all was a new one for me, but I wasn't about to kick him out in the wee hours of the morning after he'd been oh-so-good to me.

I woke up wrapped in his strong arms, my head resting on his chest. His heartbeat was steady, his skin was warm and comforting, and, when I began to stir, his grip on me tightened. I burrowed closer to him, seeking more of him.

As my sleepy brain finally caught up, I froze.

Not normal.

We weren't supposed to be cuddled together like last night was more than it was.

I rolled over quickly and sat up, pressing a hand to my head as knives danced behind my eyes. A low moan left me, and Johnny mumbled something as he turned towards me.

"Bathroom, go back to sleep," I whispered.

My hand reached out and traced his cheek before I could stop myself. He turned into my touch and murmured something before rolling back over and sighing into the pillow. I launched myself off the bed before I continued to sit there staring at how adorable he looked. I peed, then splashed some water on my face, driving the last bits of sleep out of my brain.

Alarm bells that had been chiming before started ringing in full force.

This had to be it. One and done.

Sometimes, if the chemistry was good and I didn't hate the guy by the next morning, I'd add his number to my phone and double dip. I'd thought that Johhny would be a good candidate to keep on deck, but after waking up so close to him and not wanting to leave I knew I'd have to cut it off here.

This couldn't happen again.

There was nothing that caged a woman more than a man. More than a relationship. And when I'd told Johnny that what I wanted the most in this world was freedom, I hadn't been lying.

I had always been a wanderer. I was the middle of five. Not the perfect oldest, not the baby. Just right smack in the middle. And while my childhood had been good – roof over my head, food to eat, clothes, education, family trips, gifts at Christmas, all that jazz – I was the kid my parents usually forgot. I'd grown up trying to not cause trouble, to be a good daughter and sister, to fade into the background. I guess I'd gotten pretty good.

When I was seven, my parents had actually left me behind at the aquarium on a family trip. I'd been watching the sharks, thinking how sad it was that they had to keep swimming in circles. They were trapped. The volunteer had told us that all of the animals at the aquarium were rescued and couldn't live in the wild on their own or they would die. But, as I'd watched those sharks swim in the same endless loop, I remembered thinking that maybe death would have been a better alternative. Here were these incredibly powerful creatures, kings of the largest open space on the planet, and they were stuck in this glass box swimming around and around. I thought, *Isn't it better to die free than exist in a cage?*

I hadn't even noticed my family had moved on and left me. Apparently, they'd been halfway home before my oldest brother Marcus had asked where I was. My parents had driven back in a panic, only to find me sitting and watching the sharks, crying. They'd rushed up to me, sobbing and apologizing. When it finally registered that they'd completely forgotten me there, I think something shifted in my brain.

I never wanted to be forgotten. I never wanted to get stuck swimming in endless circles.

After that I wasn't the good kid anymore. I started acting out in school, "running away" to the treehouse in the backyard. I started trying to discover everything that life had to offer. I was in trouble constantly, which I thought would give me the attention I wanted from my family. Instead, I became a different kind of invisible. Instead of being forgotten, I was a total disappointment. My mother's constant project. And when she'd realized she couldn't

16

tame me, she ignored me. As long as I wasn't arrested or bleeding, I was left to my own devices.

Puberty only made it worse, and if it hadn't been for Addy I would have ended up going down a dangerous path. She reined in my more rebellious ideas, helped me keep my grades up when I skipped class, and kept me mostly out of trouble with my parents. I'd followed her to college. More for the experience than because I'd actually wanted to go to college. But I knew it would disappoint my parents if I didn't get some sort of degree. Plus, a part of living my life the way I wanted was to make sure I'd never have to depend on anyone. I would take care of myself, and to do that a degree and a job were a necessity.

I'd ended up auditing a business class one day. I'd stumbled into the classroom to get away from a clingy guy I'd slept with a few weeks before that I couldn't shake. Sat through the entire lecture and realized that I could get into that. Owning my own business. If I was good enough, I'd be able to eventually do whatever I wanted. Work wherever I wanted, set my own hours. It took me awhile to realize how to marry all of the things that I loved into a business. But then, when I was planning our Senior trip to Cabo, a travel agent, Jennifer, reached out after I put an inquiry in on a rental place. We got to chatting and she told me all about her life as a travel agent. Essentially, she helped people plan their trips, sorting out accommodation, transportation, entertainment. She developed relationships with some of the most expensive resorts in the country, and whenever they had an extra room she could visit at massively discounted rates. She got to travel, set her own schedule, meet new people.

I was hooked. Freedom, adventure, financial independence. It was the perfect job.

I had worked for Jennifer for a few years after graduating before starting up my own business. Within a year I was seeing success. Booking trips for wealthy families across the country and living my life on my terms, my schedule.

It was the life I'd always dreamed of for myself, and nothing was going to cage me in. But I had a feeling if anyone could, it would be the surprisingly sweet Australian laying naked in my bed.

I blinked at my reflection for a moment, getting the last memories of strong arms and filthy whispers out of my head before going back into my room.

The bed was empty.

Shit.

I had a moment of panic thinking that Johnny had also come to his senses and decided to leave. I shouldn't have been so worried. I should have been relieved.

I didn't want him sticking around. I had already decided that this couldn't be more than one night. I wasn't a clingy person.

I growled a bit at the part of my heart that had flipped out and angrily started straightening the bedding.

It was good that he'd left. He understood what this was. What we'd both agreed it would be.

And if I fluffed the pillow a little harder than necessary, it was only because it needed an extra hit. Not because it smelled like his cologne and peppermint.

"Get a fucking grip," I muttered to myself, yanking the blankets straight and flattening them.

"Woah, what the hell, Rae?" I heard Johnny's deep voice from the kitchen.

Uh oh.

I blinked as I realized that Addy must be re-meeting Johnny. I wouldn't be surprised if she didn't remember meeting him last night, she'd had more than enough drinks that her memory should be scattered at best.

I took a deep breath and forced myself to walk calmly out of the room.

"Johnny?" I called. As I turned the corner, I saw Johnny and Addy standing in the kitchen. Addy had a glass of water and Johnny was sporting an easy grin. "Oh good, you guys have met!" My tone was light. Then, just to make sure everyone was on the same page, I added, "Addy, say hi and bye to Johnny."

Addy blinked at me, embarrassment flushing her cheeks. "Raelynn, don't be rude."

Johnny let out an easy laugh. "No, it's okay love." He looked at me and there was something behind his eyes that I couldn't quite place. "We're a one-night thing, it's understood between both of us. No hard feelings."

Our eyes locked and something welled in my chest. If I was prone to self-examination, I would have called it regret. But I shoved that way deep down. This was what I wanted, what I'd made clear from the moment Johnny started talking to me last night.

One night.

One incredible night, to be fair. But one.

Johnny and I were still watching each other as Addy started to move around the room, gathering her things. As I saw her movements turn to panic, I knew exactly what she was looking for.

I finally broke away from Johnny's gaze as I went to my purse and grabbed her phone, holding it out enticingly as she looked at me.

"Looking for this?"

"Why do you have that?"

I looked at her seriously and said, "So you couldn't call Derek and do something you'd regret in the morning."

She flushed. "I wouldn't have done that."

"You didn't see the way you were looking at him as you said your goodbyes last night," I said, handing her the phone and then turning to the kitchen to make coffee. Without thinking, I placed a soft kiss on Johnny's arm as I passed him. I felt his gaze on me, but quickly shook it off. That was far too familiar for a one-night-stand. I was right, this definitely couldn't happen again.

"You were about to ask him to take you home, and as much as I'd love to see that from you, I also know it's not who you are," I said, my voice edged with frustration. Not with Addy, but myself. But it was easier to focus on Addy at the moment than to investigate what was going on with my stupid heart. "I couldn't watch it happen knowing you'd get hurt."

I turned to level Addy with a serious stare and saw her fiddling with her necklace. She did that when she was nervous. Had since we were kids.

She finally sighed and flashed me a grateful smile. "Thanks, Lynnie. I owe you."

I waved a hand and turned to see Johnny watching me carefully.

Addy followed my gaze and smirked. "I will leave you two to your morning. See you around, Johnny."

My eyes snapped to her. She wouldn't see him around. She knew that. But there was something knowing in her look as she gathered the last of her things and stepped out of the apartment.

The door clicked shut and suddenly the silence in the room was suffocating.

Johnny was still watching me, his brown eyes glittering and serious all at the same time. It felt like he was simmering, like there was this heat inside of him that was bubbling right below his skin.

I found myself examining him in the light of the morning and realizing that he was somehow even more beautiful than he'd been last night. His tanned skin seemed to glow, and his light brown hair

20

was tousled and unkempt and all I wanted was to dig my fingers back into it.

He let the silence build, just watching me with that damned adorable, easy smile, until finally I couldn't take it anymore.

"Why are you still here?"

He blinked, but his smile only grew.

"I was waiting for you to offer me coffee," he smirked.

I glared at him. "No, you weren't."

"No, I wasn't."

Back to the staring. He seemed so at ease, one hip resting against my counter with his arms gently folded.

"Then you didn't really answer my question," I quipped. I tried to bring some levity to my tone but couldn't quite manage it.

"Do you really want me to leave?" His question was genuine, as were his eyes as he waited for my answer.

My mouth opened to bite something back, but nothing came out.

I didn't want him to leave. I wanted him to stay, have coffee, breakfast, morning sex. I wanted him in my shower, on my couch, spending the day with me. I wanted to hear him say my name again.

Which was why he had to leave. Immediately.

A small, soft laugh came from him, and he moved to stand in front of me. I watched him the whole time, never one to back down. He took my coffee and set in on the counter behind him before gripping my waist and lifting me to sit on the opposite counter. He lifted me like I was nothing, and tingles erupted across my body at his touch.

As he crowded into my space, our gazes were locked. The air in my tiny kitchen was suddenly ten degrees warmer.

"Go get in the shower," he said gently.

I blinked, confused.

He lifted a hand and gently traced down my cheek, my neck, to my collarbone, before leaning in and following that same path with his lips. When he pulled back, his pupils were blown and his face was serious.

"Go get in the shower, and when you get out, I'll be gone." His voice was heavy with an emotion that I didn't want to name.

He was offering me something I hadn't known I would need when we met last night. An out.

I swallowed around the lump in my throat and watched him.

He stepped back, allowing me room to slide off the counter.

I felt his eyes on me as I made my way out of the kitchen. Before I disappeared down the hallway, I stopped.

"Johnny?"

"Yes, love?"

I closed my eyes and blew out a deep breath. I couldn't look at him.

"Thank you."

He didn't say anything, but I felt his soft smile and the way his gaze burned into my back.

When I got out of the shower, there was no sign he'd ever been there.

Just the way I liked it. At least, that's what I convinced myself.

Chapter Two

Johnny

One Year Later

The small city of Hartworth never ceased to amaze me.

Well, calling it a city was being a bit generous. It straddled that fine line between quaint small town and developing urban hot spot. But damn if it didn't do it well.

I'd first been flown into Hartworth a year ago to consult on some changes to the city layout and building upgrades they wanted to do. It was sort of my specialty.

With old towns that have a lot of history, they can't just knock down buildings willy-nilly. There are procedures that have to be followed, and having an historical architectural specialist isn't necessarily a part of those procedures, but it wasn't a bad idea.

And who just happened to be one of the most respected historical architectural specialists in the country?

Me.

Technically, two countries, but that always sounded like bragging.

I loved my job.

Traveling around the United States and Australia to consult with town governments as they tried to bring their buildings and their residents into the twenty-first century was my calling.

Hartworth stole my breath from the moment I first saw her. All old brick, Colonial buildings that screamed with the fraught history of that part of the country. And residents who clearly took pride in where they lived and wanted to continue to see it flourish. Everyone who lived here seemed to be kind, intelligent, and genuine. I'd fallen for the people as much as the architecture. But there was one resident who had stolen my stupid heart from the moment she opened her mouth.

I hadn't seen Raelynn in over a year, but the sting of her rejection haunted my dreams. It wasn't just that she was stunningly beautiful. Her soft brown hair and fierce brown eyes had lured me in, sure, but it was the seven feet of attitude packed into her five foot three frame that put a cage around my heart and locked it tight.

"I'm feral, darling."

Sometimes those words floated around my head like a tune I couldn't quite remember the rest of.

Only I did.

I remembered every single moment of our night together. And I remembered watching her disappear down the hallway in her apartment after giving me a soft, "Thanks".

If I were a worse man, I would've stayed. I would have imposed myself on her until she realized how great we could be together. Because I saw it all from our first conversation. How perfectly we'd fit into each other's lives.

But she wanted one night.

One night was better anyway. I didn't have the time or energy to pursue a relationship with anyone, let alone someone who could easily consume my entire being.

24

But I wouldn't forget that night for the rest of my life.

I'd tried. Nothing had worked.

I'd been traveling constantly, taking every opportunity to fill my thoughts with a different town. With different women. I'd never been a monk, but the rampage I'd been on the last year had put my sordid past to shame. With every new city came a few new women. Always up-front about my expectations, so it's not like I was leaving a trail of broken hearts, but nothing seemed to color in the dark spot Raelynn had left.

Finally, I had realized that I needed to just fucking move on.

I had no way of contacting her. I was never going to see her again.

I had also realized that if it wasn't with her, then I couldn't see myself settling down. Of all the women over the past year, none of them had captivated me like she had. Or understood me. Because, and I don't know how, she had completely understood me. With one conversation I knew that she had the read on me.

If I couldn't have that level of connection, I didn't want any connection at all.

My friends poked fun at me that I was getting soft in my old age, but they hadn't met her.

I had been gone from Hartworth for about ten months now, working on other projects as permits were filed and pushed through and funding was raised. Now it was time to start renovations on the oldest buildings in town, so I was back.

I made my way into the conference room in City Hall where Brett, whom I had worked with before, and an older woman were waiting. Files were laid out on the table, along with neatly rolled blueprints.

"Johnny, good to see you, man!" Brett welcomed me with a firm handshake. "This is Odette L'Evelier, from Masters, Smith, and Wemberly Construction."

"Pleasure to meet you, Ms. L'Evelier. Johnny Harris," I said, giving her my trademark winning smile. "I've been looking forward to working with your company on the renovation plans."

"The pleasure is mine, Mr. Harris." She smiled, but it didn't reach her eyes.

Consummate professional, then. I smiled to myself as I set my briefcase down and settled into a seat along with the others.

"So, where are we to begin?"

***

It was early afternoon before we broke away from the conference room table. We were finally all in agreement on budget, timeline, and plans, which was the hardest part of any historical renovation endeavor.

I stepped out of the main doors and threw up a hand to shield my eyes from the blazing Southern sun.

I'd traveled all over, and I had never experienced a heat like in the Southern U.S.

I took a few steps out, waiting for my eyes to adjust, and was about to start down the stairs when I collided with someone.

Apologies were already falling as I instinctively reached out to offer a steadying hand.

"Watch where you're going, jackass!"

I swear, my heart skipped a fucking beat.

I heard a small gasp and knew she'd recognized me too.

I don't know what I'd expected from Raelynn, if I'd ever had the chance to meet her again.

A quiet reunion. An awkward silence. A passionate embrace.

Whatever I could have imagined, it was certainly not her cocking back her fist and letting it fly to connect squarely with my jaw.

26

My briefcase dropped as my hands came up instinctively.

It seemed that one punch wasn't enough for the feral wildcat that was currently using all of her available limbs to assault me.

"Woah, woah, Raelynn!" I shouted, finally backing up enough to put some distance between us. "Calm the fuck down, woman!"

She stilled and I finally got a good look at her.

Dear God, she was just as gorgeous as I'd remembered. Even more so, with her flushed cheeks and wild eyes. Her perfectly pinned hair was falling from her attack, and her smart gray suit was frumpled. She swayed slightly in her heels as her chest heaved with an effort to catch her breath.

"Don't call me woman, asshole," she snarled, her hand curling into a fist at her side.

"Don't fucking attack me," I bit back, annoyance rising now that the adrenaline of seeing her and subsequently being beaten by her was fading.

"You deserve so much worse than what I did," she seethed.

I blinked, wracking my brain to figure out why she would be so angry with me. As far as I remembered, we'd left things on fairly good terms for a one-night stand.

"What did I do?"

"Did you know what he was?" she snapped, taking a threatening step toward me.

Even though I had no idea what she was talking about, I couldn't help but appreciate that she wasn't trying to be cryptic. Some women would talk in endless riddles when they were upset, but that didn't seem to be Raelynn.

"What who was?"

That made her stop. Her eyes ran up and down my body, taking me in. She cocked her head, and I saw calculations shifting behind her gaze.

27

"Derek was a fucking monster."

It was my turn to pause as I searched my memory for who she was talking about.

"The bloke that wanted to take your friend home? Addy, right?" My mind was racing with questions, but I was trying to tread carefully.

"Yeah," she sniffed, her face a study of raw emotion. "They dated for a while and he put her in the hospital."

I paled. "God, Raelynn, I'm so sorry. I didn't know him all that well. We'd literally just met that day that we went out and met you guys."

She glared at me, as if she didn't want to believe me.

"Is Addy okay?"

"She will be." The conviction in her tone left no room for argument.

With a friend like Raelynn by her side, I was sure Addy would end up alright. But the way that Raelynn had come after me let me know that it hadn't been good, whatever had happened.

"I didn't know," I said softly, taking a tentative step toward her. "I promise. I wouldn't have tolerated that shit for a second, if I'd known."

She continued to glare at me for a moment before she deflated with a sigh.

"I'm sorry for attacking you," she said, her tone hesitant. I got the impression she didn't apologize often. "I heard your voice, and everything bubbled up. I've got a bad temper, sometimes."

"No worries, love," I kept my voice even and light.

We stood there as an awkward silence fell over us. I'd been worried this would be the result, if I ever saw her again.

"What are you doing at City Hall?" She finally broke the tension.

"Consulting on some city renovation projects," I said with a small smile. "You?"

"Filing divorce papers for a…friend."

"You're a lawyer?"

She raised an eyebrow. "No."

I waited for her to elaborate, but she didn't. Instead, she stared me down, waiting for me to say something. But I was enjoying taking her in. The wisps of hair fluttering around her face, the bright pink spots high on her cheeks, the bead of sweat running down her neck that I wanted to follow with my tongue.

"Where have you been?" she asked, breaking me out of my trance.

"I travel a lot for work."

"Work."

"I'm an architect. I specialize in historical reconstruction and renovations. Towns bring me in as a consultant to make sure they don't lose the integrity of their buildings when they need updated."

"And that's why you're in Hartworth?"

I nodded, lapsing back into staring at her.

Flashbacks of her skin sliding against mine danced through my mind and I had to shake my head to come back to the present.

She seemed content to watch me back, though her body was stiff and her eyes guarded.

Another memory, that face and those eyes in her kitchen. Scared.

That's why I'd left. She could feel something real between us, but she had been so afraid of it that I couldn't push her.

I saw a flicker of that same fear when I took a small step towards her.

"You know, I'd hoped I'd eventually get to see you again," I said softly, my eyes locked on her face.

She swallowed nervously, but didn't avoid my gaze like most people would. God this woman did things to me.

"You were the one who left," she said.

"I know," I took another step into her space. "You wanted me to, if I recall."

Her cheeks flushed. "I did."

I hummed softly before reaching out to tuck a flyaway hair behind her ear.

"And now?"

The flush spread to her chest and I knew she was remembering exactly what my hands were capable of. Her eyelids fluttered for a moment before snapping open, her gaze piercing.

She took a step backwards, putting space between us again.

"I hope you enjoy your stay in Hartworth, Johnny." She was professional and detached. "Don't fuck up our town."

With that she turned and made her way to the door, her hips swaying.

"I'll be seeing you around, Rae," I called.

"Not likely," she shot back without looking at me.

Then the giant door was swinging open and she disappeared inside, leaving me sweating and hot, and not from the sun.

Chapter Three

Raelynn

"I need two shots, pronto."

The bartender flashed me a smile and poured two generous shots of tequila, sliding them over to me carefully and then handing me a lime wedge.

I downed them both quickly and stuck the lime between my teeth, biting down and relishing the sour combination of the alcohol and the fruit as they danced on my tongue.

Immediately I felt the tequila warm my blood. My head got light, and a sigh of relief left my chest as the knot that had been building over the past few hours unclenched.

Fucking Johnny.

After our night together, Addy had taken to calling him the love of my life, if only because she knew it bugged the ever-living crap out of me. But I liked that she teased me. She was getting better every time I saw her. And I made sure to see her daily.

There's no experience on Earth that can compare to seeing your best friend beaten and bruised, lying in a hospital bed, afraid to let anyone but a few female nurses in the room. The heartbreak and pure, vile rage that had filled me still came up every now and again, even though it had been almost a year. Nothing prepares you for that. Addy was my sister, the one person in the world that I would do anything to protect.

And I had failed her.

I'd known something was off about Derek from the jump. He was too intense. Too focused.

And my Adelaide, my sweet, cautious, logical Addy, had finally done what I'd been wanting her to do for years. She'd jumped headfirst in love with the monster. I'd tried telling her to take it slow, to feel him out some more. But, as usual, she didn't listen to me.

I shouldn't have been surprised. Over the course of our relationship, I wasn't the one we listened to. My ideas were impulsive, sometimes dangerous. Addy knew best. She'd always known best.

I had very few regrets in my life. I always tried to take anything that turned out badly and use it as a lesson, something to learn and grow from. I didn't want to be on my deathbed, looking back on my life, filled with regret for the things I'd done.

I would regret not keeping Addy away from Derek for the rest of my life.

I had sensed it, that first night, and I'd done nothing. Too focused on myself. On a handsome Australian who promised to do wicked things. Addy and I were both working to put that night in the past. For different reasons, obviously, but it was a shared effort, nonetheless.

Then, out of nowhere, Johnny appeared again.

It wasn't his fault, what happened with Derek, but when I saw him, everything from that night came rushing back. My suspicion and protectiveness, my guilt for not doing something that night to save Addy from the pain she went through.

32

My mother had always hated my temper. My father had always hated that I used my fists to solve problems. I had always hated that I had no control over it.

When I saw Johnny, there was no control to be found. My knuckles were bruised where they'd connected with his jaw. His stupid, chiseled jaw, with its perfect amount of scruff that I could still feel between my legs.

He hadn't raised a hand to defend himself or to hit me back, which told me a lot about the man. He'd taken my hits until he was able to put some distance between us. As soon as I'd seen his face, I'd known he'd had no idea what had happened. It wasn't his fault. Luckily, I was able to calm down.

The rage subsided, and when it did the memories of the rest of the night crawled into my mind. The way his arms had felt wrapped around me, the way his muscles tensed as my nails scratched along his back. The sound of his voice whispering praise and encouragement into my ear all night long.

And the look in his eyes the next morning when he'd told me to go. That he'd leave.

He hadn't judged me. In fact, it had seemed like he could read my mind. He could see the fear of attachment, the indecision.

He'd known that night wasn't like nights I'd had with other men. I couldn't tell what was so different except *him*.

"Were you going to save either of those for me?" Addy's voice floated past my shoulder.

I turned and gave her a big smile. "Adelaide Jones, be still my little Southern heart," I drawled.

She rolled her eyes and smiled softly. I didn't miss the way her eyes darted around the room and her shoulders stiffened when someone brushed past her. PTSD. Her therapist had been working with her on getting out more, and Addy had tasked me with helping.

33

I held up two fingers to the bartender, who set two more shots down. I picked them up, handed one to Addy, and looped my free arm around her shoulder to guide her to the quiet corner booth I'd blocked off for us. I used my small frame as a buffer as we moved through the crowd, and Addy relaxed against me.

Venom rose in my throat as I thought, for the thousandth time, about severing all of Derek's slimy fingers at the second knuckle.

We slid into the booth and Addy sat ramrod straight against the back, looking out over the room.

I watched her for a moment as she clocked all of the exits, and the security cameras over the bar. It had become her habit after she'd spent a night in the clink for "assaulting" a guy in a bar a few months ago. I also made sure that whenever I invited her out, I only picked places with extra security.

After a few minutes, she settled back with me, and her eyes found mine apologetically.

"Nope," I declared, grabbing my shot and lifting it. "No apologies, Addy. Never to me."

She smiled and clinked her shot glass to mine. Table touch and down the hatch.

The wave of heat passed through my veins again and I sighed happily.

"So, what's new with you?" I asked, focusing back on my friend.

"Oh, same old, same old," she shrugged.

"How's krav maga going?"

"MMA" she corrected with a smirk. "You know that. And it's going fine. I'm getting stronger."

"I can tell!" I pinched her bicep teasingly and she laughed, some of the tension easing from her.

"What about you? Any stories to distract me from how loud it is in here?"

34

I took a deep breath. I told Addy everything, but something in me was rebelling against bringing up Johnny. I didn't want to trigger anything for her. But she was constantly telling me to stop coddling her, and I needed my best friend's input.

"Okay, I'm going to tell you something, but you have to take three deep breaths before and after I say it."

Her eyes narrowed, but she nodded once and then took three breaths.

"I ran into Johnny today."

She seemed confused for a moment before the memory kicked in. She had teased me for weeks for letting Johnny go. He wasn't a stranger in our conversations. Unfortunately, all of those conversations had happened while she'd been seeing Derek. Recognition flashed across her face, and then she took another three deep breaths.

She processed for another minute before her eyes found mine and I saw that she had a shit-eating grin on her face.

"And how is Mr. God from Down Under?"

I found myself choking up a little at how goddamn strong my best friend was. But I waved the tears off and laughed.

"I literally ran into him. Coming out of City Hall."

"What was he doing at City Hall?"

"I guess he's some big-shot architect and he's helping with the renovation plans for some of the historic buildings in Hartworth," I scoffed.

"Well, what happened?"

I bit my lip and let the silence linger. Building suspense. Addy hated when I did that.

"Raelynn Marie, you tell me what happened right now," she demanded.

My lips puckered at my middle name, but then I was grinning and showing her my bruised knuckles.

"I punched him in the face."

Addy's eyes went saucer-wide and she grabbed my hand, twisting it to make sure it was okay, before lightly slapping it.

"Why would you do that?"

"I don't know," I sighed. "I heard his voice, and all these memories came flooding back. I was attacking him before I could stop myself."

"It wasn't just one punch," she stated.

"You've known me for most of my life, you know it wasn't just one punch."

"Is he alright?"

"Why are you asking about him?"

"Because clearly you're fine, so I'm worried about your victim!"

"Victim-schmictim," I scoffed. "The dude is six foot four and easily two hundred and thirty pounds."

"And yet here you sit, the only harm on your little body completely self-inflicted," Addy said, her tone suddenly serious.

I looked at her and saw her eyes were dark. "I know I should be more careful," I said softly. "I didn't think. I just got so angry. And it's not like I can take it out on who I really want to." She flinched at even the suggestion of Derek, which was why I'd made sure to avoid saying his name out loud. "If it makes you feel any better, I did apologize to him. And he didn't lift a single finger to defend himself."

"He's rare, then," Addy said, a half-smile lifting her lips.

"Definitely rare."

We sat in silence for a moment before Addy let out a little gasp.

"I had completely forgotten how absolutely in love with him you were!"

36

"What in the hell are you talking about? We had one night together. I was not in *love* with him!"

"Oh, you so were!" she giggled. "Any time I would bring him up after the fact, you'd go beet red and start ranting about how men ruin women's lives and take away their freedom."

"Exactly!"

"Yeah," she said, looking at me pointedly. "Utterly and madly in love with the guy."

"I was not."

"Were too."

"Was not."

"Were too."

"Was not!"

She laughed and pointed at my cheeks. "See? Beet red. You've still got it bad, Lynnie!"

I scowled, suddenly regretting the three shots in five minutes that were keeping me from controlling my blushing.

Addy's laughter finally subsided, and she took my hand in hers. "It's okay to like the guy, you know?"

"It's not though," I sighed. "I've got a good life. I have a great job, a cute apartment, and the absolute best friend in the world. I don't need anything else."

"Look, far be it from me to pressure you to get together with a guy you don't know," she said, her eyes trained on me, "but maybe Johnny isn't something you need, but something you want. And you're allowed to want things in life."

"I do want things in life," I sniffed. "Freedom and personal space. Men just trap you. I refuse to become a trapped woman."

"Sometimes the things you think will trap you, actually are the most freeing of all."

I looked at her for a long moment before I couldn't contain my snort.

"Where did you get that, a fortune cookie?" I laughed, the tequila making it that much funnier.

"I thought it was pretty profound, but whatever," she rolled her eyes.

I let myself enjoy the feeling of laughing so freely. When I finally came back to the table, though, Addy was glancing around and fiddling with her necklace.

Time to go.

I took her hand with mine and tugged as I pulled us out of the booth.

"What? Where are we going?"

"We're going back to my place to have a glass of wine and watch a stupid, brain-melting movie. Something with Adam Sandler in it."

"Lynnie, I'm fine, we don't have to go."

I wrapped my arm around her shoulders again as I led her through the crowd.

"You're doing great, but honestly, I'm over this tonight. Indulge me, will you?"

She sighed, but her smile was grateful as I navigated us through the crowd and into a cab.

Addy was my best friend. And part of living my life for myself was making sure that I was never too distracted to take care of my best friend.

Johnny would be a massive distraction. Johnny had the potential to convince me to sacrifice everything I had been working for my entire life.

There was no way in hell I was letting that happen.

Chapter Four

Raelynn

There are moments in life that change the entire trajectory of whatever plans might have been laid.

Addy's attack was one of those for me.

Helping her through her recovery was one of the great privileges of my life, to be able to be there as her support during some of the hardest nights. She also invited me to her therapy sessions every now and then, at the insistence of Dr. Laura, who thought having someone else that Addy trusted to know what to look for when she was having an anxiety attack would be helpful.

Dr. Laura and I had hit it off. We were both straight shooters, and I loved the way she navigated the most painful moments during Addy's sessions. She was patient and kind, but never let Addy shy away from the truth of any situation.

In speaking with Dr. Laura outside of Addy's sessions (which I learned was okay because I wasn't actually a patient), I found that she was just a genuinely good human being. She and her wife volunteered at various places, offering free therapy sessions, handing out meals, donating clothing and food and their time to whoever needed it.

One of the non-profits they worked with, that she was a founding member of, was called Angels Are Around, which was an organization that helped battered women escape abusive relationships. They provided counseling, divorce services, armed escorts, and relocation services. The more I learned about it, the more I knew I had to get involved.

I started working with the Angels to help relocate women, free of charge. The organization paid for plane tickets, the first few months of housing, setting up new jobs and new lives for these women who needed to disappear to stay safe. Being a travel agent gave me some amazing connections for discounted tickets and discreet hotels, and the more I worked with Angels the more connections I made. I knew people in local governments all across the country who were happy to help the women get settled, and I knew airline personnel from every major airline that operated in the country who would help them travel incognito.

Over the past year, I'd helped several women escape from truly horrific situations, and my soul felt a little lighter with every person that I helped. The only thing that sat a bit heavy in my heart was that I had never told Addy that I was volunteering with them. I wasn't sure why I hadn't. Maybe I thought I was protecting her? After everything she'd been through, I didn't want to burden her with stories of more battered women. I wasn't sure how it would affect her, and I used that as an excuse. I figured I would tell her eventually, but I had always told her everything so I hated keeping it to myself.

Sometimes I just wanted someone to talk through cases with, especially the tricky ones.

Stephanie Jenkinson was one of these cases. Alcoholic husband who worked for a local construction company and routinely beat his wife. More than the physical, he had also gaslit her to the point that she was convinced her entire family hated her and that she had nowhere to go.

Her mother had called Angels and explained the situation, and Stephanie had been willing to come in and meet with Dr. Laura a few times a month until she finally realized what had been done to her. Now, we were working to get her out. Which meant a lot of paperwork on my end to make sure nothing slipped through.

I elbowed my way through the door as my phone rang. I dropped the stack of research files I was carrying on the kitchen counter and fished the phone out of my pocket, glancing at the name on the screen. My brother, Marcus. I sighed and answered, tucking my cell between my ear and my shoulder as I shrugged out of my blazer and heels.

"Marcus, what do you want?"

"You ever hear of manners, Rae?" he sighed. This was an old argument.

Marcus, being the oldest, was the perfect one. He'd had to grow up too fast, helping raise four younger siblings. He'd always been the rule-follower; uptight and responsible. He was the one Mom and Dad relied on the most. He was also the one who realized I had been left at the aquarium. Marcus and I usually got along fine, but he had never understood why I went batshit sometimes. And he definitely didn't approve of most of my life choices.

"Suck a dick, Marky," I sniped back. Okay, so I didn't make it easy for him.

"It's Mom's birthday Sunday." I could hear him rolling his eyes. "We're taking her out to Casa Nostra. Seven. Don't be late, bring a gift, and not something you think is funny."

"Sir, yes, sir," I mumbled, wandering over to the fridge and grabbing the half empty bottle of Pinot I hadn't finished yesterday.

"Don't gripe at me, Raelynn," he sighed again. I was the best of our siblings at pushing his buttons.

"I'm not griping," I promised. "But do I have to come? Nobody would notice if I wasn't there, and I'm super busy."

I thought I could get him with that. While Marcus didn't respect most of the things I did in life, my career was the one that he understood and was proud of me for.

"It's her sixtieth birthday, you have to be there," his tone was soft.

He knew how I had felt growing up, and he did do his best to make me feel included. It didn't usually work, but I did like that he tried.

"Okay, fine," I sighed, resigned. "Casa Nostra, seven o'clock."

"Don't forget."

"I'm putting it in my calendar right now," I lied.

"You're not, but don't forget anyway."

I rolled my eyes and wrote it down on the back of a receipt that was sitting on the counter. I stuck my tongue out at the phone.

"Don't forget a gift, either," Marcus was saying.

"I wouldn't even know where to start shopping for Mom," I whined, uncapping the wine and drinking straight from the bottle. One of the perks of living alone.

"She's been wanting to read more," Marcus said thoughtfully. "You could get her a book or two."

"What does she even read?"

"No clue," he chuckled. "Just…nothing dirty, okay?"

I smirked as a million ideas flashed through my head. But my brother knew me well, and said, "Raelynn, nothing dirty. Understood?"

"Yes, boss," I sighed. My eyes fell to the pile of folders I need to sort through tonight. "Marcus, I really am tits deep in research, so I have to go."

I could feel him cringe at my language. "Go save the world, Rae. See you Sunday."

Before I could say goodbye, he had hung up.

**

Casa Nostra was an intimate Italian restaurant on the outside of town. It was nestled a bit back in the pines, looked like an upscale cabin, and served the best food in the state. There was an outdoor patio they used for bigger groups that glittered with a million lights woven through the trees and the fences, making you feel like you were surrounded by stars. Musicians always played softly in the corner of the restaurant, and it was small enough that you could hear the music wherever you sat. It was beautiful. The perfect spot for an awkward, forced family get-together.

I showed up at exactly six fifty-nine. When I saw Marcus waiting out front, I tapped my watch, and he rolled his eyes as he came over to give me a hug.

"We're on the patio," he said, turning to lead the way.

Of course, even when I was on time my family had to make sure they were all early just to spite me.

We turned the corner to the patio, and I took a deep breath to steel myself for the coming emotional roller coaster.

The big round table in the center of the patio fit our group perfectly. Mom and Dad sat next to each other, looking as dressed up as they ever did. Mom had a nice blue dress on, and Dad was in a polo and jeans. They were chatting and looking at the menu. Then there were the rest of my siblings.

In order, we were Marcus, Bella, me, Carol Anne, and Bradley. Marcus' wife Amber was there, and so was Bella's husband, Robert. Carole Anne and her fiancée, Margaret. And Bradley with his girlfriend, Heather.

We approached the table, and nobody even looked up.

I shot Marcus a look that said, "told you". I knew nobody would have missed me if I had stayed home.

I sighed and went to my mom to give her the wrapped bundle I was carrying.

"Happy birthday, Mom," I said with false cheer.

She looked up and blinked in surprise. "Raelynn! When did you get here?"

"Just now," I smiled, trying not to roll my eyes. "I wanted to give you your present. Open it later though."

Mom's eyes widened and she carefully took the package like it might have been a bomb.

"It's books, Mom, nothing bad," I sighed. I had found a very vanilla series of romance novels set in France that I was hoping she'd like.

Her face lightened and she smiled at me. My mom had the prettiest smile. It made her whole face light up. I hadn't been on the receiving end of it very often, so I soaked it in while I could.

"You can't blame me for being worried," she laughed. "Remember the time you got me a hive full of very angry honeybees?"

"I was ten. And you'd told me you wanted local honey for your birthday," I protested.

"Still," she grinned. "I'm glad you're here. Where's your date?"

I clenched my teeth.

"No date, Mom, just me."

"Oh," her smile fell a bit, but she tried to hide it. "Well, thank you for coming."

"Of course," I said softly.

She turned to talk to Amber, and I was quickly forgotten.

I sighed softly. It was always like this, and even though I knew that, I was somehow always hurt. I turned to go when I felt a hand on my arm.

"It really is good to have you here, sweet pea." Dad's voice was soft, and he barely looked at me, but I knew he meant it.

Dad wasn't demonstrably affectionate. He preferred to keep to himself and let Mom do the majority of the parenting. But we always knew that he loved us, and that he enjoyed having us around. Over the years, as I'd acted out more and more, Dad was a sort of steadying presence for me. He never got mad, never yelled. He was always there to help me clean up whatever mess I'd made, though, no matter how badly I'd screwed up. Parents aren't supposed to have favorites, but I think I was his. From the few stories I'd heard growing up, it sounded like I was a lot like him when he was young. He always made sure to try to spend time with me when everyone else seemed to forget about me. He wasn't perfect, but I appreciated him trying.

I leaned down and kissed his cheek. "Thanks, Dad."

"Enjoy dinner," he chuckled. "Get whatever you want, Marcus is paying for it."

I grinned as he winked at me, and I found my way to my seat.

Bradley waved at me before launching back into conversation with Carole Anne about the inconsistencies in the latest superhero movie from the franchise they loved.

I looked around, and everyone was deep in conversation.

Whenever I got together with my family, it didn't matter how much I'd changed from childhood. I'd become an entirely different person – stronger, smarter, more confident – and then the second I was back with them I was twelve again.

I never felt more alone than when I was surrounded by my family.

I sat for a few minutes listening to everyone conversing around me until I couldn't take it. I wasn't twelve anymore. I stood up and headed to the bar. If I was going to survive this dinner, I needed wine and I needed it fast. I leaned against the cool wood as the server grabbed a chilled bottle of white.

"Let me guess, tequila shots?" An accented voice from behind me made me jump.

I turned and found myself wanting to melt into two warm brown pools. How the hell did this guy keep showing up?

"They don't serve liquor here, otherwise the answer would be yes," I sighed as the bartender handed me my wine.

I knew I should sip it, be a lady for once in my goddamn life, especially with Johnny standing there watching me curiously. But I needed to get a buzz going before heading back to my table, so I downed it in one. I set the glass on the bar and tapped it, not caring what either of the people watching thought of me. While I waited for a refill, I turned back to the mysterious Australian who seemed to be following me.

"What the hell are you doing here?" There was no venom in my voice. I was genuinely curious. This place was off the beaten path and mostly only patroned by locals.

He flushed and cleared his throat, uncomfortable. Interesting. I'd never seen Johnny anything less than casually confident.

"I'm not stalking you, I swear." There was a light tease in his voice, but his eyes darted behind me.

I turned to grab my wine and, as I did, I saw a woman sitting at a table in the corner, her eyes trained on Johnny.

She was gorgeous. Tall, tanned, long blonde hair and big, bright blue eyes that I could see from here. My stomach dropped and I suddenly felt flushed.

I turned back and took a drink.

"You're on a date," I said, watching him.

He shrugged one shoulder and wouldn't meet my eyes.

"You sure do work fast, don't you," I snipped, anger warming my blood. I didn't know why I was getting so worked up, but I wanted to fight with someone, and Johnny was here. "How long had you been in town when we met? A day? A few hours?"

"It's not like that." He got defensive, his eyes flashing as he finally looked at me. "She works in the same offices I'm in, and she asked me. I couldn't very well say no."

"Why not?"

"I don't have a good reason not to," he said pointedly, his own anger bleeding through.

Silence hung in the air as we stared at each other, quietly fuming. He was right. I had no right to be upset that he was on a date. He had every right to say yes when a runway model asked him out.

"She's stunning," I said acidly, taking another drink of my wine. "Enjoy your night, Johnny."

"Why are you here?" He stepped in front of me as I tried to walk away.

"You're not the only one with a hot date," I said, flicking my hair over my shoulder as I shoved past him.

I don't know why I did that. I didn't need to lie. I could have just told him I was with my family. But seeing him out with that cover girl made something squirm inside me. I didn't like it. I wanted him to feel the same.

As I got back to the table, I saw that the waiter was taking the menus from everyone. They'd ordered. Without me.

The waiter had the decency to look confused as I approached the table, and Marcus at least looked ashamed that he had forgotten me.

I rolled my eyes and ordered quickly. A chicken parm and a bottle of wine, just for me. It was going to be a long fucking night.

***

I was right.

By the time dinner was done, I had barely touched my food but had polished off one and a half bottles of wine. I couldn't stop thinking about stupid Johnny on his stupid date with his stupid Victoria's Secret model. It helped that my family largely ignored me.

Amber and Margaret attempted to talk to me a few times, but they would quickly get pulled back by their partners, leaving me with my enraged, drunken thoughts.

Finally, it was time to say goodnight. As we got up from the table and turned to leave, we saw that our path out was blocked.

Johnny stood in the doorway, his head cocked, his eyes sparkling, and an infuriating smirk on his lips.

"This is your hot date?" he asked loudly.

Blood rushed to my face as my entire family stopped talking at once and turned to me.

"It's quite literally none of your business," I sniffed. The wine was buzzing through my head, making everything a little fuzzy.

Johnny watched me for a moment and then his eyes grew concerned. He glanced at the table and saw the empty bottles.

"You good, love?"

He was talking to me like my entire family wasn't watching our every move. He hadn't so much as glanced at them. He was entirely focused on me, and for some reason that made a part of me roar with delight. For once, everyone was watching me. Everyone was seeing me.

They were seeing me swaying slightly in my heels, but still. They couldn't ignore me when this god of a man was giving me his undivided attention.

"I'm fine, Aussie," I sighed, grabbing my jacket. I was trying to play it cool, but my heart was pounding furiously.

As I turned back around, I lost my footing and stumbled. Johnny was right there, his strong arm catching mine and steadying me.

"How much of that did you drink by yourself?" His voice was pitched low, only for me.

"I'm a big girl, Johnny. And it's only wine."

He raised an eyebrow and let me go. I felt myself swaying, even though I was ordering my body to stand still.

Shit. I couldn't drive like this. And if I had to ask my siblings for a ride it would be just another anecdote about Raelynn the fuck-up. Got so drunk at Mom's birthday dinner that she made a big scene and had to be driven home.

"I'm fine," I sighed. I could still feel my family watching me, and when I glanced over to them, I saw I was right. They were all staring at us. Mom's jaw was almost hanging open, probably a side-effect of Johnny and everything about him. My Dad's eyes were wary, and so were Marcus'. Everyone else looked confused and slightly amused.

Johnny followed my gaze, and a new light of understanding passed over his face. He wrapped an arm around my waist, so I didn't fall as he turned to the group.

"I'm sorry, I'm being rude," he said, his voice back to the casual charm he carried so easily. "I'm Johnny Harris, a friend of Rae's."

I saw Marcus blink at him calling me Rae, and I fought back a blush. There was a long, increasingly awkward silence building. Finally, Marcus stepped forward and offered Johnny his hand.

"Marcus Rogers, Raelynn's brother," he said. I could tell his grip was probably firmer than necessary, and I tried not to die of embarrassment.

"Did I interrupt a family event? I'm so sorry."

"We were just finishing up," I said softly, starting to get uncomfortable with everyone staring at me. I was so used to being ignored by them that having their undivided attention went quickly from exhilarating to off-putting.

"Were you?" Johnny looked down at me, and I realized that I rather enjoyed having *his* undivided attention.

"We were," Marcus said with a small laugh. "We were just about to head out. I hadn't realized how much Raelynn had...celebrated, tonight." He turned to me and went full big-brother mode. "You can't drive home."

I bristled at his tone. I hated being told what to do.

"That's actually why she called me," Johnny swooped in.

My head whipped to him, wondering why he was lying and where he was going with it. I deliberately ignored the way to room spun in my periphery.

"She asked me to come pick her up and take her home."

"I bet she did," Carole Anne snickered. My mom swatted her shoulder, but still never took her eyes off Johnny. At least her mouth was closed now.

Marcus' eyes flicked between me and Johnny.

"How long have you known Raelynn?" Marcus asked.

"Shoot me before the inquisition starts," I groaned, shoving myself out of Johnny's arms. I waved to the group as I headed for the door. "Happy birthday, Mom."

"We'll talk soon," she said. Her tone was happy, but it sounded like a threat.

I rolled my eyes and stumbled through the restaurant and out to the parking lot. Fumbling with my keys, I finally hit the lock button enough times to find my car. I knew I couldn't drive yet, but I could lay down in the backseat until I sobered up. I had an early morning tomorrow, and knew I'd regret the second half bottle.

As I reached for the door handle, an arm suddenly blocked my path.

"You are not driving home," Johnny said, his voice firm.

I turned and leaned against the door, letting his body tower over me and cage me in.

"Who's gonna stop me?" I challenged. "You?"

His eyes flashed, and even in the dark I could see his jaw clench.

"Why did you drink so much tonight, Rae?"

I sighed. "You met my family."

"I did, they seemed lovely. Not like you'd have to be ripped to get through a dinner with them."

I clenched my teeth. I couldn't look at him.

"Those five minutes they were talking to you was the most attention they've paid me in years," I bit out. "I was forced to come out of familial obligation, they ignored me, so I drank to entertain myself."

"Was that the only reason?" He took a step closer, and his cologne filled my nose.

I wanted to lean in and bury my nose in his shirt. The top button was undone and there was a delectable patch of chest hair sticking out that looked so soft. I found myself swaying forward, and then stopped myself just in time.

"Yep, just my family. Nothing else," I muttered, distracted by how overwhelming his presence was.

"Nothing else," he repeated, his voice soft and dark.

"Nope." I couldn't take my eyes off that patch of hair. "Definitely nothing to do with the European goddess you were on a date with." Shit. The alcohol in my blood was making me say stupid things. True, but stupid things.

He chuckled and I thought I could feel it in my bones. He was so close.

"I knew it," he breathed. His free hand that wasn't holding my car door shut came up and cradled my chin, forcing me to look at his face instead of his chest.

"You were jealous."

I scoffed. "I don't do jealous."

He lowered his face until his lips were hovering over mine. "If you weren't so drunk, I would show you exactly why you don't need to be jealous."

I swallowed around the rock that was suddenly in my throat as my heart pounded. I couldn't look away from his eyes as they traced my face and down my body before coming back to my lips.

Then, he pulled away and dropped his hand, sliding it down my arm to take my keys.

"Say the word, Raelynn," he said softly, looking at me for a long moment.

I didn't understand, and he must have seen that on my face. He sighed and scooped me up, carrying me to the passenger side. He put me down and helped me in, buckling my seat belt for me. His hands didn't linger, even though I wanted them to.

And then he was getting in behind the wheel. I didn't tell him my address, so I was surprised when, twenty minutes of full silence later, we pulled up outside my apartment. I glanced over as he folded a piece of paper that had Marcus' handwriting on it. Traitor.

"What about your car?" I finally asked, breaking the tension.

"I take cabs," he said, not looking at me. "Let's get you inside."

"Johnny, I can get myself inside," I huffed. The wine was starting to wear off, and I could feel a headache building. "I don't need your help."

"But do you want it?"

He turned to look at me, and I was trapped in his eyes. I wanted him so badly. I wanted him to take me inside and hold me until I fell asleep. I wanted him to save me from my family over and over again. I wanted him to see me every day, because with him I felt truly seen. But I didn't want everything that came after that. The resentment, the compromise. The restrictions.

"I'll be fine," I muttered.

"Of course, you will be," he sighed. "I'm going to make sure of it."

I blinked and then he was opening my door and helping me out. He handed me my keys and led me to my door. We were quiet for a moment, neither of us willing to break the silence.

"You're afraid of me," he said, finally.

"I'm not afraid of anything," I said tersely, fiddling with the keys. I couldn't look at him.

"It's okay." He reached out and turned my face to his. He was so intense. His gaze stole the breath from my lungs. "I'm afraid of you, too."

I blinked, my brain short-circuiting.

He smiled softly and dropped my chin, sticking his hands in his pockets and backing away.

"Have a good night, love."

And then he turned and walked away. I was stunned and confused, so I just stood there for a few minutes trying to get my bearings before slowly making my way inside.

I had known tonight was going to be something, but this was not what I had expected. My wine-soaked brain tried to catch up with all the feelings that were swirling around my nervous system.

The bitterness and resentment of being largely ignored by my family was nothing new. The flares of jealousy over a guy I'd had a one-night stand with, definitely new and decidedly unwelcome. The erratic beating of my heart every time I looked into Johnny's warm, brown eyes was a bit alarming.

I downed a huge bottle of water before dumping myself into bed, choosing to ignore all of these feelings and sleep. I just prayed tomorrow would be easier.

Chapter Five

Johnny

I woke up with an empty bed and a pounding headache.

Fucking Rae.

I'd been in town for months after she'd kicked me out of her apartment last year and had never run into her. Yet here I was, seeing her twice in less than two weeks. No wonder she thought I was stalking her.

My mind went back to the way her eyes had flashed when I'd had her trapped against her car last night. The way she'd mouthed off, wanting me to react. God, how I'd wanted to show her exactly how good I would take care of her, if she'd let me.

I hadn't been lying when I'd told her I was afraid of her.

I was so afraid of how that woman made me feel. Like my blood was on fire. Like my head was going to explode if I didn't see her.

I rubbed a hand over my face and blew out a long breath. I sounded insane, even for me.

I was known to be hot-blooded, rushing into things headfirst. But this...this whatever it was with Raelynn was something else entirely.

She was explosive. Dangerous.

And I wanted that danger. Like nothing I'd ever wanted before.

I swung my legs over the side of the bed and sat up, waiting for the blood to stop pounding in my ears.

Vanessa had been understanding when I'd all but blown her off last night. I hadn't lied when I'd told Raelynn that I wasn't in a position to turn down the offer of a date. It was the last thing I'd wanted to do, and that's exactly why I'd done it.

Over the course of my life, I'd found that when I felt very strongly that I didn't *want* to do something, it was usually because I was afraid. I hated being afraid. I had held myself back for far too long because of fear, and I was determined to never let myself do that again.

My parents divorced when I was five. Nothing unusual about that. Theirs had been a sort of whirlwind romance. They'd met when Mum had visited Australia for the first time. She'd run into my father at the beach. It was a month of romance, laughter, and adventure. When she'd returned to the States, she'd realized that she had brought home more than just fond memories and a few knick-knacks. Her parents kicked her out. My dad, thinking he was doing the right thing, had offered to bring her back to Australia, but she had wanted me to be born in the U.S., so that I could have dual citizenship.

That was the first sacrifice my father made for my mother, and I think it was the one that fostered the most resentment in him. He uprooted his life. Moved across an ocean to be with a woman he barely knew and raise a child when he was barely out of adolescence himself.

When I was born, Mum could never shake the postpartum depression. I think that logically Dad knew she had no control over that, but the funny thing about anger is that it doesn't care about logic. She could barely function. So, Dad did everything. I know he

56

tried, but there's only so many things a person can take before they have to give up.

For him, that was when he'd spent weeks planning my fifth birthday party, only to have my mother fly into a rage at the thought of having people over at the house. She'd torn down all the decorations, thrown cake all over the back lawn, and burned the gifts Dad had bought for me before passing out for two days.

I'm not sure how some people fail to realize that children are, in actuality, much more perceptive than most adults give them credit for. They just don't have the words or the understanding to make sense of what they see. I knew Mum wasn't okay, and I knew Dad hated her. I knew they both hated me.

He left after that. Packed it all in, filed for divorce, and when that was finalized, he moved back to Australia. I didn't see him at all for two years. Finally, my maternal grandparents insisted he become a part of my life, which was rich considering they were barely a part of it. I visited him every summer but spent the rest of the year with Mum.

She was a bad mother.

It wasn't her fault.

I was still angry with her.

It took me years of therapy to reconcile those three thoughts.

She *was* a bad mum. I took care of myself, for the most part. I used to blame her, as a child. When I didn't fully understand depression or mental illness. When there was no part of my brain that could compute how she must have felt getting pregnant at nineteen from a vacation fling. I would have felt like my entire future was ripped away from me. I would have been angry and resentful too. She couldn't have known how to cope with those feelings. It wasn't her fault. But that didn't mean that I wasn't still angry with her. That I didn't still have nightmares of her tantrums. That I'd hated having to be her parent when she was supposed to have been mine. I hated that I loved her, but I couldn't stop. When she was good, she was wonderful. Attentive, kind, sweet. But those weeks weren't frequent, and over the years they became farther apart until finally there were no good weeks anymore.

I was fourteen when she killed herself. I suppose she thought I was old enough to survive on my own at that point. She wasn't wrong, I'd been surviving on my own for a long time by then. But no fourteen-year-old should have to find their dead parent.

After the funeral, my absent grandparents shipped me off to Australia to live with my perpetual bachelor father. It felt more like living in a frat house than living with a parental figure. He didn't much care what I did or when I did it, as long as he saw me once a day to make sure I was still alive. Besides that, we lived completely separate lives. I went to school, played sports, joined clubs – anything to keep me from having to go home. He worked and spent his nights at the bar, bringing home whatever tourist wandered in that night. That's not to say he wasn't a good person. He was fun, jovial, and light-hearted. He was always up for a good chat, or an adventure. But he wasn't a dad. I don't think he ever wanted to be.

It was like going from living in a mausoleum to a carnival. Neither place had rules. Neither had room for genuine love or connection.

After living through that, I knew I was a wreck. I knew that I never wanted to be in a position where I'd have to find out what a shitty partner or father I'd be. So, I kept my relationships superficial. No real feelings, just good times. I was my father's son, and I was usually in danger of jumping headfirst into some stupid situation, so I tried like hell to make sure the women I was with knew that nothing would happen. I wasn't a boyfriend, or, God forbid, a husband.

Love was just a four-letter word for me. Flirting was a fun game to entertain myself with, maybe get some good sex from, and then move on.

Raelynn shouldn't have broken my heart that morning.

She shouldn't have stolen it the night before.

But something about her made me think that maybe I wasn't so broken after all. I mean, she was clearly just as terrified of anything real as I was. Maybe that's what was so different. She played the game, and she played it well. I'd finally met my match, and that was intoxicating.

I sighed and dropped my head into my hands.

Hartworth wasn't a big city, by any means, but it was big enough that I could avoid running into Raelynn again.

I knew that's what would be best for the both of us. But something in my blood sang for me to find her. To make her mine.

"Idiot," I muttered to myself.

That could never happen. I wouldn't let it.

***

The old warehouse on the corner of the downtown strip was in desperate need of a facelift.

It had been around since the late nineteenth century and had originally been a textile mill, taking in the cotton produced from plantations around the area and turning it into fabrics for clothing. As with most industrial buildings at the time, it was primarily steel and brick, but it had some quaint Southern features that gave it a nostalgic, timeless look. The tall windows were framed by arched red brick, and the interior was in surprisingly good shape for its age and history.

A bird fluttered through a hole in the front façade as I walked through, taking in the space.

A fire in the eighties had gutted the place, and it had stood vacant pretty much since. I guess, from what the town records showed me, a few businesses had tried to move in, but hadn't had the capital to fix it up.

Because of its age and historical significance, it had come into the care of the city a few months prior to my return, and as soon as I went to look at it, I knew I wanted it to be my first project. It would be the perfect building to become the template for the rest of the historical renovations the city was planning.

"What do you think?" Brett asked, leaning against the door frame that led to a back-office area. It was a few days after my disastrous date, and we were doing a walk through of the property to see what needed to be done.

At first, I had thought Brett would be a good friend, but I was wary of him after what Raelynn had told me about that guy he'd brought with us on our night out. Brett was constantly inviting me out, and I think he was starting to get hurt when I rejected his offers. I just didn't know how to bring up my concerns without it turning into something bigger than it needed to be. But we were partners on this project, and I couldn't let this weird tension continue to grow between us.

"It's got good bones," I said, gazing at the high ceiling. Large windows on what would have been a second floor let in light that filtered through the exposed steel beams.

"In the right hands, it could be something great," Brett sighed. "The only problem is, no business in their right mind would move in as it is."

I nodded, letting my gaze drift around the space.

"Then let's get it fixed up," I smiled at Brett. "We'll restore the exterior, patch the problem areas, reinforce the frame, replace the roof. Restore it to its original glory. Hopefully that'll persuade a good business to move in."

"Where should we start?"

"I'll do a more thorough investigation on its history and get an inspector in here to take a look at the foundation, and we'll go from there."

An awkward silence fell over the cavernous space.

Finally, Brett blew out a breath.

"Look, not to get all touchy-feely, but did I do somethin' to piss you off?"

I blinked. I guess we were having this conversation now, then.

"Nah, mate, you didn't," I hedged. "I just…do you remember when you took me out last time I was in town?"

He cocked his head, trying to remember. Finally, he nodded.

"Yeah, we met up with Em and Jo, right?"

"Sure," I said. Raelynn was the only woman I really remembered from that night. "But there was another guy from the office that went out with us. Who was that?"

Brett thought for another moment and then said, "I think it was Derek. Weird guy."

"How do you mean?"

Brett shoved away from the wall and walked toward me, his hands in his pockets. We made our way towards the door, ready to head back to City Hall.

"He had just started around the same time you came around. You were working in different departments, so I'm not surprised you didn't hear much about him after," Brett explained. "That night, I figured, since you were both new, I'd take you out. That was fine, but he literally stopped showing up to work like two weeks later. Just completely dropped off the grid."

"So, you weren't friends with him then?"

He laughed. We were at his car now, and he unlocked it so we could escape the oppressive heat.

"No, man. Dude was weird energy even before that." He looked at me curiously. "Wait, was that why you didn't want to hang out with me? You thought I was friends with that guy?"

I nodded. "I ran into the girl I went home with that night, and she told me that Derek beat on her friend."

"Shit, really?" Brett winced.

"If you were still friends with him, we'd have had some issues, mate," I said softly.

"No, I had no clue."

Another silence fell over us, but this time it wasn't awkward. It was tinged with sadness, and a bit of anger.

"I'd have beat his ass if I knew," Brett finally said, his voice serious.

I glanced over at him and saw that he was white knuckling the steering wheel.

"My dad beat my mom real bad for years before she finally got the courage to leave. To get us away from him," his voice was quiet.

I let his words sit. He didn't have to tell me that. He was trusting me.

I reached over and squeezed his shoulder briefly.

"It's alright, mate," I said. "My parents were right pieces of work themselves. It doesn't make you a bad person. You didn't know about this Derek guy until I told you, so you can't take any of that on yourself."

Brett blew out a long sigh. "It sucks."

"What does?"

"How are you supposed to know?" he asked. "If I'd known, I wouldn't have brought him that night. That girl wouldn't have been hurt. I know it's not my fault, but I feel like I should have seen something."

"You knew the guy for all of five minutes, Brett. You couldn't have known. You were just trying to be a nice guy. That's all you can do."

"Right."

"You're a good guy, buddy," I said softly. "How about we go out tonight? I have a feeling, now that I know you're not a complete piece of trash, that we'll be good friends, yeah?"

Brett laughed, which was what I'd been hoping he'd do. "Yeah, let's go out. Do you like clubs? There's this new one that just opened the next town over. I hear it's supposed to be a great time."

"Let's do it," I laughed at his enthusiasm.

"Perfect," Brett was excited. "Dress nice. I don't want you to embarrass me."

"Wouldn't dream of it, mate."

Brett glanced over at me, and then we both broke out in laughter.

Chapter Six

Raelynn

Loving what you do and liking every aspect of your job are two very different things. Especially in my line of work. There was nothing easy about the kinds of cases I handled. They were gut-wrenching. Painful. Emotional. Heart-breaking.

If I were a different person, I wouldn't have been able to do my job. But I loved helping these women. I knew every night when I went to sleep that I was making a difference in the world.

Of course, I still had my ways of coping with the stress and anger and sadness that threatened to overwhelm me every day. One of those ways was dancing. Not ballet or any kind of dance class. No. Good, old-fashioned, dirty club dancing. Sometimes, when I told people this, they made assumptions about me. That I was a party girl, chasing some high or something like that. But those assumptions were wrong.

Having spent so much of my life fighting for attention from my family and not getting it, my comfort zone was being invisible. It's why I forced myself into situations where I wasn't. Comfort zones were for pussies. However, when I was stressed, or losing hope in the state of the world, becoming invisible again felt safe. And there was no better place to be invisible than in a throng of sweating bodies and heavy basslines.

Addy had always hated clubs, so clubbing was something that I was used to doing alone. I was always safe. I never drank, never accepted anything from strangers, and I always wore sensible shoes and carried pepper spray in my bag. I was reckless, sure, but not an idiot.

This case was getting to me. It was causing me to sink into this state of hopelessness that there were no good men in the world, and that they were all cheating, abusive scumbags. Pepper in the weird tension from family dinner a few nights ago, and the way my mind wouldn't stop wondering what Johnny was doing, and I was in desperate need of a night of no thinking. So, instead of wallowing in pits of despair about things I couldn't change, I had pulled on a form-fitting, sparkly dress that clung to my curves and my favorite pair of skater shoes and had driven myself the next town over to Blink. It was a new club, so they were still running specials and pulling out all the stops to bring people in.

I texted Addy when I dropped my car off at the valet, and then stuck my phone in my clutch and turned to wait in line. It was still fairly early, so the wait wasn't too bad, and within ten minutes I had a stamp on my hand and was ushered inside.

Immediately, I could feel the bass vibrating the floor. My adrenaline kicked up, and the knots in my shoulders began to unwind themselves. I made my way through the hall and the bouncer pulled aside the curtain for me with a sexy smile. Bouncers loved me, but who could blame them? Plus, it was always good to have the massive guys doing security keeping an eye on me. I also liked to do a walk around of a new club to familiarize myself with the layout, emergency exits, VIP sections, and whatnot. As I made my way around, sticking to the walls, a wide smile grew on my face.

This particular club had three rooms. Their main room was the classic club experience. Heavy bass-filled music that invaded all of your senses and left you in a state of numb bewilderment. The second room was filled with pounding reggaeton music, the beat somehow languid and energizing all at once. The third room was more EDM, electronica music. Music that was its own kind of chemical running through your blood and altering your perception of reality.

I liked the variety but knew that EDM wasn't my mood that night. Reggaeton would have been great if I'd been looking for someone to hook up with. The only problem with that was that the sensual dancing happening in that room made me think about strong arms pinning my hands to the bed and whispering filthy things in my ear in a silky accent. Hard pass.

Classic it was.

I let myself wander through the crowd until I was in the middle of the room. I closed my eyes and felt every pulse of sound reverberating through my bones. My feet were solid on the ground. I was here. I existed. I was alive. I was making a difference in the world.

I let the music move my body, lifting my arms, swaying my hips.

The press of bodies caged my existence into this singular moment. The smell of sweat, hormones, and adrenaline flooded my bloodstream. My thoughts were drowned out by the bass, leaving me floating on a different plane of existence.

This was exactly what I needed. To drown out the world. To forget that there were truly horrible people mixed in with the good ones. To be forced to exist outside of my body while being unbelievably present within my bones.

I don't know how long I had been dancing, losing and finding myself over and over, when every hair on my body stood to attention.

Electricity zipped down my spine, and when I turned my head, my eyes locked with two brown ones across the room.

Johnny.

My chest was heaving as I came to a stop in the middle of the dance floor. The people around me didn't care that I'd stopped and kept dancing, their arms jostling me. It didn't matter anyway. They all fell away as I held Johnny's hungry stare.

I didn't know how long he'd been watching me, but the look in his eyes told me it had been a while. And that he'd enjoyed the show.

Holding my gaze, he gave me a slow, heated smile. He nodded his head, asking me to come to him.

I had no control over my feet as they slid through the crowd, my eyes never leaving his. Something in my chest was drawing me to him. It could have been against my will, but I wasn't sure I had any willpower at that moment. Everything in the world was focused on my heart pounding in my ears, synched with the music, and the heat in his stare.

Somehow, I arrived in front of him. He reached out a hand and traced my cheek gently, as if he couldn't believe I was real.

Fear shivered through me.

I was real. I existed. I was alive.

But was I?

Whenever I was around Johnny, I wondered if I'd ever really existed outside of his stare. I wondered if anyone had ever really seen me. Perceived me.

If a tree falls in a forest and no one is around to hear it, does it make a sound?

If someone lives in a world ignored by everyone around them, do they really exist?

Johnny was a drug. His attention was addicting. I hated it. I was terrified of it. I felt trapped by it. I craved it.

The air left my lungs.

I couldn't breathe. I couldn't think. I couldn't stand the weight of his fingers on my skin.

I ran.

That's why I wore sensible shoes, after all. In case I needed to run. When I first started going to clubs alone, I'd thought I might have to run from some would-be attacker. I'd never had to run in my sensible club shoes.

I ran for my life out of that club, bursting out the front door so suddenly I knocked the bouncer off his feet.

Mumbling an apology, I jogged to the valet.

"Raelynn," Johnny's voice was muted in my ears from the music in the club, but I could hear the panic and concern as his hand gripped my elbow and spun me around to face him.

I couldn't speak. My eyes were wild as I looked at him. I'm not sure what he saw in my face, but his fingers curled into my skin as his eyebrows furrowed.

In his typical fashion, Johnny didn't say anything. He simply cocked his head and examined me. His hand on my elbow was steadying and burning all at once.

My breath was coming in pants. I needed to get out of here.

Where was my damn car?

I shook Johnny's grip and wrapped my arms around myself.

"I'll take those." I heard him say to someone. I turned and saw him holding my keys. He gave me a cheeky grin and said, "I think you just like having me drive you home."

"You're not driving me home," I snarled. Jesus, where was my control? At least I'd managed to speak.

If he was upset by my tone, he didn't show it. He simply led me to the passenger side of my own damn car, again, and opened the door.

I stared at him, shaking.

His eyes darkened and he leaned down so that his lips were at my ear.

"If you don't get in the car right now, I'm throwing you in the trunk."

I pulled back to stare into his eyes, not believing him. But he was deadly serious.

Huffing, panicked, and sweating, I dropped into the passenger seat. My fingers fumbled with the buckle, but luckily, he didn't help this time. I'm not sure I could have taken another round of his skin touching mine.

I was still shaking slightly, though the panic was receding. As the adrenaline left, shame and embarrassment took its place.

What a fucking mess.

Johnny slid into the driver's seat, the sound of his door closing like a gunshot in my ears. Heavy silence filled the car, pressing into my head. A shiver ran through me again, and Johnny wordlessly reached over to turn the heat on. It was the end of summer and the air outside was still warm and humid, but the dry heat coming from the car was oddly comforting.

There was an unintended consequence of the heater though. His cologne exploded through the air and invaded my nose, fogging my brain and making my mouth water and thighs clench.

I had always been a sucker for a good cologne. There was something about a man's scent that drove me insane. I'm sure it had something to do with the pheromones – the combination of the cologne with whatever was the essence of Johnny speaking to something on a molecular level within me.

It didn't matter. My psyche was already on edge from the intensity of whatever had just happened in the club, and I wasn't sure

I could take a forty-minute drive trapped with his scent wrapping around me.

I turned the heat off, which earned me a glare.

"You're shivering," Johnny admonished, turning it back on.

"Not because I'm cold, jackass," I sniped, flipping it off.

"I know," he sighed. Heat on.

"I don't need you to take care of me." Heat off.

"Well, you're obviously doing such a bang-up job of it yourself." On.

"What the hell is that supposed to mean?" Off.

"Why is it that every time I run into you, you're drinking to excess or engaging in what most would call high-risk behavior?" His tone was hard. I'd never heard him sound so serious.

I also resented the implication that I wasn't completely in control of my life.

"You don't know me, Johnny." My voice was quiet. Deadly soft.

"Tell me I'm wrong, then."

A knot rose in my throat. I didn't need to justify anything to this man. It was none of his business how I lived my life.

But he was here. In my car. Driving me home, again.

He was present. Not only that, but he was worried about me. I wasn't sure of the last time someone was genuinely worried about me. Besides Addy, of course. He didn't have to stay. He didn't have to voice his concerns.

If I really thought about it, he wasn't wrong. Aside from our brief encounter outside of City Hall, he'd only ever seen me taking shots or chugging wine. How was he supposed to know that I didn't drink when I went clubbing?

I blew out a long breath and dropped my head back against the headrest.

"You're wrong," I said, letting my eyes slide over to him.

He was focused on the road, but dear God his profile was mouth-watering. That strong jaw with just a hint of stubble. His nose had a bump that you couldn't quite see from the front but gave him a very Grecian silhouette. And his lips had this perfect cupid's bow, plump and soft.

His eyes drifted over to me, and his cheek quirked in a grin, flashing that dimple, before he looked back at the road.

"You're staring, pretty girl."

Fire flashed up my spine and I squeezed my eyes shut.

His hand reached over to take mine gently. I let him.

"Why am I wrong?" He brought me back to the topic.

"I haven't been drinking tonight," I explained. "I don't drink when I go out alone. It's dangerous. I know the monsters that hide in the shadows of this world. I'm not stupid. Reckless, sure. But not stupid."

"And the other times? You sure you don't have a drinking problem?" He said after a pause. His tone was light, and I could tell he believed me.

"The first night we met we were all drinking," I reminded him, digging my nails into the back of his hand for emphasis. I heard a small growl escape his throat and smiled to myself. "And I have a... complicated relationship with my family. It necessitates wine. I'll grant you that I didn't anticipate drinking that much that night. But it was a rough one."

He was quiet for a while as the night raced past us.

Finally, he gave my hand a final squeeze and let go. His fingers moved to turn the heater back on, and I sighed but didn't fight him.

We sat in amiable silence for a long time as he drove. When we got closer to Hartworth, I began giving him directions. My voice was barely more than a whisper.

I was taking this time to try to reason why I'd had such a visceral reaction to seeing him in the club. Part of me wished I'd been driving. I did some of my best thinking while I drove. It was meditative. Allowed me to sort through my thoughts without getting overwhelmed by them.

I couldn't come to any sort of reasonable conclusion. I had been in a different state of consciousness, regardless of the fact that I was sober. That's the only thing I could think to blame.

That, and whatever unnamed thing was growing between myself and the infuriating Australian beside me.

I couldn't believe he'd been in that club. I'd specifically chosen to leave Hartworth because I didn't want to run into anyone I knew. How was it that we'd managed to occupy the same random spaces so often lately? Was it some conspiracy set by the Universe? Was he stalking me?

I risked a glance at him and shook my head. No. I may not have known all that much about him, but he didn't trigger any of my bad man spidey senses. In fact, he only seemed to trigger the parts of me that weren't used to being seen. He seemed hell-bent on taking care of me, and that made me ridiculously uncomfortable.

I had no idea how to let people take care of me. I'd been taking care of myself and other people for so long. It felt alien to be taken care of. Something foreign and bitter rose in my throat at the thought of being the complete center of someone's attention simply because they wanted me to be.

And Johnny seemed to have no other motus operandi.

My eyes, without my permission, found their way back to him. He was holding the wheel lightly with one hand, the other arm resting against the window. He was relaxed, his eyes focused on the road, but I was sure he knew I was staring at him.

My mind flashed back to meeting him for the first time last year. He'd played the game so well. Known exactly how much to give and how much to take. He'd figured me out quickly. Almost too quickly. It was comfortable to be with him. Normally, if I were stuck in a car with a man that criminally attractive, my pulse would be pounding, and I'd be constantly thinking of the next thing to say to keep a flirtatious banter going. But I didn't feel the need to do that with him. I felt…calm.

I blinked at that realization. Calm wasn't something that I ever felt. Righteous outrage. Heated lust. Arrogant over-confidence. Those I was intimately familiar with. But calm?

"We're here," Johnny's voice was soft.

I looked out the windshield and saw we were parked in front of my apartment. I fiddled with one of my rings. I needed to get out of the car and never see this man again. He was turning my nervous system upside down, and I didn't like it. But I couldn't make myself leave.

Johnny made no move to get out of the car either.

"I guess I should say thank you," I sighed.

"No worries," he said softly.

I looked at him for a long moment and then steeled myself again. I got out of the car wordlessly. He followed suit, walking me to my door like a perfect gentleman. He handed me my keys, and I resolutely ignored the static that sparked between us when our fingers met.

"I'll see you around," he said with a small smile.

"I wouldn't count on it."

He looked at me for a moment and again I had this feeling of being exposed. As if he could see right through the walls I was trying so hard to shore up.

His smile was warm and understanding when he winked at me.

"I'll see you around." He sounded so sure.

I watched him walk back towards the parking lot, pulling out his phone to no doubt call a ride-share or something. He'd driven me back with absolutely no qualms about spending money to get back to his home.

What was with this guy? He was sweet, and kind, and sexy, and emotionally intelligent, and for some reason seemed to be into me of all people.

I shook my head, my hair falling around my face and hiding the blush I'm sure was there. I escaped into my apartment and immediately headed for bed.

I would sleep off this weird night, and in the morning, it would be like nothing had ever happened.

I made a pact with myself to stop thinking about Johnny, and pretended it was someone else's deep brown eyes that I saw as I drifted off to sleep.

Chapter Seven

Raelynn

I loved a good farmer's market. One of the only days I enjoyed getting up early was a farmer's market day.

Hartworth Farmer's Market was every other Saturday during summer and once a month in winter. We were on the last few weeks of the summer hours, and I was determined to go as much as possible.

I couldn't explain why I loved the market so much. Something about the crowds of people milling around, everybody engaged in conversation on topics they were passionate about, and the *smells*. There were always fresh pastries, seasoned meats, and ripe fruits that captured your nose first. Then there were the undertones of floral soaps, luxurious candles, and sharp oils and lotions. And, running as the base that every other scent layered on was the Town Green, which was always freshly cut and watered, giving an earthy tone to everything.

The chatter and the energy were infectious, and I loved it. Which meant that I usually dragged Addy with me, but since the attack she didn't feel safe in the crowd. I would never blame her for that, and, luckily for me, I was fine with doing things myself. I did miss perusing the stalls with my best friend, but I wouldn't lie and say that I didn't enjoy being by myself.

There was more freedom in doing things solo. I never had to wait on anyone, I could go wherever I wanted, leave whenever I wanted, talk to whomever. I wasn't bound by anyone else and their social battery. I loved it.

This particular Saturday was the perfect mix of end of summer and beginning of fall. The morning was crisp and refreshing, but I knew the day would heat up quickly. The cool air felt like water on my skin, invigorating me and putting a smile on my face that couldn't seem to go away.

The last two weeks had been wildly productive for me. I had finally finished up the case for Angels I had been working on, I had booked several expensive vacations for a few well-off families in California, and I had not spared a single, solitary thought to the entire country of Australia, let alone a singular citizen. Okay, maybe a few had slipped through here and there, but I had resolutely shoved them way in the back of my brain and refused to acknowledge them.

I hummed a bit to myself as I wandered between booths and stalls, chatting with people, buying odd bits and bobs. I was having a beautiful morning, and nothing could ruin it.

One of my favorite stalls was an assortment of fresh vegetables from a small local farmer. His wife was usually the one manning the booth, and over the weeks she and I had become friendly. She was an older woman with bright white hair and sparkling lavender eyes. Sharp as a tack and one of my favorite people at the market. She was always sneaking me extra produce and making sure my bag was never empty when I left. Today, I was looking at a variety of carrots in stunning purples and whites as well as traditional orange.

"Cynthia, these are gorgeous," I gushed.

"Like little flowers, no?" she winked, deftly bagging someone else's cabbage.

I laughed and gathered a few in my hands and held them up like a bouquet. Cynthia laughed as I gave a twirl and pretended to walk down an aisle at a wedding cadence.

"Who's the lucky bloke?" Johnny's voice stopped me dead.

I turned and he was leaning against the tent post with an easy grin on his face. For some reason, it caused the smile that had been on my face all morning to drop.

I rolled my eyes and turned back to Cynthia.

"I'll take the bundle, please."

"Not even a hello? I'm wounded." Johnny came up beside me with his hand covering his heart and a puppy dog look.

"Hello, Johnny," I sighed. Part of me was annoyed that he kept showing up wherever I was, but another part, a traitorous part, thrilled at his attention. "I see you're taking the stalking to the next level."

"What can I say, I heard this was the best way to pick up chicks." He shot a wink to Cynthia who gave him a saucy one back.

"What? Things didn't work out with Hartworth's Next Top Model?"

His levity dropped for a moment as he looked at me. "It was one date, Rae. Nothing serious and only because I didn't want to be rude."

"Be rude next time." I gave him a shrug as Cynthia bagged my carrots. "Can you throw in some Romaine hearts too, please, Cynthia?"

"Of course, dearie."

Johnny edged closer to me as we watched Cynthia work, and my skin tingled at the proximity.

It wasn't fair, the physical effect this man had on me. My body remembered everything about our night together, even if my mind tried to wipe it from existence. The way his hands skimmed my sides. The soft kisses he trailed down my sternum. The weight of his body holding me down so that I couldn't escape the onslaught of attention. My blood started pumping just thinking about it and I nearly growled in frustration.

I glanced over at the infuriating Australian and saw that he was watching my face curiously. Our gazes caught and he grinned as if he knew exactly where my thoughts had been.

"You alright, Rae?" he feigned concern. "You're looking a little flushed there."

"You are a little red, honey," Cynthia chimed in as she handed me my bag. Her eyes were sparkling as she watched Johnny and I, as if she knew everything from the short interaction.

"I'm fine," I snapped at Johnny. Turning to Cynthia, I gave her a bright smile. "I promise, I'm fine. The day's just heating up and I turn bright red at the first hint of sun. Thank you for the beautiful carrots!"

I gave her a wave and turned sharply to continue perusing the market. It seemed, however, that'd I'd picked up a new shadow.

"Seriously, though," Johnny said, "of all the gin joints in all the world, I run into you at a farmer's market. Seems like fate, if you ask me."

"I don't believe in fate."

I kept my gaze firmly on the stalls ahead of us. Body oils, definitely not stopping there. I wasn't hungry yet, so the crepe stand was out. Knick knacks? Perfect. I kept my pace casual as I made my way into the stall, delighting in the tiny wooden figurines and puzzles that were displayed.

"I believe in making your own fate," Johnny said. He picked up a puzzle box and tugged at it for a moment.

I watched him as his eyes squinted and just the tip of his tongue peeked out over his bottom lip as he concentrated. It was adorable. How was this man both infuriatingly sexy and adorable?

"Making your own fate is an oxymoron," I said to distract myself. It was easy to bicker with him, even over something as silly as this conversation.

"I live in oxymorons," Johnny grinned widely as he solved the puzzle. "Look!"

He waved it in front of my face like a little kid and I couldn't help but smile at his enthusiasm.

"That's actually pretty impressive, Aussie." I gave him a grin and his eyes glazed over for a moment.

"Thank you," he said softly. His excitement was gone, replaced by something smaller.

Before I could look any deeper into it, he was grinning at me again and handing me a different puzzle.

"Your turn."

My eyes narrowed and I contemplated him for a moment. I was never one to back down from a challenge, and I could tell that he knew it. I bit my lip and then dove right in, twisting and pulling the pieces of wood until they untangled themselves and formed a perfect star.

"There." I tossed it back to him with a smirk and flicked my hair over my shoulder.

"Do you know the legend of the star puzzle?" Johnny asked as we slowly made our way around the stall.

I shook my head and found my gaze refusing to leave him.

"It apparently goes back to a small village in India several hundred years ago. A poor farmer was getting married, but he had nothing to give his wife on their wedding day. So, he flew to the heavens and plucked a shooting star from the sky. On the way down though, he dropped it and it shattered. He had to put all of the pieces back together so that he could give it to his bride. It was never perfect again, but it was a symbol of his love for her."

"That's surprisingly romantic," I said softly, feeling my cheeks heating again. I didn't know if it was the story, his accent, or the way his eyes never left my face as he spoke.

"You know, I can be surprisingly romantic myself."

"I have no doubt," I said, rolling my eyes but finding myself grinning.

"I'd definitely fly to the heavens to give you a shooting star."

I stopped so abruptly that Johnny ran into me. His hand caught my elbow, and he pulled me into him to keep me from falling.

Heat bubbled under my skin where he touched me, and I had to quickly step away.

"You'd give me a shooting star?"

He nodded and then looked thoughtful. "I think I'd give you everything I could, actually."

My breath caught in my throat, and I looked around to see the vendor watching us bemusedly.

I growled and grabbed Johnny's shirt, pulling him out of the stall and across the Green to a tree that nobody was occupying.

"What are you saying to me right now?" I demanded.

The smile that grew on his face was somehow sweet and sinful all at once.

"I'm saying that I think I'm falling in love with you, and I want to date you and someday, probably, marry you."

If I were a weaker woman, the ground would have dropped out from beneath my feet in that moment. I would have swooned and let myself get caught up in the pretty words coming from that mouth. Because it sounded lovely.

I could see it, being married to Johnny. I didn't think I would ever get tired of his eyes lighting up when he saw me, or the way his skin felt against mine.

"You don't even know me." My voice was a harsh whisper.

"I know you better than you think I do, Rae," he shrugged. "Look, I've been trying to get you out of my head for a year now with no success. Then I run into you three times in two weeks the second I'm back in town. And then again today? I mean, there are coincidences but come on."

"It's not like I've been going out of my way to run into you."

"Exactly."

"But that doesn't give you any reason to say you're falling in love with me. That's ridiculous."

"In case you hadn't noticed, Raelynn, I'm a bit ridiculous," he laughed. "Look, I'm not saying we rush into anything, but life's too short not to be honest with people about how we feel."

He was looking at me so earnestly that I wanted to jump right in. God knows I'd jumped into stupider relationships. But the feeling of snuggling deeper into his embrace that morning haunted me.

"Well, you can save your shooting stars and marriage proposals," I said, keeping my tone as icy as possible. "You'll come to your senses soon enough and forget all about me."

"Aren't you listening?" He was exasperated with me now. "I can't forget about you. Don't you think I've tried?"

"I don't know what you've done," I shot back. "You left that morning and then I didn't see you again until more than a year later. I don't know anything about what you've been doing, or the kind of person you are."

"So that's the issue? You need to know more about me?"

"I don't want to know more about you," I huffed.

His eyes burned as he took slow, deliberate steps towards me. "See, I don't think you're being completely honest, Rae. I think you do want to know more about me. I think you do see a future with us. I think you're just as drawn to me as I am to you. I think that you are two breaths away from falling in love with me too."

My back hit the trunk of the tree, and a flush was creeping up my chest. Tingles ran down my entire body at the look of pure devotion and arousal in his eyes. I would never deny that my body wanted this man more than anything in the world, but my head and my heart were screaming at me to run.

"You don't know shit about me, Aussie."

"But I want to," his voice was soft as his eyes traced my face.

"Then you'll have to try harder."

I smirked as a semblance of sense came back to my body and I ducked around him. I could feel him watching me as I walked away to my car. I refused to look back. Let him get a good look, because this was the last he was going to see of me if I had anything to say about it.

Chapter Eight

Raelynn

I think you're two breaths away from falling in love with me too.

Johnny's voice echoed in my dreams. I tossed and turned the next three nights, unable to escape the sincerity and hope that had been laced in those words.

I believed him when he said he was falling for me. He seemed like the kind of man who felt things deeply and wasn't afraid of his own emotional shadow, like I was. But I didn't think I was ready for anything as intense as falling in love. I couldn't even bring myself to admit that I *liked* Johnny. It was slippery slope from liking him to loving him, and I couldn't love him. I wouldn't love him.

My life was good. I'd worked damned hard to make a life for myself that I adored. Falling in love, especially with someone like Johnny, would inevitably change my life. A man had never been worth sacrificing my life for, and I wasn't about to start now.

I was exhausted when I pulled up to my little office. The lack of sleep was starting to get to me, and I had to blink a few times to focus. I was convinced I was seeing things, because strewn across the sidewalk in front of my office were flowers. Bright yellows, oranges, pinks, and purples covered the concrete and the frame around my office door. Dahlias, sunflowers, carnations, and roses, with baby's breath and other foliage to fill them out. Huge bouquets.

My eyes were wide as I got out of my car and slowly made my way through the petals. It smelled heavenly. I drifted to the door, trying not to disturb the pieces of art that adorned the walk. There was a note taped on the glass.

I carefully pulled it off and opened it, a laugh of disbelief bubbling out of me involuntarily.

One breath down? I thought that you might like actual flowers instead of carrots, you weirdo.
XO, Johnny

The absolute nerve of this man. I had no idea how he'd managed to find my office, but it wouldn't have been hard. My business information was one quick internet search away. Then to actually wait for the office to be empty, buy all of these flowers, and assemble them in such a picture-perfect way? The man was insane.

That was the only explanation.

I read the card a few more times, and with each pass something in my stomach tightened.

He was determined to make me fall in love with him. He wasn't going to let me go easily, and I was afraid I wouldn't be able to hold my resolve. If this was his starting move, what would come next?

Then, I remembered the night we met. I'd never met someone who knew the game I was playing and could match me as well as Johnny had. He'd seen through all my moves but still let me play them, giving them right back to me. A smile crept across my face as I realized that he knew I wasn't going to be an easy sell. He was going to have to work for it, and this was him letting me know that he was ready to play for all the marbles.

In that case, game on.

***

The smell of the flowers was far too overwhelming for me to keep them locked up in my office, so I piled as many bouquets as I could fit into my car and decided to spread the concept of love around a bit.

I wound my way through town to the nondescript brick building that housed Angels Are Around's headquarters. The office was small, but it was really more to have a physical address for the mail to go to. More often than not, all of the volunteers were out in the field, helping women. They had several safehouses all over the county, and always made sure to have at least one volunteer at each house at any given time, in case someone needed a refuge. But, whenever we had volunteer meetings or trainings or simply needed to connect with each other about the various moving parts of what we did, we met at the office.

Dr. Laura was there today, and she rushed to help me when she saw me carting several dozen flowers out of my car.

"What in the world is all this, Raelynn?" Her voice was always steady, even when she was surprised. I think it's what made her such a good therapist.

"I was given these as a gift, but they were stinking up my office, so I thought I'd share."

She laughed and held the door open before taking a bundle out of my arms. Together we moved all the bouquets into the office and spaced them around, separating some to take to the safehouses.

When we were finished sorting, Laura looked at me with a soft, knowing smile.

"Who exactly gifted you so many flowers? It must've cost them a pretty penny."

I sighed, knowing there was no way to get around the subject.

"I have an admirer."

Her gaze grew serious, though her tone stayed light. "Is the attention welcome?"

"Yes and no," I said with a laugh. "It's this guy that I met a little over a year ago. We slept together, he left, and now he's back in town and convinced himself he's in love with me. So, I guess he's courting me?"

"Do you like him?" Her gaze was steady.

I shrugged. "He's a nice enough guy."

She was quiet for a moment, studying me. Then, she grinned.

"You like him a lot, don't you?"

Ugh. Was it really so obvious?

I sighed, deciding that if I couldn't be honest with myself, I could at least be honest with Laura.

"Yes. I like him a lot and could very easily see myself falling in love with him."

"So, what's the problem?"

"I don't want to love him," I said softly. I both hated and loved how easy she was to talk to. "Love is constricting. It's compromise and forgotten dreams. I like my life. I like the freedom I have to do whatever I want. And I'm happy. I don't need someone to come in and fulfill any hole or need in my life. I don't want to be trapped by someone. And I don't want to eventually be forgotten by them."

Laura was quiet for a moment as she watched me. Then, her gaze turned to the flowers around the room. She smiled softly as she landed on one bouquet in particular, full of dahlias in different shades of pinks and oranges.

86

She drifted over to it and ran her fingers across the petals, before turning slightly to me.

"This is very similar to the bouquet Zarah got me for our first date," her voice was lost in the happy memory before it focused back on the present. "You know, I was a lot like you. I was just starting to get my practice off the ground, had a full and engaging social life. I could never imagine being married happily. Of course, my parents were no help in that department. They've been divorced thirty years. Zarah terrified me."

I blinked at that word. Terrified wasn't a word I liked to use to describe myself, but it was how Johnny made me feel. Overwhelmed. Terrified.

"Why?" I asked.

"The connection I felt to her was so strong. She was everything I hadn't known I'd wanted in my life. Because, like you, I didn't need anyone. I was perfectly content on my own. But after spending time with her, I realized that I *wanted* her. She challenged me, and comforted me, and understood me in a way nobody had been able to before."

I was quiet, thinking of the way Johnny seemed to see right through me but chose to play my game.

"So, you married her?"

"When we were able to, yes," Laura smiled happily. "And, let me tell you, nothing in this world could have prepared me for the life we get to live together. There is always compromise and consideration when you blend two full lives into one, but instead of closing doors like I had thought would happen, so many more opened up."

Laura looked at me with a gleam in her eyes. One that, I noticed, was always there when she spoke about her wife. Then, her look turned conspiratorial as she leaned in.

"I'll tell you a secret, Raelynn. True love doesn't hold you back. It pushes you to become better than you've ever been."

She turned her attention back to the bouquet, giving me time to collect my thoughts.

"Thank you, Laura," I said softly. She gave me a smile. "So, how much do I owe you?"

That broke the strangely quiet atmosphere that had settled between us.

"First session is free, how about that?" she laughed.

We chatted for a few more minutes before I said my goodbyes and headed for home, one bouquet sitting in my passenger seat.

***

I couldn't get out of my head the rest of the night.

Since the morning I woke up and found myself burrowing deeper into Johnny's arms, I had been vehemently pushing away the possibility of anything real between us.

I wasn't built for that life. I couldn't do commitment. It would infringe on my freedom. I wasn't going to compromise my life for anybody.

I had never once stopped to consider the possibility that being with Johnny could be a good thing. That, instead of losing parts of myself, I could uncover bits I hadn't even realized existed. That, maybe love didn't have to be synonymous with mundane.

What would that life even look like?

I didn't know Johnny all that well, but I knew he was dedicated to his work. That he loved it and was proud of the work he did. He liked his independence; I could tell that too. So, how would two people who were so used to operating as a single entity come together? How would that work?

I couldn't picture Johnny being content living in the suburbs with two point five kids, a dog, and a lawn to mow every weekend.

I *could* picture Johnny stretched out on a veranda, the view of the ocean behind him. Or wandering through a crowded market in Thailand. I could picture him bribing a tour guide so that we had five minutes alone at the top of the Eiffel Tower.

I could picture adventures with Johnny. But how long would that last? How long would it be before he got bored of me? Before he realized that I was never going to be someone that he could tame or who would give up her dreams for someone else? Before he forgot how much he'd once loved me and I became invisible to him?

The thought of having Johnny and losing him hit me harder than the thought of never having him at all.

I was a strong woman. That was never in question. But if I let my heart love someone as deeply as I knew I could love Johnny, and then he left? I wouldn't recover. Not for a long time.

My phone buzzing broke me out of my stupor, and I realized I'd been staring at the wall for the past two hours. My head hurt.

"What?" I snapped into the phone, unaware of who was even calling.

"Ouch. Take it you didn't like the flowers then?"

My breath caught in my throat for a moment, which only served to make me angrier. His voice shouldn't have the power to stop my breath.

"Rae?" Johnny sounded worried, and I realized I'd been silent for a beat too long.

"The flowers were nice," I forced out.

"Hmm, you don't sound that impressed," he mused. "Guess my next gesture will just have to be bigger. I wonder how much it would cost to hire the high school marching band for an evening?"

"You wouldn't dare," I said, but my tone had no venom.

"I'm telling you, Rae, I'm going to get you to realize that you're just as in love with me as I am with you. I'm not stopping until you admit it, and if the wooing has to get bigger and bigger each time, well then that's on you."

I rolled my eyes but found myself smiling just a little.

"To my earlier point, Johnny," I kept my voice business-like, "I don't even know you. How can I be in love with you if I don't know anything about you?"

"That can be remedied. Let me take you on a proper date."

"Counteroffer. You tell me anything I want to know, and then I decide if we go on a date."

"Sounds like I'm wearing you down, love."

"How did you get my number, anyway. I know for a fact I've never given it to you."

I could hear the grin on his face as he said, "Let's just say I've got an ally in my romantic endeavors."

My eyes narrowed as Addy's sly smiles over the past few weeks popped into my head.

"Adelaide Jones," I growled under my breath.

"Girl after my own heart," Johnny laughed.

When I was silent, fuming, Johnny's voice gentled.

"C'mon, Rae, don't be mad at Addy, she just wants you to be happy."

"I decide what makes me happy."

"So, decide it's me then."

"Johnny." I was suddenly very tired. I think he could hear it in my voice. The energy on the other end of the phone shifted, became less intense.

"I'm not trying to put any pressure on you, really. You know enough about me to know that I'll push and joke, but I need you to know that my feelings for you are real. I'm a patient man, and I want falling in love with me to be your choice. I want you to choose me."

I knew I was supposed to say something, but I couldn't make words come out.

"You want to know me, Raelynn?"

I took a deep breath. I hated how easily this man threw me off my game and got in my head. He could go from playful and flirty to direct and sincere with a snap of his fingers. I hated how he could read me from across the city.

He waited for my answer, giving me time to collect my thoughts. "I think I do, Johnny."

He laughed and the sound made my heart beat faster. Dammit.

"Have a good night. Get some rest."

Two beeps told me that he'd hung up.

I set my phone on the counter and pressed the heels of my hands into my eyes. I wasn't sure what I'd just agreed to, but I knew I needed to get my shit together.

This wavering, unsure, fluttery person was not me. Raelynn Rogers was a fucking badass who ran circles around men.

She was not a woman who was going to change her entire life because a gorgeous Australian covered her office in flowers. If he wanted to win my heart, he was going to have to give it a hell of an effort.

Chapter Nine

Johnny

It had been pure dumb luck, running into Addy at the grocery store. She'd been surprised that I had recognized her, but that head of curls was hard to forget. I hadn't wasted a second running up to her. I'd been overly excited, though, and had seen the effects of her experience with that Derek guy firsthand.

She had immediately squared her feet, and her eyes had widened in panic. Once I explained who I was, she was still wary, but less overtly defensive.

"What do you want?" she'd asked.

"This is going to sound crazy, I know, but could I get Raelynn's phone number from you?"

She'd watched me closely for a moment, her eyes narrowed. "What do you want it for?"

"I want to woo her." I'd cracked a smile that grew when Addy had laughed and rolled her eyes.

"Oh, she'll hate that," she'd said, only hesitating a moment before smiling. "Fine."

The shock must have been evident on my face, because she had sighed as she pulled her phone out.

"Raelynn doesn't know how much she deserves to be loved by someone like you," she'd said softly. "Just don't fuck it up, okay?"

As I had programmed Rae's number into my phone, I couldn't help feeling like the universe was on my side with this. Like it was fate. Because for all my big talk at the farmer's market, I had no idea what play to try after the flowers. Then the gods had sent me her best friend, and immediately I knew what to do.

The first call had gone about as well as I'd expected. Rae was guarded. I wanted to show her who I was, but it was never really going to work if I couldn't get a little bit of insight into the woman.

***

My fingers lightly tapped the coffee mug that was steaming in front of me. The early morning light was just starting to break through the clouds and light up the coffee shop I was sitting in. I was waiting for Addy, who had agreed to meet with me before she went to work.

I knew I should have been at the office already, looking over blueprints. I was balls deep in restoration planning for that warehouse, and the knot in my shoulders was well-earned. City ordinances could be a bitch, and Hartworth, for all its charm, was no different. A thousand different little pieces of red tape were hanging up the project. To be fair, this was why they paid me the big bucks. I was usually a genius when it came to navigating tricky ordinance situations, citizen concerns, and the actual restorations themselves. It sounded conceited, I knew, but my track record spoke for itself. For some reason, though, this project was killing me.

I knew that if I could just focus for a minute everything would become clear. I'd find the path through the maze, and we'd be able to break ground. The only problem was my focus was trained entirely on a woman who was putting up a helluva charade that she wasn't in love with me.

Hence the reason I'd asked Addy to meet with me. She was the closest person to Raelynn, and I knew that if I could get her on my side, she'd help me out. I had a feeling it wasn't going to be a hard sell, considering she'd given me Rae's number like she was a phone book. But I also liked Addy. She was a sweet girl who'd been dealt a hard hand, and if she was friends with Rae then I wanted to be her friend too.

I knew love was a strong word, and if I didn't know deep down that Raelynn wasn't so easily scared, I never would have used it so quickly with her. But I did love her. And if that was all it took to scare her off, then she wasn't who I thought she was.

She was right, of course. We barely knew each other. We'd had one night together over a year ago, and a few run ins since I'd been back. But every time I saw her it was as though more pieces settled into place.

She was fiercely independent. She hated relying on anyone and would rather put herself in harm's way than ask for help on her behalf. But she *gave* her help and her attention freely. She felt invisible in her family, which was probably why she tended to thrive as the center of attention. But I'd also seen her blend in seamlessly into the background, content to observe others. She craved control, but when we'd been physically intimate, she had relished letting me take care of her. She was paradoxical, quick-witted, with a barbed tongue and eyes that melted my heart.

I didn't want to love her.

Love for me had always been a taboo word. Something that didn't truly exist. The illusion of love had killed my mother and estranged me from my father. I had never once let myself believe it was something anyone could really feel.

94

That being said, it was the only name for the pull I had to Raelynn Rogers. What else could it be when I wanted to be around her all the time? To hear every one of her stories and learn every one of her quirks? To see her on her worst days? I wanted to break through the façade she presented of the put-together, independent woman and make her realize she didn't have to be that with me. I wanted to burn down the world for her and lay it at her feet.

I was a logical man, despite my raging emotions, and the only logical answer to any of those questions was love.

I watched as the bus arrived and Addy walked up to the coffee shop. Her eyes were wary as she glanced both directions on the sidewalk before opening the door.

I watched her gaze sweep the room before finding me. She smiled, but it didn't light up her face. I waved her over and she made her way, her body tense right up until she settled into the booth and tucked her back into the corner of it. I wasn't even sure she was aware she was doing it, but it broke my heart.

"Hey, Johnny, how are you?" Her voice was steady and warm.

"I'm good, Adelaide," I gave her a soft smile back. "Thanks for meeting me."

"My pleasure. I've been curious to get to know you better, after all I've been hearing." Her grin turned mischievous. "I'm assuming you're going to try to convince me to give you dirt on Raelynn?"

"Not dirt, per se," I hedged, keeping my tone playful.

"Good, because that's not why I showed up."

"Oh? What's the reason for accepting my invite then?"

She smirked before waving over the waiter. "Tea, then talking."

She ordered a large black tea, which honestly surprised me a bit.

"I thought you'd be one of those super sweet coffee girls."

She scrunched her nose. "Not anymore."

She didn't offer anything else, so I didn't push it.

The waiter came back with a steaming cup, and she took a long drink before sighing contentedly. Then, her gaze met mine and she looked positively wicked. I swallowed, suddenly nervous.

"Raelynn is my best friend." Her voice was even as she set the cup down and studied me.

"I know."

"She really likes you."

I smirked. "I know that too."

Her eyebrow twitched and her smile lingered. "She's never had a serious relationship in her entire life."

I blinked at that.

"Didn't know that one, then?"

I could see now how the two women, who seemed so diametrically opposed in personality, had managed to stay best friends for so long. Addy was sharp, loyal, and observant. She didn't miss a trick. I had a feeling she'd been keeping Raelynn safe for a very long time.

"Look, Johnny, I'm not trying to scare you off," Addy sighed. "I'm just trying to level with you so that you can understand a bit of the resistance you're facing."

"I really didn't invite you here to try and get any of Rae's secrets from you," I said sincerely. "I just wanted to get to know you a bit more and see if you had any advice for me."

"She told me that you said you were in love with her?"

I nodded, but kept my mouth shut.

"How could you possibly know that already?" Her gaze was sharp, and the tension was back in her shoulders.

"I just do," I shrugged. "I want to be around her all the time. I want to see her smile. I want to make her life easier. I want to learn everything I can about her. I want to keep her safe."

Addy barked a laugh at that. "Keeping Raelynn safe is akin to strapping on a parachute and jumping out of a plane. You can only hope that you reach the ground in one piece, and there are no guarantees you will."

"I'm starting to gather that," I chuckled.

"Raelynn lives for her freedom." Addy was serious again, her voice soft. "My concern with your so-called love is that it's more of an obsession than real love."

I cocked my head at her choice of words, but her eyes held mine as she continued.

"I know about obsession. Obsession is ugly. It's restrictive and possessive. It's dangerous." Her face darkened and she seemed to retreat back into herself. "Obsession is quick, too. It shows up like this gasoline lit bonfire. But eventually it burns out, and all you're left with is something dark and dirty. Ashes."

She looked back at me and my gut churned. I knew what she was talking about. I'd read my mother's diaries from her summer in Australia. She was convinced her and my father were in love about three days after meeting. It wasn't quite the obsession that had put Addy in the hospital, but it had led to my entire existence and the worst moments in it.

"I can't let Raelynn get hurt, Johnny. And I think you're a good guy. A great one, possibly. But we don't know you. If Rae is going to let go of her most prized possession, she'll need to know she's putting it somewhere safe. It's your job to prove that to her."

I nodded. Amazement and warmth trickled through me as I really took in the woman sitting across from me. After everything she'd been through, she was using her experience to make sure her friend stayed safe.

"Rae's very lucky to have a friend like you, Addy."

The corner of her mouth lifted, and she took a sip of her tea before saying, "She damn well knows it, too."

I laughed and took a long drink of my coffee. We sat in silence for a moment, both of us watching each other.

"So, hotshot, what's the plan?"

"Plan?"

"To woo my best friend? Come on, this thing is gonna have to be airtight if you want Raelynn to fall for you."

"Oh, don't worry," I smiled. "I've got about a million ideas, and if she needs more than that I'll come up with a million more. I don't care how long it takes. Raelynn is a woman worth waiting for."

***

The flowers had only been the beginning. Raelynn was a woman who deserved not only gestures, but grand ones. I knew she was probably a little irritated, but I had this feeling that deep down she craved someone showing her that they cared.

But, according to the relationship podcast I'd been binging, love also meant listening to your partner and really hearing what they were saying.

Raelynn's biggest concern was that she didn't know anything about me. She didn't realize that she knew more than most, but I wasn't about to let that be the reason she kept her walls up.

My hand shook a bit as I dialed her number, and I had to roll my eyes at myself. Seriously, in what world was I so nervous to talk to a woman that my hand shook? But Raelynn was upending everything I thought I'd known about myself.

She picked up on the third ring with a heavy sigh.

"Hello to you, too, beautiful," I said with a laugh in my voice.

"Hi Johnny." She was trying to play it cool, but I could hear a glimmer of something in her voice that gave me hope.

"I was on seven different clubs in high school."

There was a pause on the other end of the line. When she didn't say anything, but hadn't hung up, I kept going.

"Drama, obviously, debate, maths, ceramics, climbing, cycling, and rugby."

"Why is drama obvious?"

"Because I'm clearly meant to be the center of attention," I joked.

She hummed, but didn't say anything.

"My favorite was debate, strangely enough."

I was sitting on the couch in the apartment I was renting, so I laid down and stretched my legs out, one arm behind my head. If I was going to travel down memory lane, I might as well be comfortable. I wondered where I'd caught Rae. If she was still at work, her fingers drifting across her keyboard as she listened to me ramble. Or if she was home, curled up under a blanket and cozy sweater. God, I just wanted to be with her already.

"There was something intoxicating about proving my point, regardless of whether it was the morally correct point or not. Because that wasn't the goal in debate club. The goal was to win the argument."

"So, what I'm hearing is that talking to you at length about any topic will prove to be confusing and annoying?"

I laughed and a thrill went through me when I heard her soft chuckle.

"Absolutely the opposite. In fact, my love of debate is what keeps my mind agile and my perspective open. We don't have to agree on everything or anything at all, but if you're willing to hear me out and if you've got a solid argument for your point, I'm more than willing to concede the topic. I like to keep an open mind about things. It's always okay to change your opinion about something."

"Or someone?"

I nodded and then realized she couldn't see me.

"Yeah, or someone."

We were both quiet for a moment.

"What are you doing, Johnny?" she asked, her voice soft.

"You wanted to get to know me."

"Well, yes, I did say that –"

"So, until you agree to let me take you on a proper date, I'm going to call you. Every day."

"Every day?"

"Every single day. With a new fun fact about me."

"What will you do if I don't answer? I do have a life, you know." She was teasing me, playing the game she loved so much.

I let my tone drop and my desire pour into my voice. I wanted her to know how much I wanted her. I didn't want there to be any doubt in her mind where I stood.

"One day soon, I'm going to be an everyday part of that life," I promised her. "I know you need proof of that, so regardless of whether you answer my calls or not, I will be calling you and you will be getting a fact about me."

"Johnny." She sounded breathless. Good.

"Sleep tight, Raelynn." I smiled into the phone. "I'll talk to you tomorrow."

When I hung up, it took me a solid minute to calm my heart back down. Consistency and proof. That's what she needed, so that's what she was going to get.

Chapter Ten

Raelynn

My favorite part of my job was helping people take trips that they'd only dreamed about. As someone who loved to travel myself, I could give personal recommendations for some of the more common trips like The Bahamas, Hawai'i, Alaska, and the top spots in Europe. But my favorite to plan were the trips that were more unique.

Jessica McBride wanted to go to Morrocco. I didn't get a lot of clients that wanted to travel to Africa, so there was a lot of research that I needed to get done. I prided myself on getting my clients the best deals and curating a completely unique experience for them.

I was currently on the phone with one of my airline contacts, Brendan. He had been *everywhere* and was one of the best resources I had when planning trips to places I wasn't as familiar with.

"Is your client going by herself?" Brendan was asking.

I had my feet kicked up on my desk and was jotting down notes as we spoke.

"She'll be meeting up with a group of girlfriends, but they're all flying separately to Marrakech. They're coming from all over the place."

"Understood. I was going to warn against traveling around Morrocco alone. It can be done, but it's a conservative country, so if she was solo there'd be more safety precautions I'd advise her to take. But a group should be fine. They're definitely going to want to stay in some riads, but there are great mainstream hotels I can recommend as well."

"What about trips to the desert? She specifically mentioned riding a camel as a bucket list item for her."

"Totally doable in the timeline you've given me. Just be aware as you're booking experiences that from Fez to Merzouga is about a seven-hour drive. Fez is a must visit, so it should definitely be on the itinerary. Merzouga has some amazing desert camps, and usually they'll pack you in on camels, so couple of birds one stop."

I heard the bell over the front door jingle as he was talking, but I was trying to write so I didn't immediately look up.

"Brendan, you're the love of my life, have I told you that lately?" I flirted, knowing how much Brendan loved when I flattered his ego.

"You could always stand to tell me more, babe," he joked back.

"I love, love, love you," I laughed. "I've got a client that just came in, but I'll give you a call if I have more questions or run into anything that requires your specific brand of expertise."

"Alright, I can tell when I'm no longer needed," he sighed dramatically.

"I will always need you, silly," I said, rolling my eyes. "Give Jaime my love."

"He says hi." I could hear Brendan's smile through the phone, the way he always did when his partner was mentioned.

We gave kisses and then both of us hung up.

I swung my legs down and turned my chair to look at my little waiting area.

Leaning against the wall was six feet of breathtaking Australian.

"Johnny?"

"Didn't mean to interrupt," he said softly. His eyes were dark and he seemed upset.

"You weren't interrupting." I waved a hand and stood up to meet him. "I was just getting some info from a friend for a trip I'm planning for a client."

"A friend, huh?" He watched me carefully as I came up to him.

I smirked. He was jealous. Something in me thrilled at the thought. It wasn't one of my better kinks, but something about a possessive man made me melt.

I let my eyes drift over him. He was delicious, dressed in his work slacks and a white button down. His hair was a little longer than it had been when he'd first reappeared in my life, and I found my fingers itching to run through it.

"Yes, Brendan is just a friend," I said. My voice dropped without my permission, and I relished the flash in his eyes.

"Not the love of your life?"

"I thought that was supposed to be you?" I said, cocking an eyebrow at him.

His smile was slow and sweet.

"Is that you finally admitting what I've known all along, love?"

"In your dreams, Aussie."

"Every night, Rae."

Silence enveloped us as we watched each other.

A thousand questions were running through my head. How could he be so certain of his feelings for me? How was I supposed to trust his intentions? Why couldn't I take my eyes off of him?

"What are you doing here?" I finally asked. The easiest one to get an answer to.

"I wanted to see you," he admitted softly.

"Why?"

He grinned and walked past me. He was comfortable in the space, or at least acting like he was. All confidence and certainty that I wasn't going to kick him out.

"Where are your flowers?" He looked back at me with a small frown.

"You mean the wholesale store? They're in good homes, I promise."

"You didn't keep any of them?"

"I didn't say that." The smallest bouquet was livening up my kitchen counter, but he didn't need specifics.

His face lit up as he turned around. He stuck his hands in his pockets and studied me.

"I don't know how, but you seem to have become more beautiful since I saw you last."

"Shut up," I rolled my eyes.

"No, I swear." He held a hand over his heart and the other up in the air.

His eyes sparkled and I knew he was loving that I was engaging with him. I had to admit, I enjoyed the banter. It wasn't often that I met someone who knew how to push all of my buttons while still somehow making me feel special.

"I donated most of the flowers to this charity I work with," I said, offering him something.

"Oh, yeah? Which charity?" He turned and began exploring more of my office space. I found myself following him instead of trying to stop him.

"They're called Angels Are Around. They help women escape from domestic abuse situations."

His gaze leveled me when he turned around again. There was understanding and something soft and warm in his smile.

"That's a worthy cause," he said. "I'm glad I could help, even if my intention was to sweep you off your feet."

I laughed and shook my head. "I don't need you to sweep me off my feet, Johnny."

"You don't need me at all."

He said it so casually. So matter-of-factly. He said it without an ounce of resentment. It stopped me in my tracks.

"No, I don't," I said slowly.

He hadn't stopped watching me, and I was starting to feel uncomfortable with the attention. I found myself fiddling with my watch. I forced myself to settle and meet his unwavering gaze. I decided when I was uncomfortable, and being the sole focus of this baffling man was not the time.

He laughed low in his chest and walked over to me. He lifted his fingers to cup my chin and studied my face.

"You're incredible," he breathed.

"I know."

"I want to kiss you so badly, right now." The confession cut through the still air between us.

I wanted him to. At least, my body did. My heart did. My head wasn't as sold. I knew that the moment his lips touched mine I would lose all my resolve.

He had to earn my kisses. He had to earn my trust.

"Tell me something about you," I demanded. I didn't move, keeping my chin in his grip. I wanted him to know that I wasn't going to back down, but that I was still calling the shots here. I wanted to see how he played this.

He smiled before tracing the tip of his pointer finger across my cheek and bopping me on the nose.

"Greedy little thing, aren't you?" He laughed as he stepped away from me and over to my desk.

He picked up a photo of Addy and me. We were sixteen and dressed as vampires for Halloween. What should have been stereotypical teenage girl costumes were instead historically accurate Italian Renaissance gowns that were tattered and bloody. Vampires were cliche, but Addy had been obsessed with them that year, and the corset had looked great on me.

"I grew up in the States," Johnny said, still looking at the picture. "I never liked Halloween. Still not the biggest fan. We don't really celebrate it in Australia, you know?"

"I didn't know that." I watched him curiously. "Why didn't you like it growing up? Most kids live for Halloween."

"When you're afraid every day, it makes it a little hard to understand why people would *want* to be scared."

He wasn't looking at me, so I couldn't tell what expression he wore, but his voice was soft. Clearly, there was more to that statement, and a part of me was ragingly curious. The other part didn't want to pry. He was offering bits of himself to me, and I didn't want him to feel as though he had to share more than he was ready for.

Hearing the residual pain in Johnny's voice broke my heart. What could possibly frighten a little boy so much that Halloween seemed silly?

My feet moved without my permission, and I found my hand resting on his forearm. He turned those deep eyes on me, and I saw a thousand emotions floating through them.

"Halloween was my favorite holiday because I got more attention that day than the rest of the year," I said, a little surprised at my own confession.

"What do you mean?"

I shrugged, crossing my arms over my chest. Defensive posturing, Laura would tell me.

106

"As soon as I was old enough, I would come up with elaborate costumes," I explained. "I actually made those outfits in that picture for me and Addy. The more I did it, the better I got. I think it was the thing my mom was proudest of about me, actually. She waited months for me to reveal my costume. It was something that none of my siblings could do. It also had the added benefit of keeping me out of trouble for a bit. She would gush over my creativity and skill. Then, November first, it was like the day before had never happened. I was the forgotten child again."

Johnny was quiet for a long moment, and then he gave me a smile that was so sweet and warm, and I saw it for the first time. Love.

I blinked as a rock lodged itself in my throat.

This whole time I had thought Johnny had been exaggerating his feelings for me, but in that look I knew. He really cared for me.

"Thank you for sharing that with me, Raelynn," he said softly.

I swallowed around the lump and nodded. "Don't get used to it," I huffed.

My walls had slammed back up, but Johnny didn't seem fazed. He seemed content to take whatever I was willing to give him, and he could read me almost better than I could read myself.

He set the picture down and strode casually over to the front door.

"So, dinner tomorrow?" He asked as if we'd done it a thousand times before.

It made me laugh, even as my hands shook a bit from the whiplash of emotions I was feeling.

"You're incorrigible, you know that?" I asked as I followed him.

"Someday soon, Rae, you're not going to run away from whatever you saw on my face that made you clam up." His voice was light, and I wondered how he could know exactly how to speak to the parts of me that were terrified of him.

When I didn't say anything, he simply smiled at me. He swooped down and kissed my cheek before walking out the door.

"I'll call you later, love," he called.

And then the door shut, and my office felt empty and even smaller than usual.

***

Addy had managed to drag me to the park for a run. First thing in the morning. That's how I knew I loved her, because nobody else could have achieved that.

It was a nice morning and the sun was lighting the clouds with pinks and oranges that lifted my soul. Even though I hated the burn in my lungs, I loved seeing Addy running. It was the only time these days that the tension left her shoulders.

She turned to me with a broad, teasing smile.

"Hurry up, slowpoke," she called, casually jogging backwards.

I forced my feet to move a bit faster until we were side-by-side. Addy laughed as I wheezed out an expletive at her.

"You really should do more cardio, Lynnie," Addy said with fake reproach in her voice. "It keeps you young."

"I get plenty of cardio, I promise. Just not running," I winked at her, and she laughed.

"Try any Australian workouts lately?" she said archly.

"Shut up," I grumbled.

She was quiet for a few moments, and I could practically hear the wheels turning in her head.

"Alright, spit it out," I said, trying to keep my breathing steady.

She grinned softly. "You know, he invited me out for coffee the other morning?"

"What?" I stumbled and stopped running, my hands landing on my knees to keep me steady as I stared at her.

"Down girl," she laughed, coming to a stop a few feet in front of me. "Believe it or not, he wasn't prying for info on you. I think he wanted to get to know me because he knows I'm important to you. It was sweet. He's a good guy, Lynnie."

"I know he's a good guy," I groaned.

Addy started walking, giving me no choice but to follow her.

"So, are you gonna tell me what the problem is? From where I'm sitting, he's sweet, funny, ridiculously handsome, and totally into you."

"He's all of the above, and that's the problem."

"What are you talking about, woman?"

"I think I could fall in love with him."

The confession hung in the air. A pair of squirrels chittered, and our shoes crunched the gravel, keeping the silence from getting too heavy. It still seemed stifling to me.

Addy slowed her pace and leveled me with a serious stare.

"Would that be such a bad thing?"

"Of course it would."

"Lynnie," she said softly.

"Don't do that," I sighed. "You know me. I'm not the person that does commitment. I'm the detour that men take when they need a good time and a spank bank memory to look back on thirty years into their boring marriage. And if I fall in love with this man, I will inevitably end up hurting him and getting my own heart broken, and neither of us need that. Johnny is a good man, and he doesn't deserve to be put through me."

Addy watched me through my entire little speech, before rolling her eyes, scoffing, and taking off at a jog again.

I blinked. Addy wasn't the type to react like that when I was trying to be vulnerable, which was a rare occurance. Confused, I raced after her.

"Excuse me, miss missy," I called. "What the hell was that?"

"Me?" she laughed harshly. "What the hell was that whole 'I don't want to put him through me' shit?"

"You've literally known me longer than anyone that I care about," I huffed. She hadn't slowed her pace and was forcing me to keep up with her. "You know I'm no good as a long-term partner."

"No," she snapped angrily. "I don't know that."

"What? Have you been blind our entire relationship?"

"That's exactly it, Lynnie." She was exasperated with me now and stopped abruptly. I wheeled around and tried not to double over to catch my breath again because Addy was glaring at me.

"What's exactly it?"

"Our entire relationship." She looked at me pointedly. "I do know you. I've known you for fourteen or so years, at this point, and I've known you to be nothing but loyal, kind, and a fierce protector for those you love. You're an incredible person and you're not afraid of commitment. You and I have been in a committed relationship for years now. So, it's not that you can't do it, it's that you're scared to."

The stitch in my side flared and I snapped, "Of course I'm fucking scared."

Addy's gaze softened. "What are you so scared of that you can't even bring yourself to talk to the man?"

"Addy, I woke up cuddling with him."

She was quiet for a beat, and I could see her trying not to smile.

"Stop it," I warned. "That is a very, very bad thing for me!"

"What's so bad about waking up next to an Australian demigod and wanting to be held by him?" She cocked an eyebrow. "I want specifics, Raelynn. What specifically was so bad about it?"

"It…the physical aspect of it wasn't the bad part." I tried to corral my thoughts. I hated when Addy got pragmatic on me. It made it so much harder to keep my defenses up. I knew I wasn't being logical, and when she forced me to look at things logically all my arguments sounded silly. "It was the concept of feeling comfortable enough with someone to want to stay in bed with them, okay?"

"Why is it so scary to feel comfortable with him?"

She wasn't going to let this go. God, I loved the girl, but she was annoying as hell sometimes. Especially now that she'd been going to therapy and facing her own demons. She seemed bent on getting me to confront mine. I knew it was coming from a good place, but damn.

She must've seen the frustration on my face, because she sighed and looped her arm through mine.

"You deserve to live the fullest, happiest, most amazing life, Lynnie," her voice was soft. "You've been taking care of me for so many years, and you've been taking care of yourself even longer. I don't want you to lose something that could be an amazing addition to the wonderful life you've made for yourself just because the kid in you is scared of being forgotten at the aquarium."

I blinked as my eyes burned. She'd nailed it, as usual.

"It's easier to be the one that does the forgetting than to be the forgotten one," I said quietly.

"I know." Her hand soothed down my arm as we walked. "Trust me, I know how it feels to be paralyzed by your mind."

"How do you deal with it?" I'd never asked her before.

I never wanted to bring up the hurt and the pain that she'd been through. But Addy was the strongest person I knew. She got out of bed every day and was rebuilding her life brick by brick.

"I finally realized that I would hate myself if I let my life and decisions be ruled by fear." Her gaze didn't leave my face and in her eyes was pure fire and resolution. Strength. "If I let that happen, I would always be scared and weak. Two things that I am decidedly not."

"No, you're definitely not that," I laughed softly with her, and she squeezed my arm.

"Neither are you."

We walked in silence for a long time, each of us wrapped up in our own thoughts.

"How do I let him in, Addy?"

Smiling, she said, "You make his ass work for it, obviously. But you have to choose to let him get close to you. You have to choose to let your feelings for him grow and deepen, otherwise it'll never work no matter how much effort he puts in."

"I have to play the game," I nodded.

"But a different game than you're used to playing," Addy said. "Similar rules apply: both parties need to put in the work, everyone gets what they deserve, and you have to be honest."

"Johnny is winning at this point, isn't he?" I sighed.

"Oh, definitely," Addy laughed. "Are you gonna stand for that?"

Oh, she was good. I was far too competitive to even think about letting Johnny win this game of love.

Shooting Addy a look, I untangled our arms and took off at a sprint.

Johnny wanted to win me over? Fine. But two could play that game. And, if I knew anything about Johnny it was that he was a master. I'd seen it the first night we met.

He wanted to make me fall in love with him. I already was, and I was finally able to admit that to myself.

It was time that I showed Johnny just what it meant to be in love with me. Let's see how well he could keep up.

Chapter Eleven

Raelynn

My packed bag was staring at me from my bed. Taunting me. Mocking me.

You're really going full hopeless romantic, aren't you? It seemed to say. Maybe I was. But if I was going to go all-in with Johnny, then what was the point of waiting around?

I picked up my phone and found his number right near the top of my recent calls. True to his word, he'd been calling me every day, offering me insights into his past. He'd talked to me about his ongoing feud with vegemite, which was apparently a staple of Australian cuisine but one that he still wasn't able to stomach. He'd told me about his favorite place he'd ever traveled - Florence. He'd gone during university as a part of an exchange program studying classical architecture and had completely fallen in love with the place. His favorite sport was rugby, his favorite musician was Paloma Faith, his favorite artist was Monet, and he still couldn't understand the electoral college.

Every day he was proving to me that he was a man of his word. Every day he asked me out on a date – coffee, lunch, a walk.

Something innocuous and no pressure. I never said no, but I hadn't said yes either.

I bit my lip and pressed Call.

The line rang twice before he answered, and I tried not to smile.

"Beautiful, breathtaking, gorgeous Raelynn," his voice was warm. "To what do I owe the pleasure?"

"I was thinking," I started.

"Are we sure that's safe?" he teased.

I rolled my eyes. "Safer than listening to you rattle off compliments like you're reading them from a thesaurus."

"I'm hurt, Rae," he put some sadness into his voice. I could picture him with big puppy dog eyes and a hand over his heart. So dramatic. "I would hope you'd know me enough by now to realize that I have a comprehensive list of compliments ready to unleash on you at any given moment. I don't need a book to help me with that."

"Yeah, yeah, you went to college, big whoop."

He laughed and the sound sent a thrill down to my toes. Dear God, I needed to get myself together.

"So, before I so rudely interrupted you," he said. "You were thinking?"

I took a deep breath. Now or never.

"Coffee and lunch seem so…blasé, don't you think?"

He paused for a moment before responding, "I would have gone with traditional. Where are you heading with this?"

"I really enjoy Mexican food."

"So, dinner then?"

"That was where my mind was going." I bit my lip, hesitating.

"It sounds like you've got a spot in mind, love."

Here went nothing.

"There's this little restaurant on Isla Mujeres, down in Mexico. Great margaritas, and it's right on the beach so the seafood is really fresh. What do you think?"

He wasn't breathing. I could tell. I could practically hear the gears whirring as he tried to make sense of what I'd said.

After a very long, tense moment, I heard him chuckle. The sound was deep and low, with a darker edge to it. It made a smile creep onto my face.

Gametime.

"Are you whisking me away to Mexico?"

"Well," I drew the word out and found myself leaning up against the counter, like I would if he were standing in the room with me. "I was whisking myself away to Mexico and thought you might not be terrible company."

I expected him to laugh in that carefree way that he did, but instead the energy over the phone intensified.

"Raelynn." He drew my name out, which sent tingles down my body. This was going to be fun. "Are you asking me on a date?"

"I'm asking you to accompany me on a quick trip to Mexico for the weekend," I sighed, pretending to be annoyed. "If you're not up for it, that's fine."

"Oh, I think you'll realize soon that I'm up for anything when it comes to you."

"So, am I booking two tickets?"

He was quiet for a moment, letting me wait.

"Book them."

I grinned but tried not to let it come through in my voice.

"You sure you can handle an entire weekend alone with me?"

"Raelynn, I've been trying to get some alone time with you for weeks now. If your crazy ass wants that to be in Mexico, there's no way I'm saying no."

I couldn't keep the excitement out of my voice anymore. "Meet me in front of my office Friday. Can you get Monday off?"

"I might just come down with something over the weekend," he laughed. "The boss doesn't have to know. I want all the time with you that I can get."

"Trust me, you'll be sick of me by Saturday."

"Putting me through the ringer then? Bring it on." I could hear the smile on his face and knew that it matched my own.

"I'll send you your ticket tomorrow morning once I book everything."

"Let me know what I owe you. I'm good for it." If he were here, he would have winked, I just knew it.

"I'll cover flights and lodging if you cover meals, how about that?"

I wasn't one to keep a tab. The way I figured, if someone was in your life long enough then it all evened out in the end. I blinked when I realized this was me assuming Johnny would be around awhile.

"You know I'd pay for the whole thing if I didn't think you already had the hookup for great ticket prices and hotel rates."

"Don't get your gentlemanly knickers in a twist," I teased.

"Excuse me, I don't wear knickers. I am a proud briefs man."

I couldn't stop myself from laughing. Johnny joined me, and as I listened to his warm baritone something in my soul settled. It felt right, this moment. Talking and joking and laughing with this man as we planned an impromptu trip to Mexico.

Johnny was unlike anyone I had ever met. I was terrified of my growing feelings for him, but I had never been one to let myself be ruled by my fears.

I was a woman who grabbed her fears by the balls and twisted until they ran back to the insecure caves they came from.

116

Our laughter subsided and a comfortable silence fell between us. There was so much I wanted to say, but I knew it wasn't the time. That's not how this worked. Johnny seemed to recognize it as well, because he let out a sigh.

"I'll call you tomorrow, yeah?" he finally said.

"I just might answer," I bluffed. We both knew that I hadn't missed a single one of his calls.

"Goodnight, Rae," he laughed and then hung up before I could say anything.

I stared at my blank phone screen, a million thoughts running through my mind. Finally, I couldn't stop the huge smile that broke out across my face.

I dialed another number and waited for them to pick up. When they did, I didn't waste any time with pleasantries.

"Brendan, I need two tickets to Cancun for this weekend. We'll be staying on Isla Mujeres."

Ten minutes later, the tickets, hotel confirmation, and itinerary were in my email.

***

Trying to stay focused at work with the upcoming trip proved to be almost pointless. By Thursday, I was so wound up that I had considered not going into the office at all. What was the point in owning your own business if you couldn't decide when you worked, right? The problem with that line of thinking was that I wouldn't have any money if I never went in to work. Discipline and self-control won out, and I found my feet dragging into the office.

I'd just set my bag down on my desk when the bell over the door jingled.

I looked up and Laura was there. I gave her a big smile, which dropped when a young woman stepped out from behind her.

She was in her early twenties, petite and delicate. My throat closed when I saw the signs of abuse that marked her body. Her cheek was swollen, with stitches holding the skin together, a dark purple bruise surrounded her eye, and one of her lips was puffy. There were faint bruises along the side of her neck that instantly enraged me, and sporadic cuts and marks in several different shades along her arms. She glanced around the room quickly before her eyes settled on me. They were tired and wary.

"Come on in ladies," I said, regaining my composure.

The girl went to sit in one of the chairs in front of my desk, but Laura stopped her.

"We're going to go to the back office," I explained, giving her a warm smile. "Laura, can you take our guest to the back, and I'll make some tea."

Laura squeezed my arm as they passed me, and I took a steadying breath. It was always hard for me to see a woman in that state, but she didn't need pity in this moment. She needed support and action.

After locking the front door and putting out the closed sign, I quickly boiled some water and steeped some chamomile tea with honey. Balancing the three cups carefully, I made my way back to the more secure office that I kept.

It had been a decently large storage closet, which meant it was small for an office, but the clients that I met with here were usually in a rush, so efficiency was more important than space.

I handed the ladies their tea and closed the door behind me. I secured the three deadbolts and booted up the television on the wall that was linked to the security camera I had outside. I'd placed the TV so that everyone in the room could see it.

The extra deadbolts and security feed had been a hard lesson. I'd been working with a woman to relocate herself and her children, and she had come to the office to pick up her travel documents. Her husband had followed her, and when he'd seen her come into my office, he'd lost it. He smashed through the door and would have put his wife in the hospital again if I hadn't pepper sprayed him.

After that, I fortified my back office to give everyone a little more peace of mind. The women that came to me from Angels were usually terrified, exhausted, and distrustful, so I tried my best to show them that they had support and that they were safe.

"I hope you like chamomile," I said gently. "It helps with anxiety, and it should help the inflammation as well."

"Thank you." The young woman's voice was scratchy.

"This is Jenny," Laura said. "Jenny, this is Raelynn. She helps us out with relocating women in situations like yours to safe places around the country."

"Nice to meet you, Jenny," I smiled.

She lifted her gaze from the steaming tea and searched my face.

"He only did it once," she said. Her tone was defensive, and I knew her guard was up.

"You're brave for leaving," I said, keeping eye contact. "Many women stay."

She swallowed and her eyes got watery. "My dad hit my mom a lot. I swore I'd never let myself be in a relationship like that."

I nodded, not pushing for anything more.

"Do you have any family that you can stay with where you'd be safe?" I asked.

Usually, if they were sitting across from me the answer to that was no. If it came down to me finding a place for them, they were usually going through the entire terrible ordeal alone and needed a completely fresh start.

"I have an aunt," she said slowly, as if she weren't sure she wanted to say it. "She lives in Maine, and she's been no-contact with my mom for the majority of my life. She didn't approve of my mom staying with my dad and raising me in that house. Can't say I blame her."

"Do you have a way for us to contact her?"

Jenny shook her head, her hair falling over her face. She winced and moved it back, and I saw handprint bruises around her wrists.

If I ever saw the man who did this to her, I'd kill him myself.

"That's not a problem." I gave her a confident smile. "If you can give me her full name, I'll track her down and reach out to see if she'd be willing to take you in."

When Jenny looked at me again, tears were tracing down her cheeks.

"You'd do that? I thought you just set up travel arrangements?"

I gave her a confidential smile. "I am going to do whatever needs to be done to keep you safe, Jenny. Don't you worry about a thing."

"Jenny, you'll stay in one of our safe houses until Raelynn can contact your aunt," Laura said. "Does that sound okay?"

Jenny nodded, and then her eyes got big. Her breathing shallowed, coming in quick gasps.

"I can't let my job know that I'm leaving, because he could go by and ask about me," Jenny choked out. "And I can't go home to get any of my clothes, or my things. I'll have no money, nothing to my name. He's taken everything from me."

I moved over to kneel in front of Jenny, my hand resting on hers. I rubbed a soft circle across the back of her hand until I saw her breathing start to match the pace of my thumb. Laura held her shoulders and spoke gently to her, coaching her through the panic attack. After a few minutes, she was calmer.

She looked at me with pure desperation.

"Jenny, as long as you keep fighting him and taking care of yourself, he doesn't win. You are brave and strong and a fighter, and those are things he can never take from you."

I watched her process my words before she broke down in tears again, throwing her arms around me.

Laura and I held her as she cried, and when Jenny was finally ready to let go, neither of us moved far.

"Annie Rose Fitzgerald," Jenny said. "She lives in Wiscasset, Maine."

I smoothed her hair back from her face gently. "I'll find her, I promise."

"I don't even know if she'll take me."

"Trust me, Jenny, Miss Raelynn is exceedingly persuasive," Laura said, earning her a soft laugh from Jenny.

I got a few more details as Jenny sipped her tea. I checked the security camera before we left the office. Nobody had come by, and there were no cars on the street other than Laura's BMW.

Laura said she'd call me as she guided Jenny out the door and into the back seat. I hoped that Jenny felt better after meeting with me. I hoped that she knew she was on the path to safety.

I watched Laura pull away with a small wave, and then turned to go back into my office and nearly had a heart attack.

"Johnny, you scared the crap out of me," I admonished.

Johnny was leaning against the entrance, a concerned look on his face.

"Sorry, love," he sounded sincere. "Who was that?"

"Some clients," I said shortly.

"That poor girl looked like she'd been beaten to hell and back." His demeanor was calm, but his voice betrayed his anger.

"Let's go inside."

We were quiet as we went into the office. I didn't feel like dealing with the general public at the moment, so I locked the door behind us and led Johnny to the small kitchenette. It was behind a wall, so anybody that passed by wouldn't see anyone inside the office.

The problem with this plan, I quickly learned, was that the space was far too small for two people. Johnny's presence overwhelmed me, but I found myself wanting to escape into it instead of run away.

"What exactly is it you do for this charity?" Johnny asked.

His expression was soft, but I could see the concern lingering in his eyes.

"I help relocate women who need to get far away from their abusers," I said softly. "Either they can't afford a lengthy court case, or the police didn't take them seriously. These women know that their abusers will hunt them down wherever they go, so many of them need to disappear."

"And with your connections in the travel industry, along with your fierce protectiveness and tenacity, I'm sure you work miracles for these women," Johnny said quietly.

I gave him a tired smile. "I wouldn't go that far."

"You're doing more than most people would," Johnny pressed. "You care. And that in and of itself is a miracle these days."

His eyes were warm and full of wonder as he looked at me, and it made my stomach turn. He didn't know enough about me to be looking at me like that. He didn't know the troubled I'd caused, the life I'd led. He saw me as a bleeding heart hero.

"After Addy was attacked, I blamed myself," I said.

Johnny looked quizzically at me, but didn't say anything.

"I should have known what Derek was. I had a bad feeling about him from the jump, but I didn't stop it because I wanted Addy to be a little reckless. Like me. I've always been the risk-taker in our friendship, and I just wanted her to follow her heart instead of her

122

head. Just once. And I fucked it up. I know that taking the trauma that someone else went through and making it about me is possibly the most horrendous thing I could do, but it wrecked me to see her so broken. Every time I watch her enter a room, my heart breaks for her."

"I noticed that," he said.

"And I blame myself for it, still," I whispered, my throat tightening around tears I wouldn't allow. "I met Dr. Laura through Addy. She's part of the governing board of Angels Are Around. I started volunteering, just little things. Cleaning up the safe houses, helping to stock them with clothes and toiletries, running donation campaigns, that sort of thing. One thing led to another, and suddenly I found myself helping to discreetly relocate a few women because I was the only one that could. It hasn't made my guilt go away, but at least I feel like I'm doing something to make a difference."

Johnny was quiet for a long moment. With anyone else, the silence would have gone too long to be comfortable, but I appreciated that he was letting my words settle.

Finally, he reached out and took my hand. He watched me carefully as he gently pulled me towards him. I didn't stop him as he wrapped his arms around me and held me close.

It was more comforting than anything he could have said. Sometimes words weren't what was needed. I found myself relaxing into his warmth and I was rewarded with him holding me tighter.

Maybe he did know me. Or maybe I wanted to be the person that Johnny thought I was. My emotions were all over the place, and when he pulled back to look at me I thought I might pass out. His eyes were burning. No one had ever looked at me like that before.

Men had looked at me with lust, desire, fascination, greed, hunger, and rage, but never had a man looked at me like he was ready to fight the world to protect me.

123

My eyes drank in his expression, and the moment they dropped to his lips he let out a small sigh.

I couldn't stop myself as I pushed myself up onto my toes and kissed him.

I really had been trying to hold off on physical affection until after this weekend. I wanted this to be different than relationships I'd had in the past, almost all of which were based on pure physical attraction. But I doubt any woman could have resisted that face with those burning eyes.

It took less than a second for Johnny to take control of the kiss. He growled in victory as his hands framed my cheeks and he tilted my head. He traced my lips with his tongue, and I was helpless to resist. He tasted like mint and honey as he explored my mouth. He stole my breath, and when he finally pulled away it was to rain soft kisses along my cheeks and nose, before resting his forehead against mine.

"Just as perfect as I remembered," he whispered.

I wanted to laugh, or say something snarky, but my head was dizzy. Johnny was the only thing keeping me upright.

Finally, my dignity came back to me, and I pushed away from him a bit. He didn't let me go, but he allowed the space.

"I didn't mean to do that," I admitted.

"I could tell," he laughed. "Though, I won't lie to you, I've been wanting to do that for weeks."

"This doesn't go any further than that though," I said sternly. "This weekend is not some sex-cation just because we've kissed."

"I'm shocked you think so lowly of me, Rae."

"It's not a low opinion, it's a blanket rule for the both of us." I rolled my eyes, and he laughed.

"I understand," he grinned cheekily at me. "You're reminding yourself to keep your greedy hands off the goods, is that it?"

"You call me greedy an awful lot."

"I call it like I see it, love."

I was going to end up with a constant headache from rolling my eyes at this ridiculous man.

"Don't worry," his voice dropped, and he pulled me close again. "You be as greedy as you want. I'll never stop giving you everything I have."

I gazed up at him and tried to take in the fact that he was completely serious. He was all in on this, which was mind-boggling to me.

He was watching my face intently, so he saw the exact moment I began to panic. He laughed softly and dropped a sweet kiss to my forehead before letting me go.

"I originally dropped by to see what I needed to pack," he said. He opened a cupboard and began perusing my mug collection.

"Clothes."

He stuck his tongue out at me and eyed a light pink mug that said "You Go Girl" on the side.

"Preferably more than a few," I quipped.

"Life with you will never be boring, will it?"

"Life doesn't come with guarantees, but that's a pretty sure bet," I laughed.

"Alrighty then." He closed the cupboard and turned back to me. "Speedos and long-johns it is."

"You didn't come to get a packing list."

He chuckled low in his chest and gave me his best innocent look. "Guilty."

"So, why did you come by?"

"Would it be cringy for me to say that I just couldn't wait until tomorrow to see you?"

"Ugh, yes, so cringy," I fake gagged and he laughed.

"Well then, I guess I'm just gross like that." His voice was warm.

"I've been really excited about this weekend," I admitted.

"Oh, really? I'm starting to wiggle my way into that ginormous heart of yours, then?"

"I'm excited for the beach and the food," I sniffed.

"Ah, well, that makes perfect sense. I did some reading on this little island you're whisking me away to, and it looks heavenly."

"It's one of my favorite places on the planet."

"See, what I love about that phrase in your mouth, is that I believe you," Johnny said, going back to opening drawers. "When most people say that somewhere is their favorite place on the planet, they've never gone further than their town line. But you have actual experience to qualify that statement."

"I could say the same about you."

"Peas in a pod, darling."

"You throw around a lot of endearments for someone so chronically single."

"Well, the plan is to end that streak sometime soon, so I think I'll continue to play heavy-handed with the well-deserved pet names, pet."

I wrinkled my nose, and he caught the look and laughed.

"Okay, not pet then."

"Never pet."

"Some chicks are into that sort of thing."

"I'm not just some chick, though, right?"

He turned and gave me his full attention. My tone hadn't changed, but he'd still managed to hear the very real fear that prompted my last question. I didn't know how he knew, but he knew.

He came over to where I was leaning against the opposite counter and boxed me in with his arms, his eyes level with mine.

"You're unlike any person I've ever met, Raelynn."

126

I tried not to make my gulp too obvious, but his smirk told me I'd failed. It turned into a full-blown grin as he leaned in and kissed my cheek quickly before turning and heading back to the front of the office.

I sat for a moment, trying to process. In one breath he'd been reassuring me, and the next he'd disappeared. Whiplash.

"I'll meet you here tomorrow at three, right?" He called, forcing me to walk quickly to where he was making a beeline for the front door.

"That's what's on the itinerary," I snarked.

"I'll see you tomorrow, Rae."

"Make sure you pack appropriately please," I sighed.

"Speedos only, then, got it!"

And then the bell over my door was jingling and he was gone.

I looked at the clock and it was barely ten in the morning. My day had hardly started, and I was exhausted. I couldn't wait for this well-deserved vacation.

Chapter Twelve

Johnny

The fact that I had to wait until Friday afternoon to see Rae again was torture. After seeing how emotional she'd been talking about her work with the charity, and the fact that she was actually beginning to open up to me, I was going crazy for the woman. I had already known she was fiercely loyal and protective of the people that she cared for, but to see that her love extended to perfect strangers. She was truly remarkable.

I could see that her opinion of herself was tarnished by her past, but I was hoping that this trip would allow her to see how genuine I was in my feelings for her.

I could almost hear my dad mocking me as I thought about feelings. He'd always told me that real men hid their feelings. That it was our job to be strong, stable, and resolute. He was all for that old school macho man crap, and my entire life I'd resented him for it.

It had taken me years to be comfortable expressing myself, and I knew that a lot of the time my expression was still too flirty or sarcastic.

I had never been as real with anyone as I was with Rae. There was something about her, and I knew that if I wasn't completely and totally honest, she'd see right through me. That was it. When she looked at me, I knew that she saw through the years of defenses that I'd built up to protect myself. She flayed me open, and if she was already doing that then what was the point in hiding myself from her?

More than that, I didn't want to hide. I wanted her to know every single part of me, even the ones I hated.

I was beyond thrilled that she'd invited me to Mexico. I'd heard the anxiousness in her voice when she'd called and had been worried that she was going to tell me to fuck off. Instead, she'd offered an impromptu trip out of the country. I felt like it was test, of sorts. She was telling me who she was. Someone who got a craving for seafood on a little island and took off for the weekend. I had a feeling most of the men who'd courted her hadn't been able to keep up, but she was in for a surprise. I'd renewed my passport the year before and got double miles on my black card. It had taken every bit of my self-control not to take over the trip planning. I would have to ease her into being taken care of. She'd been taking care of herself a long time, but once we were all in on this I wanted to show her that I was more than happy to take some of that weight for her. Raelynn was about to learn what being spoiled meant.

I chuckled to myself thinking about her face when I'd mentioned only packing a Speedo. I did have one. It had been a gag gift for my birthday a few years ago from my buddy.

I threw it in my suitcase just to fuck with Rae.

I also packed some light linen pants and nicer button-downs, my favorite tee shirt, and the other essentials. I wasn't the most stylish guy, but I knew how to pull together a few looks. In my work, I had to be presentable, and I enjoyed going out dancing, so I wasn't a complete slob in the wardrobe department.

I wondered what Raelynn was going to pack. My mind immediately created an image of her lounging on the sand in the world's smallest bikini. God, I had no idea how I was going to get through this weekend without touching her. But I had to.

She was setting the pace for this. I was still reeling a bit from that kiss in her office. I'd waited so long to taste her again, and it was torture when we'd pulled away. A knife in the gut when she'd said this weekend wouldn't progress past that. But I wasn't going to push her. My feelings for her went so far beyond just a physical attraction, and I knew that wasn't her history, so it was my job to behave. I stayed up way too late the night before, running through every possible scenario this weekend might bring. I didn't want to be caught off guard and lose myself.

When I woke Friday morning, my head was groggy. Not the best way to start the day.

I looked at my phone and saw the countdown I'd put on it. Ten hours, twenty minutes, and seven seconds until I would meet Rae outside her office.

What to do until then?

***

I ended up at the warehouse we were just beginning to break ground on. After a few miserable weeks of jumping through every governmental hoop imaginable, we were finally moving forward. I technically was off work, but I liked to check in every so often on current projects to make sure they were going smoothly.

The interior was gutted, only the structural beams showing. It was a little painful to see such a wonderfully old building broken down like this, but I knew that the end result was going to be beautiful. This was such a great space, and if the right business moved in it would be an amazing addition to the town. I could imagine people gathering to eat and drink. It'd be the perfect spot for a local watering hole.

I ran my hand along the brick windowsill. I was a firm believer that buildings held energy. Dad would say to knock it off with that woo woo shit, but what else could explain the feeling of gravity that settled over me whenever I walked into an old building?

I'd worked on a lot of projects over my career, but historic buildings were my favorite. Especially in a place like Hartworth. There was no denying the history of this place. Hundreds of people over the past few hundred years had lived and worked and existed there, and each of them left a bit of themselves in the wood and the brick and the stone floor. It was a privilege to be able to preserve and restore as much of that history as possible, and it was a task I didn't take lightly.

"Hey, Boss," Ferndando, our foreman, greeted me.

"Fernando, man, how many times do I have to tell you not to call me boss?"

"Well, if you're not the boss then it's Brett, and his ego is big enough as it is," Fernando laughed.

"What do you call Brett then?" I asked.

"Amigo."

"There are worse alternatives," I laughed with him. "How's the structure looking?"

"It's got some good bones." He cast his gaze up at the exposed beams. "There's still a lot of demo we need to get through, especially in the back space. There was some fire damage at some point that wasn't fully addressed, just patched up and repainted."

"You're kidding me," I groaned. "Anything structural?"

"Luckily no. We should be able to get everything cleared out by the end of next week."

"That's great, I can't wait to see it."

"You going to be checking in over the weekend?" Fernando asked. He knew my habit of stopping by even when I didn't need to.

"You're free of me this weekend, mate," I laughed. "I'll be out of town."

"Where are you heading?"

"Mexico, actually. I'm going with a girl."

Fernando got a sly grin on his face. "No better place to woo a woman than my homeland."

"We're going to Isla Mujeres and trust me I fully intend on taking every romantic advantage I can," I gave him a wide smile and a wink.

"Good man." Fernando clapped me on the shoulder. "Now, get out. My men need to work without the boss looking over their shoulder."

With a wave to the rest of the crew, I made my way outside. The warehouse was in Downtown Hartworth. There was a big town green that ran along the back of the buildings, with a fountain that kids would play in on hotter days. There was always something going on, and today it was a small craft fair.

I wandered through the booths, taking my time and enjoying chatting with vendors. There was a burly, bearded man who made scented soaps, and a group of kids who were selling jars of wildflower seeds.

I spent a lot of time looking at handcrafted, blown glass flowers.

"Each individual flower is fifteen, but you can put together a bouquet of eight for eighty," the guy selling them said after he'd watched me peruse for a moment.

"Oh, that's great."

"The lilies and daisies look great together."

132

"I appreciate that, mate," I gave him a smile. "I'm thinking of getting some for my girl. I went overboard buying her live flowers, and she gave them all away. I wanted to try again with something that showed a bit more…permanence."

"You'll want to go with these then." He reached down behind the table he was standing at and pulled out an intricate bouquet of blue irises. "They're a bit more expensive, but they're a symbol of trust in a lot of cultures."

I couldn't take my eyes off them. They refracted the light beautifully. The edges were sharp and pristine, almost lethal looking, but the petals themselves curved softly and created beautiful movement. They reminded me so much of Raelynn that I had to laugh.

I didn't hesitate. I pulled out my wallet and bought them without a second thought.

I'd taken as much time as I could, but I found myself buzzing with a need to see Raelynn.

Ten minutes later, I was parking in front of her office. I carefully took the boxed flowers from the car and tried to hide my smile as the bell jingled when I went inside.

"You're early."

I could practically hear her rolling her eyes as she came around the corner from the kitchenette.

"Do you ever actually sit at your desk?" I asked.

"Shut up, Aussie," she laughed. I wish I could have bottled that laughter to take out when I needed a pick-me-up.

"I take it you're not ready then?"

"You're *two hours* early!"

"Well, I got you something and I couldn't wait to give it to you," I winked as I set the box down on her desk.

"Will this something fit in a carry-on?" She cocked an eyebrow at me.

"It's for your office."

"Do I get a hint as to what's in the box?"

"Let's just say it's take two."

Her brow furrowed and my heart stopped when a sweet, excited smile flashed across her face.

Her delicate fingers untied the ribbon, and the walls of the box fell to reveal the bouquet, complete with a stunning matching vase.

Her eyes widened and her jaw dropped into an adorable O shape. She traced the shape of a petal with one fingertip, and then her gaze shot up to me.

"You didn't like that I gave away your other flowers, did you?"

"No, I didn't," I laughed.

I walked around her desk to stand next to her, loving how big her eyes got when she glanced up at me.

"Irises are apparently a symbol of loyalty," I said softly. "I wanted to get you something that would never fade or die."

"The symbolism wasn't lost on me." She was trying to be snarky, but her tone was too soft.

I swooped down and planted a quick kiss on her cheek, and she swatted me away.

"If you throw these away, I'll just have to escalate next time," I warned.

She rolled her eyes, and I bit back the urge to grab her and kiss her senseless. For some reason, whenever she decided to sass me, the lizard part of my brain threatened to take over and treat her so well that she wouldn't even think about being anything but sweet to me.

I settled for sneaking another peck to her other cheek, which earned me a smile.

134

"Are you all packed?" She asked, her gaze drifting back to her flowers.

"Seven varieties of Speedo are cozy in my carry-on."

"I hope you're joking."

"You'll just have to find out."

She looked up at me and her eyes were sparkling. She liked me, and I was determined to get her comfortable with that idea this weekend.

She gave a small sigh and looked around the office.

"Well, I'm clearly not going to get anything more done today. Want to head to the airport early, maybe get something to eat? I know the head chef at Parisienne, so the food will be free."

"I was never really one for French food, but whatever my girl wants she gets." I winked and then turned and started packing her things up for her.

"Excuse me, sir, you have no idea what needs to come with and what needs to stay." When I looked at her, she had one hand on her hip. God, that attitude was going to be my undoing.

"Then get packing." I stepped back and watched as she began grabbing the same things I'd been going for and sticking them in her bag.

She whirled around the room, flicking switches and grabbing various items, until finally she stopped in front of the flowers. She cradled one in her hand, and I didn't think my heart could take the look of wonder on her face.

"These are the most beautiful gift anyone has ever given me." Her voice was small, and she didn't look at me when she said it, so I knew it was an important admission.

"You deserve so much more," I said softly, moving next to her and cupping her face so that she met my gaze. "This weekend is just the start, love. I'm going to shower you with gifts and compliments and love until you're dizzy."

She was quiet for a long moment, her eyes searching my face. Finally, she rolled her eyes and laughed.

"If you didn't have that accent, you'd almost sound like a stalker, weirdo."

I laughed with her and looped her arm through mine.

"Let's get this weekend started." My excitement was barely contained as I reveled in three full days of uninterrupted time with my girl.

Chapter Thirteen

Raelynn

Isla Mujeres was one of my favorite places on Earth. The water was always crystal clear and the most vivid shade of blue. The air was humid and warm and felt like a cozy blanket instead of oppressive, like the heat of the South often did.

I'd been four times before, but going with Johnny was like seeing everything for the first time.

He didn't hide his excitement. He took in everything with a huge grin on his face, and when he turned it on me it felt like my heart was glowing. He also didn't let me do anything.

I thought this would annoy me, but he didn't lord it over me or make me feel inferior. Instead, he made it clear that he was taking care of things because I deserved to be taken care of. He carried my bags, opened doors, hailed the cab, and even got us discounted ferry tickets by conversing with the desk agent in fluent Spanish. He was full of mysteries, confident, and doting.

By the time we made it to the hotel, I was fighting the swoon. Hard.

Johnny scanned the key and opened the door, sweeping his arm to usher me in. He was so over-the-top sometimes, but I found myself thinking it was charming instead of obnoxious. What was this man doing to me?

"What do you think?" I asked, watching him as he set our things down and beelined for the balcony.

"Rae, it's gorgeous," he said, flinging open the French doors. A pleasant breeze swirled through the room, ruffling the skirt of my sundress that I'd put on as soon as we'd landed.

Johnny turned around and his eyes grew wide. His mouth dropped open a bit, but instead of saying anything he just stared at me.

I held his gaze, and as I did the thousands of thoughts that had been buzzing through my brain suddenly stopped. The only thought that was still bouncing around in there was the fact that Johnny and I were alone in a room with a bed for the first time in a long time. My skin flushed as my horny brain remembered exactly how it felt to be the center of Johnny's intense attention. His fingers skimming up my thighs, his lips tracing their way down my neck.

A shiver trickled down my spine.

Johnny's gaze sharpened as he tracked the movement.

"I can close the door if you're cold," he smirked, knowing full-well that the breeze was too warm.

"Shut up."

"One of these days that sass is going to get you in trouble." His tone left no room for argument, so I busied myself with hoisting my suitcase onto the bed and beginning to rifle through it.

Silence permeated the room, and I felt it settle on my shoulders. I was suddenly regretting suggesting this weekend. There was nowhere for me to run. I couldn't hide anything from this man, and being under his scrutiny terrified me. I didn't know what he would see of me this weekend, but I hoped it wouldn't be a disappointment.

"You don't have to be afraid of me," Johnny said softly.

I'd been so wrapped up in my head that I hadn't realized he had come up behind me. His voice was soft, and when I turned to look at him, he had a small smile.

"Who said I was afraid of you?"

His gaze warmed and he took my hand, leading me over to the couch.

He didn't let go of my hand as we settled, our knees brushing.

"I can't imagine what your past has been," he started. "You're clearly an exceptionally intelligent, independent, indescribably attractive woman, so men must have thrown themselves at you your entire life. You have nothing to go on with me that would tell you I'll be different. But I want to prove it to you. I'm not going to ask you for anything, there are no expectations on this trip. I just want to be with you. The only thing I ask is that you're honest with me. Can you do that?"

The knot in my chest tightened for a moment, but the longer I held Johnny's hand and let his warmth run through me, the calmer I felt.

Maybe that was why Johnny never annoyed me. For all his machismo and jokes, at his core he was a good man who, for some reason, truly cared for me. When he was around, something in my soul settled.

"Honest?" I asked.

He laughed softly. "I don't really think that's too much to ask, is it?"

He was right. The only way this would work was if we were totally open with each other. No secrets, no hiding behind games and wordplay. Vulnerable.

"Well, honestly," I blew out a long breath, "I want you to kiss me again, but I'm afraid that if you do that then I'll lose all of my resolve, and we'll spend the entire weekend in this room."

"While I wouldn't say no to that, it doesn't sound like that's a resounding yes on your part." He quirked an eyebrow and his smile grew. "How about this. Let's get dinner, go for a walk on the beach, and then we'll reevaluate the kiss."

I bit my lip, trying to hide my smile.

"There she is," Johnny grinned. "C'mon, this girl I know told me about this great shack on the beach."

He held my hand all the way down, and only let it go to open the cab door for me.

***

The sand was warm and soft between my toes. I was walking right along the waterline, the water covering my feet every few waves. Johnny was walking next to me, holding our shoes with one hand, his other intertwined with mine.

"I don't think anyone with a lick of common sense would agree with that," Johnny said, a laugh in his voice.

"You don't need common sense to understand that, objectively, Odysseus would beat Herakles in a one-on-one fight."

"Odysseus went through one thing! There were literally twelve trials for Herakles. Not to mention he had superhuman strength."

"But you forget that brains will trump brawn almost every time," I said. "Odysseus was clever, and clever is more helpful than brute strength."

"Not in a straight fist fight," Johnny said.

I glared at him and pulled my hand away to cross my arms over my chest.

140

"Aww, come on, love, don't pout."

"I'm not pouting," I said, definitely in full pout mode.

It worked exactly like I wanted, and the next thing I knew I heard our shoes thump on the sand and he was wrapping his arms around me and spinning us.

I found myself giggling as he set me down and turned me to him, his hands coming up to frame my face.

"Beautiful women shouldn't pout," he said. "It'll give you wrinkles, and then you won't be beautiful anymore."

My eyes widened and when I went to smack his arm, he wrapped me in a tight hug so that I couldn't move.

"You know I'm kidding," his voice was low in my ear. "You'll be beautiful when you're wrinkly, stooped, and bald."

"That's a bit too much," I laughed.

"Ah, but it's the truth, Rae." He pulled back and held my gaze. "I think you're gorgeous inside and out, so even if the outside changes you'll always be beautiful to me."

My heart was pounding so loudly in my chest that it drowned out the waves.

His lips quirked in a small smile as he watched a myriad of emotions run across my face, before I finally landed on sad. Then he was all seriousness.

"What did I say?" He panicked.

"Nothing bad," I said softly. "I've been called beautiful by a lot of men in my life, but you're the first one I've actually believed."

His answering smile was blinding, and suddenly my feet weren't on the ground. He'd scooped me into his arms and was racing us into the water.

"Johnny!" I screamed in surprise as he threw us into a wave.

As I came up for air, I saw him laughing a few feet away. I splashed him, which only made him laugh harder as he swam over and took me in his arms. The water came up to his waist, and while we could both stand, he made a point to hold me close as if I couldn't.

"I know you don't like me saying this, but I'm falling so hard for you, Raelynn," his words were warm in my chest.

I looked up at him. Salt water was dripping from the ends of his hair and the moonlight sparkled in his eyes. He looked at me like I was the only thing that existed. He made me feel like I was the only thing that existed.

When I was with Johnny, every little thing that I did was noticed. He saw when I had an itch on my nose. He saw when my leg was starting to go numb from sitting with them crossed. He saw when I overheard someone saying something stupid. I knew he saw these things because he'd told me throughout our travels. Moment to moment, he was always watching me, taking in my every move and mood. He wanted to know everything about me, and in a relatively short time he'd grown to know me better than almost anyone else in my life.

In this moment, he saw my eyes dart to his lips and linger, remembering their give and take against my own. I saw the hunger flash across his face, but he was staying true to his word and letting me lead.

For the second time that week, I couldn't stop myself.

My fingers laced behind his neck, and I pulled him down, crashing our lips together. He immediately caved and devoured me. My legs wrapped around his waist, and he held me so close I could feel his heart beating in time with mine.

The kiss wasn't gentle. It was ravenous, languid, possessive, and sweet. Our bodies pushed and pulled in time with the tide. When we finally broke apart, I couldn't tell if it had been minutes or lifetimes.

He ducked back and peppered kisses along my cheeks and my jaw. My eyes closed, and he lavished attention to my neck, drawing small moans from the depths of my soul.

Dammit. I knew I shouldn't have suggested this weekend.

Now there was no going back.

I lifted my head and found Johnny smiling wickedly down at me.

"C'mon love, let's get you out of those wet clothes."

I groaned and rolled my eyes. "Did you drag us in here just so you could use that line?"

"I can neither confirm nor deny," he laughed, setting me down and wrapping his arm around my waist to keep me steady as we made our way out of the water.

We wandered our way back to the hotel, dripping sea water across the lobby and all the way to our room. Our hands never stopped roaming. Light caresses and touches every few moments, as if neither of us were sure this was real.

We were quiet as we stepped inside, and I watched Johnny carefully lock the door before he turned back to me. We didn't turn any lights on, but the moon was bright enough that I could see him perfectly.

He held my gaze as he slowly lifted his shirt over his head and let it drop to the floor. He closed the distance between us and placed a soft kiss on my forehead before turning me around and unzipping my dress. The sound was like thunder in the quiet room, and I felt heat starting to creep up my chest.

He took his time, sliding one strap down my shoulder and following it with his lips. Then the other side, before he slid my dress down and let it pool on the floor.

"I thought I'd imagined how stunning you were," he breathed, turning me to face him.

He drank in the sight of me, and I couldn't stop my hands from skimming his chest. The hair there was soft and light, and the heat radiating from him seemed to travel through my bones.

He grinned quickly before sliding an arm under my knees and lifting me to his chest. I loved how physical he was with me. He understood that I wasn't fragile, and he didn't treat me like he was going to break me. He tossed me on the bed, his smile growing more wicked as he watched me bounce before climbing on top of me, caging me with his limbs.

"Enthusiastic consent, love," he breathed, tracing a line from my collarbone to the hollow behind my ear, sending shivers down my body.

"Are you seriously asking me if I want you?" I'd meant it to come out scathing, but my breathiness undercut the sass.

"You've been driving this bus, Rae." He pulled back to look at me. "You're setting the pace, and until I hear from those lips exactly what you want to happen, I'm happy to stay right here."

He accented his point by kissing along the pulse in my neck, his lips agonizingly slow.

I reached up to try to pull his face up to mine, but he caught my wrist and pinned it to the bed.

"Use your words." The command made goosebumps break out along my arms.

"Just –" I huffed, unable to form a sentence as he dipped his head and nipped my ear.

"Just what?"

I took a breath to steady myself. Johnny knew how to play the game, but so did I. I caught his gaze and reveled in the way he froze when I smiled.

"Just take your time," I breathed, relishing the way he hung onto every word. "Kiss every inch of my body. Strip for me. Tease me

144

and don't stop, no matter how much I beg. I want to feel your lips and your tongue on my pussy, and I want to come apart on them before you get close to fucking me like I know you want to."

The groan he let out was feral as he captured my lips.

He was better than I remembered. Our bodies were synchronized as he did everything I asked for. His fingers and tongue teased me, bringing me to the edge again and again but never letting me crash over it, until finally, he did.

As I was floating, he crawled up my body and kissed me again. So deeply that I could taste myself. I writhed underneath him, sated but not quite, and he chuckled when my legs wrapped around him.

Somewhere in between trailing kisses down one leg and up the other, he'd lost his pants and put on a condom, so every inch of him was hot and ready, and my needy body was impatient.

"Rae, look at me," his voice was gentle but firm, and it focused my attention, drawing me out of the haze.

His eyes were bright, and his cheeks were flushed. I reached up a hand and pushed his hair away from his head. His eyes closed at the touch and my heart melted a bit more.

He refocused on me and his gaze was a combination of sinister and sweet.

"If we do this, there's no going back, you know that right?" he asked.

I took a moment to focus on the air moving between us, the warmth of our shared breath, the sound of the ocean through the windows and the light breeze.

"I know."

His eyes never left my face as he slowly entered me. I gasped, but didn't break his gaze, letting him see everything he was doing to me.

I'd never had such an intimate moment of connection with a man before. There was nothing unsaid between us, even if words hadn't been exchanged. He knew how I felt about him now.

Like he said, there was no going back.

Chapter Fourteen

Raelynn

The weekend in Mexico had definitely been a mistake, because by the end of it I couldn't deny that I was in love with the man.

After that first night, we were ravenous for each other, but Johnny made it a point to make sure we still made it out of the room to explore the island. We went snorkeling, swam with dolphins, and feasted on as much fresh seafood as we could find. He took me dancing and bought me everything I showed even a minor interest in. I finally had to cut him off before I was forced to buy another suitcase just for souvenirs.

I hadn't realized how much he'd been holding back while he waited for me to get my shit together. He was relentless in his attention with me. He always had a hand on me. Holding mine, resting on my back, tucked around my shoulder, gently holding the nape of my neck. And he snuck kisses whenever he could.

All of this should have overwhelmed me. I hated clingy guys, and I loved my personal space. Maybe it was the honeymoon phase of it all, but I couldn't stop touching him either. I loved feeling the confirmation that he was really there with me. That I wasn't dreaming him. Though, even in my wildest dreams, I never would have pictured Johnny.

Whenever I had ever taken the time to picture a long-term relationship, which wasn't often, I had always assumed I'd end up with someone passive. Someone who would follow along on whatever adventures I cooked up, or who would be fine with staying behind.

Johnny was the exact opposite of passive. He was along for the ride but wanted to be an equal participant. For every adventure I suggested, he had one to offer right back. And when I didn't feel like leaving the hotel room, he lavished me with such attention that I was tempted to never leave the room again. He insisted on taking care of me. Bringing me coffee in bed, running baths for me, brushing my hair. He couldn't seem to stop himself.

"I'm a big girl, you know?" I told him as he hoisted my bag into the overhead bin of the airplane.

We were on our way home. I had more mixed emotions about leaving Isla Mujeres than I'd thought I would. The weekend had been perfect, but it had been a bubble. It wasn't real life. I didn't know how I'd do when we returned to the monotony of our daily lives. What if the vacation haze wore off and Johnny realized how much work it took to be with me? What if I couldn't work through my issues fast enough and he got fed up?

"Yes, you're a strong, independent woman who doesn't need anyone to take care of her," Johnny said with a sly smile.

"Exactly."

"Which is why it's so fun to force you to relax while I get to revel in the honor."

He swooped down and kissed me, hot and quick. Before the people waiting behind us could complain, he ushered me into the window seat and slid in next to me.

148

"Tell me, Rae," he leaned in so that his lips were at my ear, "isn't it nicer to have me take care of some things? Doesn't it free up some space in that big, beautiful brain of yours?"

I wanted to roll my eyes, but he was right. Him taking care of the simple things gave me space to think about everything else. It moved things along, and I was more relaxed than I'd been in a long time.

The thing that nobody talks about when it comes to being single for a long time is how much energy it takes to do everything that needs to get done.

I'd traveled solo for most of my life. I had always been the one that kept track of my travel time to the airport. The decision to check a bag or not usually came down to whether I wanted to lug a carry-on and a purse through security. If I did have a carry-on, I would usually stick it in the first open overhead spot available because it was easier to grab quickly on the way off the plane, and if I ever struggled with it a flight attendant was right there to help. Aside from the physical, I was always hyper aware of everything that was going on around me. I kept track of the other passengers on the plane, where the flight attendants were at all times. Going through the airport, I moved quickly and with purpose, taking as little time to get from point A to point B as possible.

That was just flying. There were a million other things I had to be aware of when I was somewhere new.

In day-to-day life, I was in charge of everything. Dirty dishes in the sink? My job to make sure they got done. There was always the toss-up of carrying in seven bags of groceries at once and risking not being able to open the front door, or having to make multiple trips, which was, quite frankly, exhausting. Some days, even the simple decision of what to have for dinner was overwhelming, because at that point I had already had to decide so many other things throughout the day.

I loved being single. I loved the freedom it allowed me. I loved my independence, and Johnny was right. I didn't *need* anyone to take care of me.

But I could also admit that it was nice to have someone to carry my bag if I asked. In Johnny's case, I hadn't asked, but he'd grabbed it anyway when he'd seen me rub some tension from my neck.

I twisted to look into his eyes, which were glittering with mischief.

"Just don't forget that I survived a long time without you." I pointed a finger at him sternly.

"I'm completely superfluous, understood."

I couldn't stop the eye roll that time, and heat rippled down my back when his gaze darkened. His hand trailed lightly up my arm, to my neck, before it settled, cupping my jaw.

"What did I tell you about the eye roll, love?" His voice was deliciously low in my ear.

"I don't remember."

He looked at me for a long moment before placing the softest kiss on my lips and releasing my chin.

"We'll have to remedy that later, then."

The promise in his voice sent a needy shiver through me, which, of course he saw. A grin split his face and then he swooped in for one more kiss, distracting me while he secured my seat belt for me.

We were quiet through the safety presentation, but his hand settled on my thigh. It was heavy and warm, and oddly comforting. I was by no means a nervous flyer, but Johnny was proving to me every moment that he was there for me, and that was causing all sorts of emotions to stir.

The flight wasn't long, just a few hours, but we filled it with conversation. Johnny wanted to know everything about me, and I wanted the same from him. I'd been accused in the past of being

150

pushy and invasive with my questions sometimes, but Johnny answered every single one fully and with care. He wasn't bothered by my poking, and instead would come back at me with some tough, personal questions of his own.

"Who do you like more, your mum or your dad?" he finally asked after I'd explained the family dynamics and most of my relationship with each of my siblings and parents.

I blinked. I'd never really thought in those terms, which parent was my favorite.

"It sounds horrible to pick a favorite, doesn't it?" I asked back.

"To some people, but not to me. Both of my parents were shit, but my dad at least did put more effort into building some kind of relationship with me after I moved to Australia. Mum was just..." He trailed off and seemed to disappear into his memories.

"Do you want to talk about her?" I asked softly.

He looked at me and his gaze warmed. "Answer my question and then I'll answer yours. Deal?"

I laughed under my breath but nodded.

"I think I like my dad more," I admitted. "With my Mom I always feel like I'm trying to impress her and constantly falling short. She's always disappointed in me, and I really feel like she forgets about me sometimes. But Dad always makes sure to tell me that he's happy I'm around, when I go around. And sometimes he'll sneak me treats when nobody else is looking. He was the only one in the family that called me when I opened my business to congratulate me."

Johnny nodded and laced our fingers together. He looked down at our hands for a long moment before he blew out a breath.

"My Mum had a lot of mental issues," he began. "She didn't really have any support after Dad left, and so I think she saw me less as her child and more as her sounding board. She used to fall into these lows that would last for weeks. She wouldn't eat, wouldn't

151

shower, wouldn't even change her clothes. She'd just lay in bed and cry. I remember the first time it happened I had no idea what to do."

"How old were you?"

"I was four, I think?"

"Johnny, that's so young," my voice was soft.

"It had probably happened before that, but I don't remember. That first memory of seeing her like that, though…I could never see her differently. Even when she was up, happy and sweet and caring, I always knew that a low would be just around the corner," he sighed and squeezed my hand.

"The week before she killed herself, she was the best Mum in the world. She bought me new clothes, made breakfast every day, played games with me each night."

He was quiet for a long moment, his eyes unfocused. I couldn't imagine what he must have been reliving, but he never let go of my hand.

"I hate her for making me find her like that," he admitted. His voice was hoarse.

"Johnny." I didn't know what to say.

He offered me a small, sad smile. I cupped his cheek, and he leaned into my touch, his eyes closing for just a second.

"I've worked a lot with my therapist to realize that two things can be true, Rae," he finally said, his eyes blazing into mine.

"What do you mean?"

"My Mum was a bad mother, and I loved her dearly."

My throat closed and I felt tears pricking at my eyes.

"My parents love me, and they don't really like me," I said.

He touched his forehead to mine and we sat like that until the flight attendant came over the speakers to announce we were preparing to land.

***

I looked around my apartment and sighed. Something was off.

Johnny had dropped me off with the longest goodbye kiss and a promise to call me before he went to sleep. True to his word, he'd called about an hour later. That was two hours ago now.

I'd been aimlessly wandering around my home for the past ten minutes, trying to figure out what was different.

On the surface, nothing had changed. The blanket was still thrown carelessly over the back of the couch, my shoes were lined up by the front door, the grocery list on the fridge was still waiting to be filled out. But it felt...wrong.

I huffed in annoyance and pulled out my phone to call Addy.

She picked up after two rings, sounding a bit breathless.

"Did I catch you doing something naughty?" I grinned.

"Of course not." I could practically hear her eyes rolling. "I just finished a conditioning video."

"Ahh yes, your newfound obsession with kicking ass."

"How was Mexico? You obviously didn't call just to tease me about my ongoing struggle to build stamina."

I bit my lip, not sure where to start. Addy, knowing me for as long as she had, became immediately suspicious of my silence.

"You fell in love with him, didn't you?" Her voice was soft, but there was an edge of excitement to it.

More silence on my end. How to even explain what I felt for Johnny?

"It's okay to say it out loud, you know?" Addy said.

I took a deep breath and finally spoke. "Yes, I fell in love with him. Or, realized I'd been falling in love with him this whole time, I guess?"

Addy squealed and I winced, pulling the phone back a touch.

"Sorry, I know I'm not the loud one in our relationship, but Lynnie this is *big!*"

"I feel like I've totally lost my edge," I sighed, flopping down onto the couch.

"How do you mean?"

"Johnny just…takes care of things," I started. "He takes care of me. And he's so open with his feelings for me. I don't have to work or play games or manipulate him to get a view into what he's thinking. He just tells me. And he never pushes me for more than I'm ready to give him. It's like he can read my mind, Addy. It's freaky."

"It's scary, you mean," she corrected me, right as usual.

"Yeah," I paused. "It's terrifying, actually."

"That makes total sense." Addy was back to her usual pragmatic and logical self. "You are the master at reading people, so having someone that close to you that can flip all of your tricks on you must be unsettling."

"My apartment doesn't feel right," I admitted.

Addy was quiet for a second, trying to decipher the jump in topic, before she let out a, "What?"

I laughed, a little embarrassed. "I don't know. It just doesn't feel right. It feels like something's missing that was never missing before."

"Could it possibly be missing a rather tall, scrumptious Australian man?"

"No," I protested. "It's got to be something else. One weekend away with the guy wouldn't have me pining for him to move in, that would be ridiculous."

"Love is a bit ridiculous," Addy said softly. "Real love, that is. And you can't really pretend like your feelings for him came completely out of the blue. You were three steps in love with the guy after your first night together. That's why you ran him off so fast."

"I don't pine for men, Addy."

"No, you don't," she agreed. "But you've pined for Johnny before, and it's sounding like you're doing it again. Only this time, he hasn't disappeared."

"I don't know how to do this."

Addy didn't say anything for a long time, and I was starting to get nervous when she finally sighed.

"Nobody does. But Johnny seems like he's willing to go on the journey of figuring it out with you. You have to try though."

I wanted to argue with her, but she was right. I'd suggested Mexico because I was trying to make an effort. And Johnny had surpassed all of my expectations. Not only had he agreed to the trip without a second thought, he'd made every single second of it amazing.

Addy waited for me to come to the obvious conclusion, which was nice of her. If our roles had been reversed, I would have been screaming at her to get her pretty head out of her ass and just commit to the guy already.

"Okay, fine," I finally sighed.

"Good girlie," Addy laughed. "Now, I need to get some water and stretch. Call your boyfriend."

"Gross," I wrinkled my nose at the term. "Love you babe."

"Love you, too."

She hung up and I looked around my apartment again.

I hated when she was right.

Chapter Fifteen

Johnny

The last person I'd expected to find when someone knocked on my door at two in the morning was Raelynn. Yet, there she was. Not even a full day after we'd returned from the most wonderful weekend, and she was standing outside my apartment.

Her hair was wild, and she was in her pajamas, like she'd come here straight from bed. Considering the hour, she probably had. Immediately, my heart rate kicked up and concern flooded my senses.

"Rae, what's going on?" I tried to keep the panic out of my voice. "Is everything alright?"

"I've been trying to sleep all night," she said, frustration flashing across her face. "I couldn't stop thinking about you."

The unease that had been creeping up my spine melted, replaced with a smug satisfaction and a bit of awe.

"Dirty thoughts, I hope."

"Those were peppered in," she grumbled, shoving past me and into the room.

I watched her take in the sparse décor and the cool color palette that the landlords had settled on. There were no personal items of my own. I was a light traveler, with very few sentimental things. I had one picture of my mother, father, and me when I was probably two, a photo album that my college friends had given me at graduation with photos from our adventures over the years, and a throw blanket that I'd bought my first week in Australia, because my dad hadn't had any spare linens for my room.

She glanced around and when she turned back to me her arms were crossed over her chest with one eyebrow raised.

"I pack light," I explained. "My job takes me around, and I've never had a reason to call any one place home."

She nodded, but her mind seemed elsewhere.

I approached her and slowly took her elbows, pulling her arms apart so that she would wrap them around me. I held her for a long time, until I felt her relax into my touch. I couldn't help my smile at that. I loved having this girl in my arms, and I loved even more that she trusted me.

"Tell me what's going on, Rae."

"I can't explain it," she sighed into my chest. "I mean, I can eventually, but right now I need you to just take me to bed so that I can sleep."

She looked up at me and her eyes were sparkling with so many emotions that my heart physically hurt.

"Please," she whispered when I didn't immediately say anything.

I smiled softly down at the miracle woman that had fallen into my life. Didn't she know that all she ever had to do was ask and I would give her anything she wanted?

I scooped her into my arms and cradled her to my chest, pressing a soft kiss to her forehead.

I held her tightly all the way to the bedroom and then settled her down, pulling the covers back and crawling in beside her. I tugged her until she was curled against me, her dark hair spilling over my

157

shoulder as her head rested on my chest. Her delicate fingers traced up my chest, drawing nonsense patterns.

I ran my hand up and down her back, listening to her breathing.

Finally, her fingers stilled, and her breaths became long and soft.

I glanced down and saw her eyelashes fluttering against her cheek.

I had always thought it would be exceptionally creepy to watch someone sleep, and maybe it was, but I loved watching Raelynn. She was so peaceful and relaxed.

I knew the toll it took, looking after yourself your entire life. We were two people who, though our lives had been very different, had experienced the same loneliness. The same desperate urge to prove that we didn't need anybody to take care of us. Who had been convinced, somewhere along the line, that we weren't worth loving, so we'd love ourselves enough to make up for it.

I couldn't speak for the enchanting woman in my arms, but I couldn't quite believe that I'd found someone who understood me. Who saw me for exactly who I was and hadn't run away.

Well, she had at first, but she seemed hell-bent on trying not to this time. In her defense, I hadn't put up much of a fight a year ago either.

I squeezed her tighter as I thought of all the time we'd lost because we were so scared.

"I love you," I whispered.

I knew she couldn't hear me, and I knew I'd said it before. But this time, more than ever, I meant it with every bit of my soul.

***

I didn't know what she liked for breakfast, so I decided on everything. I got up early, leaving Raelynn blissfully asleep in my

158

bed. She would never admit this, but for such a small woman she was a massive bed-hog. I'd left her sprawled out over two-thirds of the Queen-size mattress. Her hair was knotted, her legs were tangled around the blankets, and she had one arm tucked under a pillow and the other draped over the edge of the bed. She was beautiful chaos, even in sleep.

I was just finishing scrambling some eggs when I heard her soft footsteps down the hall. I turned and watched her rub her eyes, and I thought my heart would explode.

"Good morning, gorgeous," I sang, pulling the pan off the stove and dumping the steaming eggs onto a plate.

"How are you so chipper this early in the morning?" Her voice was groggy and cranky. Not a morning person then. Good to know.

"I thought you might be hungry when you woke up, so I made breakfast."

I brought the eggs and the pitcher of orange juice over to the table where the rest of the meal was laid out.

"You realize that two people can't possibly eat all of this?" She eyed the spread.

"I'll admit, I might've gone overboard," I chuckled.

Pancakes, waffles, bacon, sausage, toast with butter and jam options, eggs, bagels, raspberries, and strawberries decorated the kitchen table. I'd also managed to find some flowers outside, which sat neatly in the center.

Raelynn stood with her hands resting on the back of a kitchen chair, staring at the food. She looked lost.

"You don't have to eat it all," I said softly. "You don't have to eat any of it if you don't like."

She was quiet for a moment before she turned to me.

"Nobody has ever done anything like this for me before," she said.

No wonder she'd looked so bewildered for a second there. I crossed the room and took her in my arms, kissing her deeply.

Kissing Raelynn was my favorite thing in the world. The way she immediately surrendered to my lips, letting me devour her, never failed to drive me crazy. But, it *was* first thing in the morning, so I tried to control myself. I pulled back and then kissed her once more, chastely, before catching her gaze.

"You deserve to be treated like a queen," I said sincerely.

"So do you."

I grinned cheekily at her. "Trust me, I am the biggest queen you'll ever meet, and I don't let anyone forget it."

"Smartass," she huffed, rolling her eyes. "I mean you deserve to be treated like a king."

"A pair of royal pains in the ass, that's us." I nipped at her nose and she giggled.

"I don't deserve the way you spoil me."

I leveled her with a serious look.

"I want you to hear me when I say this, okay?"

She nodded, her eyes locked on mine.

"You and I both deserve this love. We both deserve every beautiful thing that's going to come with it. You deserve all of the attention and gifts and trips and ridiculous breakfast spreads that I could ever give you. Do you believe me?"

She bit her lip, and I watched as tears welled up in her eyes. My own widened. Shit. I didn't mean to make her cry.

"Rae, what's going on in that head of yours?"

"I want to believe you." Her words came out small and I hated it. "And I do *know* that I deserve to be treated well. It's just battling the years of conditioning that convinced me otherwise."

I smiled and pulled her in for a hug, resting my head on hers.

"I know what you mean," I said. "And we'll navigate all of that together, yeah? But for today, let's glutton ourselves on breakfast foods and then work it all off."

She blushed faintly and I grinned, stealing her lips for another kiss.

***

We spent the entire day together. We weren't supposed to, both of us should have gone to work, but we couldn't tear ourselves apart. I made good on my promise and after breakfast we spent another few hours in bed, exploring every inch of each other.

I knew I'd just spent an entire weekend with Raelynn, but I wasn't sure I'd ever have enough time with her. I loved seeing her in my space. Granted, it wasn't a permanent home, but I'd grown comfortable there and it thrilled me to see her relaxing on the couch with a blanket thrown over her lap.

Raelynn was a walking contradiction of a woman. She was tender and soft and demanding and needy and impatient and wicked and shy, somehow all at once.

She was currently telling me a story about sewing all of her brother's socks together because he had tattled on her in high school.

"Marcus has always been such a goody-goody," she sighed. "Someone had to keep him grounded."

"It sounds like he was trying to look out for you," I said with a laugh.

"That's the problem, though," she pointed at me with a serious look on her face. "Everyone likes to act like they want to help take care of me, but when push comes to shove, and I actually need help nobody is around."

I digested her words as I played with the frayed edge of the blanket. Raelynn's feet were resting on my lap, and the late afternoon sun gave the room a cozy glow.

"I know what you mean," I finally said.

Her gaze sharpened and I knew she was remembering what I had told her about my mum.

"You do, don't you?"

I caught her eye and smiled, though it held a hint of the sorrow that I always felt thinking about my childhood.

"I wished so much when I was younger for a brother," I admitted. "I thought about a sister a few times, but didn't think girls were worth the trouble." She laughed and it sent warmth through my chest. "But a brother? I would have done anything for a brother. Someone who could look out for me when I needed it. Someone who understood the crazy that went on in that house. Someone who wouldn't leave me."

Rae crawled over and settled herself against my side, lacing our fingers together.

"I guess I was pretty lucky," she said. "I have too many siblings for only one to care about me like Marcus does, but at least I have him. And it's not like my other siblings don't care at all. They're just…apathetic. Like, I'm an acquaintance, more than anything. But we still all commiserate over our parents, and it does bond us. I can't imagine you having to deal with all of that by yourself."

"It made me who I am," I shrugged, giving her the nonchalant answer I'd rehearsed my entire life.

"But don't you ever imagine who you could have been if you hadn't had to go through all of that?"

"Yeah," I nodded. "I do."

"Don't get me wrong," she said, looking up at me with those eyes. "I love who you are now, but I hate that you had to go through life thinking you were all alone."

A slow smile spread across my face. She blinked at me in confusion, clearly having missed the significance of what she'd just said.

"Raelynn Rogers, did you just tell me you love me?"

Her eyes grew wide and she paled a bit. Yeah, she hadn't meant to say that. I couldn't help my growing smile as I cupped her neck and kissed her.

When I pulled away, she looked dazed and a bit embarrassed.

"It's okay," I whispered, my lips grazing hers. "I love you, too."

"Yeah, but you say it all the time," she groaned, though I could feel the drum of her pulse against my palm.

"Yes, but now we both have said it without thinking, which means we really mean it," I kissed her nose, and she sighed dramatically.

"There'll really be no getting rid of you after this, will there?"

"Not even death, my dear."

"Promises, promises," she muttered, her cheeks still red. I knew sarcasm was her defense mechanism, but I needed her to know how serious I was.

I slid off the couch and knelt in front of her, both her hands in mine.

"I do promise, actually," I said. "I know I will love you beyond the end of my life. It's okay if you're a little less sure. You love me, and that's all I need."

She was quiet for a long moment, staring at our hands. I watched her chest rising and falling, trying to keep my breathing in sync with hers so that I didn't panic that she wasn't saying anything. It wasn't a proposal, but it was a promise.

Finally, her gaze met mine and she smiled, lighting up the room and my heart.

"I am sure," she said softly. "And I promise, too. In fact…"

She slid off the couch and knelt next to me.

"This might be absolutely insane." She took a deep breath, and it felt like she stole it directly from my lungs. "Johnny Harris, will you marry me?"

Of all the things she could have said, of all the ways today could have gone, I would never have imagined being proposed to by the most perfect woman on the planet.

"Of course I will," I said.

She laughed and launched herself at me, knocking us both down in a tangle of blanket and limbs. She peppered kisses along my jaw and my neck, straddling me before taking my lips in hers. We kissed endlessly, both of us refusing to come up for air any longer than necessary.

Finally, the fire coursing through my blood was too frenzied. I flipped us over, making her squeal in delight, and traced a line down her neck with my nose. She shivered and her breaths became pants. Her hands grabbed at my shirt, lifting it. I sat up and tore it off before sliding hers off as well. I needed to feel her skin, to be close to her.

She was intoxicatingly beautiful, laid out beneath me, her body needy and wanting and craving me. She was made for me. From the roots of her hair to the polish on her toes, she was perfection.

She pulled me down and captured my lips again and again, and just as my brain was about to short-circuit from desire I pulled away.

"Get back down here," she ordered, a pout on those red lips.

"One thing I need to clarify first," I laughed.

"No thinking," she whined.

"Just a bit, I promise."

164

"Fine," she said, rolling her eyes. I became impossibly harder, and she smirked a bit. She knew what that did to me, and she would pay for it, but in a moment.

I took a breath to calm my raging hormones a bit before making sure I had her full attention.

"I'm as impulsive as the next man, you know that," I started. "But I have to make sure you really want this. My parents got married out of convenience and obligation, and I promised myself I would never do that. Now, I'm all in. I hope I've made that perfectly clear. But I need you to be one thousand percent sure."

Her hand drifted up my arm to caress my face as her eyes searched mine. I was glad she was taking the time to think it through, as painful as the waiting was.

"I know it might seem fast, or impulsive," she said slowly. "But I have never denied myself the things that I want. I see a life with you, Johnny. We've got a ton of shit to work through, obviously, but I *want* to work through it with you. I want you in my life. I believe you that you're all in. I'm all in too, more than you could possibly know. And I want it official."

"So that I can't run away from you?" I said it lightly, but I knew that was at the heart of this for her.

She wanted my promise in writing, and I was more than happy to oblige.

"And so that I can't run away from you," she said.

"Then let's get married," I grinned, leaning down to kiss her again.

It took no time for us to find our rhythm again, our bodies moving deliciously with each other as the want and need took over. Before long, I was sliding into her slowly, relishing the shudder that went through her and the way her thighs clenched around my waist.

She was utter perfection.

I watched every emotion pass over her face as she came apart beneath me. I held her through it, whispering over and over again how much I loved her. With each repetition, I felt my heart expanding, encompassing a feeling I had never dreamed to feel.

Raelynn was going to be my wife.

Chapter Sixteen

Raelynn

I stared at my pale finger for the seventh time that day. Soon, it would be sparkling with a ring that would signify to the world that I was capable of loving someone. And, boy oh boy, was I utterly and madly in love with the ridiculous Australian man that was my now-fiancé.

I still wasn't sure what had made me propose. Addy had laid into me for half an hour about how "you don't just get married on a whim". But it wasn't a whim. Johnny was it for me. We'd work out all the messy details later. Finally, Addy had calmed down enough to congratulate me.

"This was your idea, pretty much, you know that right?" I asked her.

"In what *world* could this be construed as my idea?" she'd demanded.

"You're the one who told me I had to try."

"I meant try dating the guy!"

"Well, you know I don't do anything halfway," I'd shrugged.

I'd left her grumbling to herself about booking an extra appointment with Dr. Laura.

Sitting in my office chair, I nearly jumped out of my skin when the bell above the door rang. I had to get better at paying attention, and spend less time daydreaming about my Australian.

I spun around and found Jenny looking at me carefully.

"Jenny, hi, come on in," I said, getting up from my seat and ushering her in before turning around and locking the door. I pulled the blinds too, just to be safe. "How can I help you?"

"I was wondering if my travel documents were ready yet?" Her voice was small, like asking was taking every ounce of courage she had.

"Nearly." I gave her a warm smile. "I was able to get in contact with your aunt, Annie, and she seemed happy that you wanted to stay with her. She wished it was under better circumstances, but she wanted me to make sure to tell you that she's very proud of you for leaving. For doing what your mother couldn't."

Jenny blinked at me a few times before tears began streaming down her face. I quickly handed her a tissue and went to kneel beside her.

"I haven't spoken to Aunt Annie in years, and she's just willing to take me in no problems?" Jenny hiccoughed.

I nodded, resting my hand on hers. "Some people are just full of love for us, even when we don't fully love ourselves."

She cried for another few minutes while I just held her. Finally, she straightened and took a deep breath, dabbing at her eyes with a fresh tissue.

"When can I go?"

I went back to my computer and checked a few things, making sure everything was on track.

"We'll have your new license and passport issued in about a week. We've taken care of legally changing your last name to match your aunt's, so even if he wanted to find you, he wouldn't know what

168

name to start looking with. Those documents are the last things we're waiting on, and then I'll book the flights, and we'll get you to your aunt."

"One more week," she sighed.

"I know it's hard, living this half-life in hiding, but it will be worth it once you're free. I promise."

My second heavy promise in two days. I was usually in the "make no promises, tell no lies" camp, but apparently love had turned me into a mushy optimist. Still, Jenny was safe at the Angels house, we had been collecting money through a secure donation site to get Jenny set up for a few months while she settled in with her aunt, and I had Brendan waiting on standby to book me three tickets under her new name at a moment's notice. Two would be decoys and one for her actual destination.

Jenny smiled at me and beneath the still healing bruises I saw the first glimmer of hope in her eyes. She was strong, she'd get through this.

That's when voices outside broke through the silence of the office. I was watching Jenny's face and saw the moment fear flooded her eyes.

"Andrew," she barely breathed, fear etched in every line of her face. She was ghostly pale and frozen.

I took a deep breath. Unfortunately for me, this wasn't the first time an abuser had found their way to my office. Unfortunately for them, it meant that I was prepared.

"Jenny, come on, we're going to the back office," I said quietly.

I took her arm gently and as we passed my desk, I hit the panic button that was installed underneath. The police would be here in three minutes. I hurried Jenny into the back office and settled her behind the desk.

"Don't move, okay? I'm going to lock you in, and nobody else can unlock this room from the outside but me, so you'll be safe here. The police are on their way, and I'll call Laura and have her meet us here once it's safe."

"Where are you going?" Jenny's eyes were wide with panic.

"I'm going to make sure everything is okay outside. I'll be okay, I promise." Another promise.

Before she could argue with me, I closed the door and pressed my ring finger on my right hand to the biometric lock, which locked all three deadbolts.

I grabbed the bat that I kept in the kitchen and hurried back to the front, where the voices were still yelling. But no glass was broken, so that was good.

I unlocked the door and stepped outside, pulling in enough air to try to sound as intimidating as possible.

"I've called the police, and they're on their way, so everybody stop yelling," I commanded.

"Don't you fucking tell me what to do, you bitch," a burly twenty-something year old with buzzed dark hair and arms the size of tree trunks snarled, whipping around to face me when he heard my voice.

"Mate, that's no way to talk to a lady."

My heart stuttered. Oh no.

Johnny grabbed the kid by his massive arm and locked it behind his back, effectively pinning the young guy against him so he couldn't move.

How had I not recognized Johnny's voice in all that shouting? I must have been so focused on getting Jenny to safety.

The kid's muscles weren't all for show, and he threw an elbow back, knocking the air out of Johnny's lungs. He doubled over with a groan and the kid turned to stalk towards me.

I held up the bat and refused to back down. Men like him enjoyed seeing fear in women, and I wasn't about to give him that. My heart was pounding and rage was bitter in my mouth. I tightened my grip, ready to smash the bat as hard as I could into this punk.

Just as he was about to reach out and grab me, sirens filled the street and three cop cars screeched to a stop, surrounding the sidewalk.

The kid, Andrew, immediately held up his hands, panic and fear on his face.

The air filled with shouting, and it was difficult to separate the different commands that were being thrown around. Andrew dropped to the ground, and I managed to loosen my grip on the bat, letting it fall to the sidewalk with a clatter.

Johnny and I both held our hands in the air, waiting for the mayhem to settle. After a few moments, it did. We were facing each other on the sidewalk, and I couldn't take my eyes from him.

His face was pale, his eyes wide, and he couldn't seem to tear his gaze from me. His chest was heaving and for a moment I thought he was going to pass out. Then, his mouth set in a firm line and his eyes hardened. Was he upset with *me*? He couldn't be. I must've been misreading his look.

After a long, tense moment, an officer grabbed Andrew from the ground while another two took me and Johnny aside, their grip on our arms a little too firm. It took every ounce of my self-control not to snap at the officer holding me, but I knew it wouldn't help anything.

"Tell me what happened," the officer holding Johnny demanded.

He was older, and he kept his voice even. I could tell he already knew what had happened, but he needed to make sure.

"I'm the owner of this business," I explained, holding the officer's gaze steadily though my heart was racing. "That man is the abusive ex-boyfriend of my client. We heard him show up and he was shouting and angry, so I hit my panic button. When I came out, Johnny was trying to keep Andrew from getting inside. It got heated and Andrew came after me, so Johnny grabbed him. Andrew hit him and then kept coming after me, and that's when you all showed up."

The officer's eyes softened, though the hard lines of his face did not.

"Where is your client?"

"I have a panic room inside. She's there, waiting for me."

His level gaze turned to Johnny. "What's your role in all of this, son? Random good Samaritan?"

"I was on my way to visit my fiancée," Johnny said, a small smirk on his face which he quickly tried to school. It almost made me giggle but realized that wouldn't give us much credibility with the officer.

"You're his fiancée?"

"I am, sir," I said softly. I couldn't stop the smile that stole over my face. I guess I shouldn't have been so quick to judge Johnny. It was hard not to smile at that stupid word. I cast a glance over to my Australian, but he was refusing to meet my gaze.

The officer was quiet for a moment, and then he nodded and the cop gripping my arm released me.

"We'll need official statements from both of you, and from your client, miss," the older man said. "Mind letting us in?"

I looked at the two officers and quickly made a decision.

"My client's situation is delicate, so I would prefer only one officer come inside, if possible," I said.

The older officer held my gaze before giving a single nod and turning to his comrade.

"Take this young man's statement, I'll go inside and get the statements from the ladies." There was no room for argument, and I breathed a small sigh of relief.

One cop would be easier to digest than a whole swarm, and I wanted Jenny to feel safe. As we turned to go into the building, I saw Laura running full tilt towards us.

"Wait," she called.

As she approached, another officer stepped in to hold her back. I turned and explained the situation to the officer I was with, who spoke into his radio. Then Laura was walking quickly to us.

"Raelynn, are you alright?"

"How did you know to come?" I asked. "I was going to call you in a second."

"I heard it on the scanner, and I recognized your address," she explained.

"You have a police scanner?"

Laura turned with a single raised eyebrow to the officer standing behind me. "It's not illegal, Officer…?"

"Sargeant. Hitchins," his tone was slightly amused. "And you're correct, it's not illegal, though it's a bit suspicious."

"Let's go inside and we'll explain everything," I said, suddenly very tired.

I herded the two into the office. Officer Hitchins looked at me curiously when I closed and locked the door behind us.

"I would leave it unlocked, Rae," Laura said softly. "It'll be okay, we're safe."

I shook my head. "I didn't even think about it, sorry."

I left Laura and Sargeant Hitchins in the front while I went to the back and unlocked the office door.

Jenny was curled in the corner on the floor, her knees drawn to her chest and silent tears streaming down her face. When the door

173

opened, her eyes flashed to mine full of fear before relief flooded her gaze.

"Thank God you're okay," she breathed, standing quickly. She was hugging me before I could blink, and I held her while her shakes eventually subsided.

"Jenny, there's an officer in the front office that needs to take our statements," I said softly.

Her face dropped. Then her shoulders squared and she nodded once. Strong woman.

"Sargeant Hitchins, this is Jenny," I introduced.

Laura gave Jenny a quick hug, and Hitchins offered his hand. I didn't miss the way his eyes clocked every healing bruise on her face and arms, and the anger that flashed across his face. Good. That was the only correct response.

"Jenny, I'll try to make this quick," he said, his voice warm and gentle. "I just need you to tell me what happened before the incident outside."

It took twenty minutes for Jenny and I to give our statements to the satisfaction of Hitchins. He left, but not before pulling me aside.

"Here's my card," he said. "I would love to hear more about why this young lady came to see you. Not just her in particular, but generally why someone would come to see you." His gaze was heavy with unspoken thoughts. "I'd like to help, if I can."

I smiled at him and his eyes lightened in response. "I'd love to talk with you more about what we do, Sargeant."

He grinned back at me, and for the first time I felt like I was seeing who he really was.

"Let's go see about your young man, shall we?"

Johnny was standing in front of the window, his foot tapping impatiently as a younger officer continued to question him.

"Jessup, what's the hold up?" Hitchins asked, authority back in his voice. "This young man was providing a public service. Wrap up the interview."

"Of course, sir," Officer Jessup said sheepishly. "Sorry to take so much of your time, sir."

Johnny waved a hand, a jovial but practiced smile on his face.

"No worries mate."

Then, I was wrapped in his arms. He squeezed me as if it was the last time we'd ever touch, and I melted into him. He pulled back to cradle my face in his hands.

"Don't you ever do that to me again," he demanded, his voice low and his eyes dark.

"I can't make any promises."

"Rae." His tone left no room for argument.

"I'm not being stubborn," I sighed. "But this kind of stuff happens sometimes, and I will always defend the people I care about. So, I can't promise I won't stare down some asshole and stand my ground if he's threatening me. I can't do that."

He took a deep breath and closed his eyes as he let it out.

He needed to understand that I wasn't going to turn into some frail damsel in distress just because he was capable of carrying my bags through the airport. My regard for my own self-preservation might not be as high as he would like it to be, but I'd always been this way. I wasn't changing who I was. He could either love all of me, or none of me.

"You're infuriating," he ground out. "But you're right."

I blinked up at him. His answer surprised me, which was a very difficult thing to do.

He held my gaze and his thumbs rubbed soothingly along my cheekbones.

"I don't want you to be anything other than the fierce, wild, amazing woman that I fell in love with," he said softly. "That woman is fully capable of taking care of herself. I just ask that you do your best to recognize when you might get hurt and do everything you can to not let that happen, okay?"

I laughed, something warm and fuzzy trickling through my veins.

"I'll try," I said.

He kissed me gently and it stole my breath. Not because it was intensely passionate, like so many of our kisses were. No, this was something else. He was kissing me because he was happy I was okay. He was kissing me to reassure himself that I was still there with him. It was slow and sweet and almost chaste. The kind of kiss that Victorian girls would ruminate on for years. I had never been kissed like this, and I could already hear Addy calling me a hopeless romantic, but I didn't care.

I loved this man.

"I'll get you, you bitch."

The harsh words cut through the haze of romance and doused me in cold water.

Our heads whipped towards the cop car where Andrew was being unceremoniously ushered. Hatred curdled his features, and his eyes were trained on me.

Before he could say anything else, the door slammed in his face. He kept staring at me until the car drove away, leaving a cold vice around my lungs.

I'd been threatened by men before, but I had never been afraid that they would follow through. My mind began racing.

Andrew wouldn't serve serious time for this. Nothing had been broken, nobody had really been hurt. He hadn't even come into my place of work. The worst they might get him on was a violation of a restraining order, but even then with the right judge it wouldn't be more than a fine.

He knew where I worked. He could easily find me again.

"Rae."

Johnny's voice filtered through my thoughts, and when I looked at him I realized I was breathing too quickly.

I forced myself to breathe through my nose – long inhales and even longer exhales.

"You okay?" Johnny asked, his arm solid around my waist. I leaned into him, letting his warmth and stability help calm me.

"I'm fine," I muttered. "I just have to make a few calls. Jenny needs to leave, like yesterday."

"He didn't threaten Jenny," Johnny said darkly.

"I'll be okay. She's who I'm most worried about. He found her here."

"And that's not supposed to happen."

"Right."

Johnny nodded, his eyes glued on the direction the car had driven.

"Then let's get her to safety, yeah?"

I looked up at him and marveled at the raw determination I saw on his face. He must have been scared for me. I was scared for me. But it was nothing compared to the fear I'd seen on Jenny's face when she had heard her abuser's voice. She had to be my top priority, and I was amazed that Johnny just innately understood that.

For the first time in my life, I had someone who would always be on my side. A partner.

I smiled up at my fiancé and thought that I could get used to that.

Chapter Seventeen

Johnny

Loving Raelynn was infuriating.

I knew she was headstrong, but if I lived a thousand years, I would never fully get over the panic that engulfed me when I saw her standing her ground, bat in hand, as an unhinged abuser stalked towards her.

I didn't know how to do this. I didn't know how to take care of someone who seemed to be insistent on putting herself in harm's way. I loved her so much. Every cell in my body screamed against loving somebody like that. From the depths of my soul. Especially when she seemed hell-bent on reminding me that I would never be able to keep her safe. Someday, something was going to take her away from me, and I would be powerless to stop it.

Immediately after "the incident", as I'd taken to calling it in my head, I had helped her wrap things up at the office and taken her home. I had wanted so badly to be there for her. To hold her and comfort her and let her know that we were okay. But as soon as we reached her apartment, I had started spiraling. I dropped her off with a quick kiss and nearly ran the entire three and a half miles to my apartment.

Three days later, I was still struggling to wrap my mind around how much I cared for and feared for this woman. I'd descended into a full-blown panic attack. It had consumed my thoughts, paralyzing me.

I'd made sure to send a text to Rae once a day, but I knew I'd been distant. I owed her an explanation. She had tried calling me a few times, but I hadn't heard from her in the last day. I knew that she must be freaking out, but I couldn't physically bring myself to pick up the phone and ease her worries. I was a steaming pile of shit, and that only compounded the fear and anxiety I was already struggling to work through, until I basically was a vegetable on the couch. Incapacitated with worry. It wasn't often that I got so in my head that I ceased being able to function in the real world, but I had never gone through this with someone that I was accountable to. Usually, I'd wallow in existential crisis for a bit and then come out the other side. I hated myself every hour that I didn't reach out, and then hated myself some more because I couldn't make myself.

I couldn't bring myself to tell her what was wrong. I couldn't even logically reason out what the problem was.

I didn't want her to change. Her fiery spirit was what I had first fallen in love with. She took zero shit from anybody, and it was the sexiest thing I'd ever seen. I hadn't taken the time to think about what loving someone like that would feel like, though. Some fucking fiancé I was. But I couldn't stand the thought of losing her because of her recklessness. I could protect her from a lot of things in this world, but I'd have a hard time protecting her from herself.

Maybe I just wasn't cut out to love somebody? Maybe I truly was better off on my own? Sure, it would be lonely, but I'd never have to feel the panic I'd felt for Rae. It was like wearing my heart outside of my body. I didn't know if I was cut out for it.

Finally, after three days of tossing and turning and running my mind in useless circles, I had to do something. I called the only person that I could think of who might be able to bring a little bit of sense to my increasingly panicked thoughts.

It was three in the morning for me, which meant Dad would just be getting off work. I called him up and the phone only rang a few times before he answered.

"How goes it, Johnny?" His voice was chipper, as usual.

"It goes, Dad." I couldn't help the smile in my voice.

For as many faults as I could lie at his feet, he was a good man deep down.

"Shouldn't you be asleep?" he asked.

"Yeah, I should be," I laughed, rubbing my hand over the back of my neck.

"Everything alright?"

"Nothing bad's happened, so calm down," I joked, trying to ease the concern that had edged into his voice. "I have a question for you but it's kind of a doozy to ask without any preamble."

He was quiet for a moment, and I could feel the tension over the line.

"It's about Mum, isn't it?"

"Yeah."

He blew out a breath and I heard him plop down in his chair. I could picture him in that small living room, his elbows on his knees as he stared into space. He always got the same look on his face every time I brought up Mum.

"Hit me with it, son." He was trying to keep his tone light, but I could feel him prepping as if I were going to physically hurt him.

"I just wondered..." Damn, getting this question out was harder than I thought it'd be. "I wanted to know why you left. Why you really left."

180

I heard him shuffle and then he sighed. "I never did explain it properly, did I? But why ask after all this time?"

It was my turn to hesitate.

"I met a girl," I finally admitted.

"Ahh. You worried being a royal jackass is hereditary?"

I huffed a surprised chuckle. "Something like that."

"Well, it's not." Dad's voice was firm. "You're one thousand times a better man than I was or ever will be. If you love this girl, which you do otherwise you wouldn't be telling me about her, then you'll figure out how to make it work."

"That was something you couldn't figure out with Mum?"

"Your Mum and I...I don't know if I ever told you about the first time I saw her?"

"No, not really. She never talked about it either."

"God, she was stunning," he breathed. "Coming out of the water like some kind of siren or something. Immediately stole my heart. I loved her. I loved her so damn much. It killed me when she left to go home. I convinced myself I was crazy, falling in love with a woman so fast. That after a while I'd forget about her."

"And then I came along."

"When she called to tell me she was pregnant, I really thought it was the universe giving me a second chance. When she told me she wanted to raise you in the States, I flew to America without a second thought. I was going to marry the woman I loved, raise our child together. It was a fairy tale, to me."

I was quiet, trying to picture the man I'd grown up with so head over heels in love. He'd been younger than me when this was all dropped on him, and I'd always attributed that to the pain I saw on his face whenever I brought up Mum. That they were too young and couldn't make it work. That they fell out of love. That he hadn't wanted to waste his best years on a child and a mentally ill woman.

181

The story that I'd constructed in my head as a kid was slowly shifting the more he spoke, leaving uncomfortable gaps.

"The final weeks leading up to your birth were stressful, but beautiful," he said, pulling my focus back to him. "Helena, your Mum, was so happy and full of life and hope for your future. I knew her parents kicking her out had devastated her, but it seemed like having me around was helping. I thought she loved me just as much as I loved her. Everything changed after you were born."

My chest tightened, every fear I'd ever had confirmed with that single sentence. Dad was quick to interrupt my spiral.

"I don't ever want you to think you weren't wanted, son," he said, his voice firm. "The second I laid eyes on you, I loved you more than I'd ever loved anything in my life. You were perfect, and you were ours. I wanted to give you the best life possible. I saw all of the good things in your Mum and I reflected in you, and I couldn't wait to watch you grow."

I swallowed around the knot of anger that had risen in my throat. I didn't want to hear about how much he loved me, about the great life he'd envisioned for me. He'd abandoned me. Left me with a woman so volatile that I never knew what to expect one hour to the next. It didn't matter if he'd loved me when I was born.

"I know that wasn't the life you got, son." The sorrow in his voice soothed my anger a bit, but caused a whole mess of other emotions to cascade through me. Grief, pain, and bitterness coated my tongue, and I blinked back tears.

"Your mother was never the same, after giving birth," he explained. "We didn't really call it postpartum depression back then, but that's what it was. Her brain chemistry was altered, and no matter how hard I tried I couldn't get the woman I loved back. And I tried so hard. For years, I did everything I could to keep a relationship with her while trying to be the best father I could to you and manage

182

the expenses and hold down a job. It got to be so overwhelming that one day I just broke. I looked around at the mess your Mum had made of the birthday decorations I'd spent weeks saving to get, and the presents I was so excited to give you. She'd ruined it all. She stood there in the kitchen, fuming and crying, and I didn't recognize her anymore. The woman I'd loved had disappeared a long time before that, but it was that moment that finally broke my heart."

I remembered that moment too. I'd been watching from the hallway, trying to stay out of the way while Mum had ransacked the house. I remembered watching Dad as he'd taken it all in. I'd watched the hope leave his body, and something in my little five-year-old brain had just known that he'd finally had enough.

"I left because I couldn't bear witness to the spiral your mother was going down," he choked on his words and tears pricked my eyes. "I couldn't stay and watch her destroy herself, knowing that there was nothing I could do to save her."

His words echoed my own fears, and my heart pounded.

"You could have stayed," I whispered. "For me."

He was quiet for a long moment, and I heard him trying to control his breathing.

"I will always regret not taking you with me," he finally admitted. "There's no taking back the hell that I put you through, leaving you with her. But I am a selfish man, Johnny. I selfishly wanted the fairy tale love I thought I'd been given, and when that was gone, I couldn't bring myself to have any reminders of that life around me. It's the most shameful part of my life, those years that I didn't see you."

I ran a hand over my face, wiping the tears away that had managed to escape. God, my therapist was going to get to buy a new boat with the money I'd spend working through this particular conversation.

"I understand why you hated me for a long time, and I know those first few years after you came to live with me full-time were rough," he chuckled, but it was hollow. "But if you take anything away from this conversation, Johnny, I need it to be that you truly are the best parts of your mother and me.

"You have her spirit, her lust for life and adventure, and you have my love for people. Those things together are what have made you such an incredible young man. Lord knows I had nothing to do with it. And if you've found this girl that you love so much that you were willing to confront me about this after all this time, then I know you'll do right by her. All you can do is love her, and keep loving her no matter how hard it gets. Because I guarantee you'll regret it if you let your cowardice take you away from her."

I didn't know what to say.

My entire life I'd thought that he left because he didn't love us anymore. It turned out that he left because he loved my mum so much that he couldn't bear to see her the way she was. He chose to protect his own heart instead of trying to protect hers.

I saw their love reflected in Raelynn and I. We were soul mates. So destined to be together that time and distance did nothing to change the way I felt about her from that first night.

I'd be damned if I was going to let myself become my father.

Raelynn was a risk-taker. I would just have to accept that and try to enjoy each and every minute that I was lucky enough to have her. I couldn't let my stupid machismo and selfishness take away the best thing that had ever happened to me.

I took a breath and smiled into the phone. "Thanks for the advice, Dad. I'm glad we had this talk."

He was silent for a beat, and I could hear him hesitate before he sighed.

"While I've got you, son, there's something else I need to tell you."

184

Chapter Eighteen

Raelynn

Loving Johnny was the most terrifying thing I had ever done.

That included skydiving over the Grand Canyon, and swimming with sharks in The Bahamas.

It had been three full days since the confrontation at my office, and I'd received two texts from my supposed fiancé. The first had been to let me know he'd made it home after he'd silently driven me home and then practically ran away. The second had been to say that he knew he was being distant, and that he'd explain everything soon. I'd tried to call him, but he hadn't picked up.

I tried to tell the voice in my head that everything was going to be okay. That, for whatever reason, the fight had freaked Johnny out and he just needed time to process. That's what Addy had told me when I'd called her on day two to cuss him out.

The day after the attack I'd been busy finalizing Jenny's documents and arranging her travel plans. She was all set to fly off to her aunt's house by the end of the week. Laura was going to take care of the rest. My job was done. It was always a bittersweet moment when my part was over, but I felt a surge of pride whenever I thought of how brave Jenny was being.

Day two was harder. I was in between clients, and with nothing to distract me that damn voice kept shouting at me that Johnny was done with me. I still hadn't heard more than the meager text from him, and my intrusive thoughts kept telling me that I was more trouble than the sex was worth, and so Johnny was going to leave.

There were many reasons I'd never really had a serious, adult relationship. Addy knew some of them, my family assumed some of them, and I was quite vocal about some of them. The biggest reason, though, was one that I kept closely guarded. I only acknowledged it in the dead of night, when my eyes burned from crying and lack of sleep, and my heart ached with a profound loneliness that I was sure would follow me the rest of my life. Even then, I could only vaguely put words to it, because I knew that if I fully formulated the thought, it would destroy me.

I was a "good time" girl. Pretty enough, a bit reckless and wild, all confidence and charisma. I was a great story to tell when the adventure was over and the sun rose. For the few men that had stuck around longer than a few dates, the moment I became a real person, the illusion shattered. Once, I had gotten my period and had to cancel a date because I was laid up with cramps. He'd never called again. Another time, the guy had left in the middle of a date because I'd received a call from my mother and was agitated after. The second I dropped the façade that I used to play the games with men that they wanted, I was no longer a good time.

I'd had friends in college that would get jealous because they thought that I had some magical power to be able to date any guy I wanted. They never quite understood that "date" and "sleep with" were very different. Because, yes, I could charm any guy I wanted into my bed but getting him to stick around was Herculean. The

186

people in my life thought that I used men for sex and that was all I wanted. The fact of the matter was that I had been used by so many men for sex, that it was easier for me to say that's all I wanted and move on with my life. It helped that I liked sex. I thoroughly enjoyed a good roll in the hay and wasn't ashamed to find that when I needed it. But a part of me had always hoped that one day I'd mean more to someone that just a warm body. Even if I rarely let myself actual admit that.

I thought Johnny had been different.

I'd let myself believe that he had really loved me. That he'd wanted to be with me for who I was. He'd seen me at some truly low moments. Leaving the club with him driving my car was permanently seared into my most embarrassing memories. He'd seen me like that and still pursued me. He'd made me feel so incredibly special and *seen*. Seen in a way that nobody, not Addy, not my family, had ever seen me before.

Over those three days I replayed our entire relationship over and over and saw that I'd simply let myself be fooled.

We'd slept together the first time we'd met. Par for the course for me, but I'd sworn there had been something deeper there. But he'd left. He hadn't tried to find me or contact me for a year. When we met again, I'd spurned his advances, making me a challenge. And he'd won. I had invited him to Mexico. I had rekindled our physical connection. I had fucking proposed to the guy. All the while, he was along for the ride with a smile on his face.

Johnny had played the game so goddamn well that it had taken me this long to see it.

It took three days for me to work myself into the darkest place I had ever been.

Because I was so desperately in love with this man that I was *convinced* had played me. The longer I went without hearing from him, the further I sank into a deep depression.

I was a bit surprised by how quickly it overtook me. Fits of sadness were normal for me, but this aching, immobilizing depression was new, and it came on too fast for me to even attempt to combat it.

By the middle of the second day, I was rotting on my couch, blinds drawn, and a bottle of wine deep. Addy had tried calling me again, but I hadn't picked up. I didn't want to talk to anyone. I didn't want to move. The only effort I made was to open a new bottle of wine when the one I'd been nursing went dry. I was cocooned in my biggest, fuzziest blanket. Even the television was too much, so I just sat in the dark and stared at nothing.

I wanted to wallow for a few days and then I'd pick myself back up. I knew I'd make it out of this. I'd survived everything in my life up to that point, and I was too damn stubborn to lose myself completely over some guy. Even if I'd been convinced that guy was the love of my life. I would be okay. Eventually. But goddamn if this didn't hurt like a bitch.

***

By day four, I was starving. I hadn't been shopping in a while, and I'd eaten everything in my fridge and freezer. I'd run out of wine and snacks, and that's what finally convinced me to get my ass up.

I sighed and stared at the empty bottle on the coffee table. I knew that drowning my sorrows in alcohol was the unhealthiest of coping mechanisms, but it had helped to stay just a bit buzzed over the last few days. It wasn't something I normally used to dilute my feelings – that was typically sex – but that was clearly not an option.

A bubble of shame welled up inside of me as I took in the disaster area that had become my apartment. Food wrappers and paper plates were scattered on the kitchen counter, and four wine bottles were lined up next to the couch. The air was stale and reeked of sadness.

I needed to open the blinds, let in some fresh air, clean up, and do laundry. I would feel better once that was done. I sat up and got a whiff of myself and gagged a bit, mentally adding shower to the top of the to-do list.

I shuffled to the kitchen, still wrapped in my security blanket, and began scooping trash into a bag, feeling minutely better with each pass that decluttered the counter. Wine bottles went in next, and the knot in my chest loosened a bit more. I slowly made my way to the windows and inched open the blinds. The light hit the dust that was swirling through the air and another wave of guilt washed over me.

I hated this. I hated losing my mind over a man. I hated that my apartment, my safe space that I kept meticulously clean and bright, was little more than a cage at the moment. I hated feeling so insignificant and small and stupid.

Anger bubbled through my veins, burning the sadness out and lighting a fire in my chest. Glaring, I threw my blanket onto the ground and slammed the windows open. The fresh air fanned the flames that were raking through me until I was vibrating. My teeth clenched and resolve straightened my spine.

I was a whirlwind, aggressively cleaning my apartment until there wasn't a speck of dust or a hint of depression left. The countertops sparkled, the bathroom smelled of bleach and my shampoo after my shower, the living area was tidy and there was a freshly cleaned blanket draped over the couch. I'd straightened my bedroom, washed all my bedding, deep cleaned the floors, and had

189

kept the windows open as far as they would go. I refused to let any of the energy that had accumulated over the last few days linger in my space.

I looked around as my emotions finally settled into something akin to peace. I nodded once to myself, and then grabbed the three full garbage bags. The last step in the cleanse.

I opened my door, bags in hand, to a very surprised Johnny. His hand was raised, ready to knock. The second our eyes met, my stomach twisted in on itself. Every negative thought, every worry, every fear I'd manifested over the past few days came pounding back into my body so hard that I nearly doubled over.

"Rae." The sound of his voice did me in.

Snarling, I shouldered the garbage bags and shoved past him. The dumpsters were on the other end of the property from my apartment, so it was a bit of a hike, but the adrenaline burning through me had me moving fast.

"Raelynn!" Johnny called, jogging to catch up with me. "Hang on."

I ignored him, stomping across the parking lot. The bags over my shoulder was digging into my skin and scraping my back, but I was too mad to care.

Johnny kept pace with me, evidently having chosen to wait me out instead of trying to stop me. Probably a wise choice, considering I wasn't sure what I'd do if he tried to touch me. Break his wrist, maybe?

I threw the bags down as soon as I reached the dumpster and slammed the lid open. It wasn't an easy thing to do, considering the thing was a head taller than me and those lids were a pain in the ass to open and close. I refused to make eye contact with Johnny, but I could feel his concern and anxiety.

190

I tossed the bags in, closed the lids, and turned on my heel to angrily march back to my apartment.

Heaven help this man if he tries to come in, I thought.

Johnny trailed after me, finally giving in and speaking again.

"C'mon, Rae. Just talk to me for a minute and I'll explain everything," he pleaded.

I didn't want an explanation from him. I didn't need to hear that he came to some grand realization over the last few days. I would rather he'd just disappeared and left me to pick up my own pieces, instead of being a grown-up and breaking up with me in person.

"We have nothing to talk about, Johnny," I growled.

I flung open the door to my apartment and then slammed it shut behind me.

I took a deep breath, the smell of cleaning products and fresh air soothing a bit of the fire within me.

Then, he knocked.

I whirled around, disbelief all over my face.

"Go away," I shouted.

There was a pause and then he knocked again. Three knocks. Very polite. Very innocent.

"Go. Away."

The pause this time was longer, and I thought he actually had listened to me. It sent stabbing pains through my chest, but my mind insisted this was for the best.

I raked my hands through my hair, trying to release some of the tension in my body. I walked over and plopped down on the couch, my head resting on the back with my eyes closed as a pounding headache started just behind my eyes.

Three knocks.

I growled and was at that door before I knew how I got there. I whipped the door open to see him standing there with two bags of Chinese food and a solemn expression on his face.

"Addy called me," he started. Addy's name was the only reason the door stayed open.

My heart was pounding in my ears and anger was bitter on my tongue. If Addy had called him, she must have been really worried about me, and that softened my rage a bit.

"She said she couldn't reach you, and that you probably were running out of food," Johnny explained, lifting the takeout bags with a shrug. "I'm pretty sure you sequestering yourself away from the world is my fault, so the least I could do was make sure you had something to eat."

I glared at him for a long time. My heart and my head were battling with each other. My stupid heart wanted to hear him explain himself. She was holding out hope that maybe we were wrong, that he wasn't here to break it off, but instead he had a good reason for going MIA the last few days. My head was more practical and kept up a litany of the reasons men had left us in the past.

Finally, it was my stomach that won out, letting out a horrifically unattractive rumble when the scent of the food finally wafted up to me.

Johnny smirked, though it didn't reach his eyes, and I rolled mine as I stepped aside to let him in.

"I guess Addy was worried for nothing," he said softly as he looked around my apartment. He set the food on the counter and turned to me with a sad smile. "Looks like you're doing just fine."

I went to lie and tell him that of course I was fine, but the words burned my mouth and refused to leave. Instead, I grabbed a carton of chicken and some chopsticks and stomped over to the couch, refusing to acknowledge him.

"Well," he sighed, "if you're not going to talk to me, then maybe I can convince you to listen while you eat?"

He came and sat on the other end of the couch, keeping a cushion's length between us. I think he might have actually been afraid I'd hit him if he sat too close.

"I shouldn't have disappeared like that," he said. I rolled my eyes again, but instead of speaking shoveled chicken into my mouth.

"That thing outside your office really fucked with me, Rae. I know it's an excuse, and you don't deserve that, but I promise I'll try to explain. But first, I have a ridiculously big favor to ask you."

My chopsticks dropped into the carton as my mouth popped open in surprise.

"Are you fucking kidding me, Johnny?"

"I know," he sounded wretched. "Trust me, I know how horrible this is. But I need you to go to Australia with me."

A laugh startled its way out of me, and then I couldn't stop. Of all the things I had imagined him asking me, that was nowhere near a possibility.

Finally, I caught my breath and stared at him. His face was etched with pain and sadness, and I realized that I hadn't ever seen him like this. When I really took the time to look at him, I saw that he was just as much of a mess as I had been, if not more. There were massive, dark circles under his eyes, his skin was dull, and his hair was flat and greasy as if it hadn't been washed recently.

After a long moment of silence, he ran a hand through his lank hair and looked at me with just a bit of hope.

"I fucked up, I know that," he said quietly. "And I will explain. I'll tell you whatever you want to know about what's been going on with me these last few days. But we need to do it on the plane."

"Why in the world would I go to Australia with you on a whim?" I asked, raising an eyebrow at him.

"My dad is dying."

The words were small and choked, as if saying it out loud was physically painful for him.

I blinked and suddenly my anger evaporated.

Whatever had been going on with Johnny these last few days, whatever reason he had for ignoring me and leaving me to my worst thoughts and insecurities, didn't seem to matter in that moment. Regardless of anything else, I knew Johnny to be kind and sweet, and right then he was in a world of pain. I knew his relationship with his dad was complicated, but I also knew that if he was really dying then Johnny would, of course, drop everything to go and see him.

"Why do you want me to go with you?"

His eyes were distraught as he looked at me. "Because I love you, Rae, and I need you there with me when I see him."

I swallowed around the knot in my throat.

Had I allowed myself to spiral too far? It was entirely possible. I knew I had a flair for the dramatic, but these last few days had been hell. Had I put myself through it for no reason? Did he really love me?

I sighed when I realized these were all questions that would be answered by a long conversation. And where better to have that than trapped in a flying metal tube?

"When do we leave?"

The relief that broke across Johnny's face made guilt flare in my stomach.

Johnny needed a friend in this moment. Regardless of what happened next with us, I told myself that I could at least be that.

Chapter Nineteen

Raelynn

Johnny had booked us tickets on a flight leaving that night. I couldn't believe he'd had that much faith that I would go with him after the hellish few days we'd had, but a small part of me loved that he did.

We didn't speak much as he helped me pack and we made our way to the airport. Through security, preboarding, boarding, taxi, and takeoff we were silent. Our bodies gravitated towards each other. We kept brushing arms, bumping shoulders, running into each other. It's like our bodies were trying to fix the rift that was between us through sheer forced proximity.

Johnny gave me the window seat, sitting himself on the aisle. He'd booked the middle seat out as well, so that we had the whole row to ourselves. It was a long flight. Almost twenty-four hours of travel altogether. Plenty of time to air out all of our shit.

I had planned to jump right into it, but after the plane took off I found myself dozing immediately. It turned out that three days of no sleep and intense emotion took its toll. When I finally woke up again it had been nearly four hours. We had one flight change in San Francisco, and I knew we must be getting close.

My head was resting on Johnny's chest. He had an arm draped around me and had lifted the middle armrests so that I could curl up against him. He smiled at me when I blinked up at him, trying to figure out where I was.

"I didn't want to wake you when they came by with snacks, so I got you some of everything," he said softly.

I sat up and stretched my neck. I was surprisingly not too sore for having passed out across cramped airplane seats. Johnny must have made sure I was comfortable enough and done his best to let me sleep. Warmth flared in my chest but was quickly tamped down when I remembered that we still needed to talk.

God, I hated talking about my emotions. For this conversation to work, I'd have to admit to Johnny how upset I'd been. I would have to walk him through every thought I'd had over the last few days, and we'd have to talk them out, figure out what was true and what wasn't. It sounded exhausting and I really didn't want to.

"I don't really want to talk either," Johnny sighed, glancing sideways at me.

"How do you read my mind like that?" I grumbled.

"You wear your thoughts on your face, Rae. It's easy to read you."

"Not for anyone else."

"Nobody else loves you like I do," he said. "I notice every miniscule expression of yours because I always want to know what you're thinking. So that you don't have to tell me."

"Yeah, but we can't have an entire conversation through micro expressions, now can we?" I sighed.

He laughed softly and my pulse thrummed.

"No, we can't," he admitted. "I think we might actually have to be adults and talk this one through."

"You sure you don't want to go have angry sex in the bathroom?" I was mostly joking.

He smiled at me but shook his head.

I chewed my lip, hating that he was right. Finally, I closed my eyes and blew out a frustrated breath. Time to rip the band-aid off.

"You said that the incident at my office freaked you out," I said. "Start there, please."

He took a moment to gather his thoughts. I watched his face, looking for any clues as to what he might say, but found nothing. It was endlessly frustrating that he could read me so well, but I had no idea what was going on in his head.

"For the first time in my life, I found myself viscerally worried for someone that I couldn't protect," he started. "Well, aside from my mum, and that was likely a factor in my freak out. I saw that man going after you, and you were holding your ground so resolutely. There was no fear on your face, only determination. But I'd seen what this particular man could do, and the only defense you had was that bat. I knew that even if I managed to grab him, I might not be able to protect you."

"I didn't need you to protect me," I said, a bite to my words.

"Well, tough shit, Rae," he huffed. "I'm always going to protect you to the best of my ability. I know you might not need me to, but I want to. And the thought that no matter what I do or how safe I can keep us, one day I'll lose you...it sent me into a spiral."

I stilled as his words sunk in. His worry wasn't actually about that moment. It was about a wildly unpredictable future that he saw with me.

"You're so spirited and self-sufficient and a bit reckless at times," he said, a hollow chuckle punctuating his words. "Over the course of our lives together, I can only imagine the trouble you'll manage to get yourself in. It suddenly hit me that I would never ask you to change. I love every single thing about you. So, I had to grapple with my fears. I had to decide, is loving you worth the pain I'll feel when I lose you?"

When. Not if. He seemed so convinced I was going to do something to get myself killed someday. Ridiculous man, as if I hadn't been keeping myself alive my entire life. But I could understand his worry. His fear and pain at the thought of losing someone he loved so dearly. He'd already lost his mom. He knew better than most that there was no guarantee of tomorrow.

"So, what did you decide?" My voice was small. I both desperately wanted to hear his answer and never hear him speak again if it meant losing him.

He turned and took my face in his hands, forcing my gaze to meet his.

"I would suffer every single day for the rest of my useless life if it meant getting to love you for as long as possible," he whispered.

My breath caught in my throat and tears stung my eyes.

That was a stupidly good answer.

I searched his face, looking for any sign that he was lying. Any sign he was using me like so many others had. I found nothing.

Now I had a choice to make. Believe him, or not?

Chapter Twenty

Johnny

Raelynn's beautiful eyes searched my face, desperate. I didn't know what the last few days had been for her, but I knew she must have been battling as many demons as I had. I could feel her desire to believe me, to trust in the words I was saying. To trust how much I loved her.

I'd known I'd fucked up when Addy had called me and ripped me a new set of testicles. She had never seen Raelynn retreat from the world the way she had, and I knew it was all my fault.

I hoped my explanation was enough. My declaration of my endless love for the infuriating woman I held in my hands. She was the most precious thing on this earth, and if I had to spend every day groveling to prove it to her I would.

Finally, she sighed softly. She pulled her face away and cast her eyes down where her fingers were fidgeting with her rings.

"I believe you, Johnny," she said. My heart started beating again and it took everything in me not to crush her in a hug. But there was still hesitation in her voice.

"What's holding you back, Rae?" I was desperate to fix this distance between us.

I hadn't realized how much comfort I took in holding her until she'd fallen asleep on me for the first part of the flight. Having her next to me, her head resting on my chest and my arm wrapped around her, made me feel whole again.

"I had a rough couple of days," she admitted, still not looking at me.

I knew that she wasn't big on sharing feelings, so I let her speak at her own pace, even though I was dying a bit inside with each pause she took.

"I've been used for sex by a lot of men. When they've had their fun, they just leave. It's usually when they see something that reminds them that I'm a real human being, and not some fantasy woman. They decide I'm not worth the trouble."

She looked up at me my heart clenched when I saw tears tracking down her cheeks.

"I thought that's what you'd done," she said.

I blinked and tried to swallow around the guilt that had settled in my throat.

Of course she'd thought that. The first sign of trouble and I had disappeared. Like a complete and utter jackass.

"Oh, Rae," I cradled her cheek, wiping the tears away before leaning in to kiss her forehead softly.

How could I ever fix that?

"I spent the last few days convinced everything had been a lie," she whispered. "I know I probably overreacted, but it was easier for me to think that than to think it had been all been true and you had just abandoned me."

I tilted her face up to look at me and my heart broke again when I saw the devastation on her face.

"I can't ever apologize enough, I know," I sighed. "But do you really believe that I love you? Because that's the most important thing to me in this world, that you believe that."

She nodded, but her eyes were still guarded.

"That's why you were so angry with me when I showed up."

"I wanted nothing to do with you," she laughed a little and sniffled.

"Rightly so," I murmured, relishing the sound of her laugh.

I pulled her to me and wrapped her in a hug. After a moment, her arms snaked around my waist, and she squeezed me hard. I felt her tears warm on my chest, and refused to let go of her. I would never let her feel that way again. I would never let her doubt that what we had was the most real thing either of us would ever experience.

She was beauty and adventure incarnate, and I loved every sharp, messy, tantalizing piece of her.

"We're quite the pair, aren't we?" I said, my voice warm.

She pulled back to look at me and laugh softly. "Ridiculously insecure, is what I'd call us."

"We'll work on it," I promised.

She nodded and then yawned. I smiled and smoothed her hair out of her face. If her last few days had been half as difficult as she'd described, I knew she couldn't have had much sleep. I hadn't either, but between fixing things with Raelynn and my father's confession that he was dying, I likely wouldn't be sleeping any time soon.

"You're not off the hook, you know," she said as she settled against me again. "I expect some major groveling to make up for putting us through all of this."

"I'll grovel to the end of my days, I promise." I kissed her head, and she relaxed a bit more. "Go back to sleep, I'll wake you when we need to change planes."

She nodded and within minutes her breathing evened out and she was asleep again.

Some of the tension eased in my chest. Raelynn and I would be okay. Now I just had to make it another eighteen hours or so worrying about becoming an orphan.

***

Sydney Airport, like almost every other international airport, always smelled like cleaning products, plastic, and stress. But to me it carried a hint of nostalgia that had me inhaling deeply, the cacophony of smells settling some of my anxiety.

Watching Raelynn navigate an airport was the weirdest turn-on. She was all confidence and efficiency, while still managing to embrace the nuances of her surroundings. She took my hand and refused to let go as we made our way through the terminal and to the arrivals gate, marveling at the architecture and artwork that adorned the walls. We hadn't checked bags, so we went right to the cab stand.

My dad lived in a little suburb about forty minutes from the airport, and I'd booked us a hotel that was close to his house. I wanted us to have our privacy but be close by if he needed us. He'd been vague about the exact state of his condition on the phone, so I had no idea if I was going to see a slightly ill version of the man I knew, or someone I would hardly recognize.

Raelynn must have been able to sense my tension the closer we got to the hotel, because her grip on my hand would tighten every few minutes, as if to remind me that she was still here.

I had no idea how I had gotten so lucky, but I was glad she was with me. My mind had a tendency to find the darkest plot lines and follow those until I was given evidence to the contrary. My therapist called it "worst-case scenario thinking" and assured me it was a

202

pretty normal trauma response to finding your mother dead as a preteen. Didn't make coping with it any easier though. The more exhausted I became, the harder it was to filter those thoughts out.

Finally, after nearly two and half full days of travel, we were checked in to the hotel. Rae swiped the key to our room, and I realized I had no idea how we'd gotten there. I didn't remember getting out of the cab, or the lobby of the hotel. I didn't even remember the elevator ride. Rae's hand in mine dragged me into the room, and when she let go, I felt empty.

She closed the door behind us, locking the deadbolt and security bar, and stashed our luggage in the closet. Then she was opening the blinds to an admittedly lackluster view of the hotel parking lot, before she turned and watched me.

"You need to call your dad, and then we need to sleep," she declared after a long moment.

I blinked at her, my brain trying desperately to focus. She sighed and gave me a playful smirk before slinking over and wrapping her arms around me.

I held her tightly, breathing in the scent of her shampoo and that sharpness that was just her. My body relaxed and my mind finally caught up.

I laughed softly and pulled back to look into her beautiful face.

"What would I do without you?" I breathed, not fully intending for the thought to be vocalized.

"Well, you definitely wouldn't have made it this far, I'll tell you that much," she said, winking as she wagged my phone in my face. I hadn't even felt her take it out of my pocket.

"Call your dad."

I nodded and took the phone. My heart seemed frozen as the line rang. It was almost four o'clock, so he might have still been at work, but that didn't stop my brain from picturing him dead on the floor as the phone rang and rang with no answer.

I swallowed nervously before dialing the office where he worked.

"Dinkum Marketing, this is Rachel, how can I help you?" A cheery woman answered the phone.

"Hey, Rachel, my name is Johnny. I'm calling for Richard Harris. Is he available?"

"May I ask what this is in regard to?" Bloody receptionists. I understood it was her job to filter calls, but my head was pounding with worry.

"This is his son, and I can't seem to reach him," I ground out. "Is he available?"

"Let me check, sir. One moment."

Rae was watching me closely as she unpacked her bag. I knew she was just as anxious as I was but was trying not to show it. She wanted to be strong for me. The look of love and support on her face almost broke me as I listened to kitchy hold music. I had to choke back the tears that were threatening to run down my face.

"Mr. Harris is currently in a meeting," Rachel the receptionist came back with. "Would you like to leave a message?"

I sighed and pinched my nose. "If you could just let him know that his son is home and to give me a call at this number when he's free, that would be great."

"Will do!" she chirped.

"Thanks," I mumbled, hanging up without a goodbye, even though I knew it was rude.

My hands dropped to my lap and the last bit of my energy left me.

And there Raelynn was.

She took my phone and placed it on the nightstand. Then she knelt down and took my shoes off for me, her hands cradling my legs as she worked her way up my body. A shiver of desire ran through me, but my head was foggy and even that didn't clear it.

"Come on, you," she said softly, pulling my arm so that I moved up the bed.

I tried not to let myself fully collapse as she settled me beneath the blankets and crawled in next to me. She snuggled into my side, and then the world disappeared.

***

"We'll be over in about an hour, then."

Raelynn's voice woke me. I blinked wearily as my brain ran at hyper speed to remember where we were.

Australia. Dad.

Fuck me, I was still exhausted.

And then it registered that Raelynn didn't know anybody in this country, so who in the hell was she talking to?

She was sitting up against the headboard, my phone in one hand. Her other hand was playing with my hair, running her fingers through it gently. She looked down at me and smiled.

"Good morning, sleepy head," she whispered. "It's your dad. Do you want to talk to him?"

I was wide awake now. I nodded, sitting up quickly as she handed me the phone.

"Dad?"

"Johnny, you didn't have to book a flight you dag," he laughed.

"You tell me you're dying and don't expect me to come see you? What kind of son do you take me for, old man?"

"Alright, alright, keep your knickers on," he said, and I could hear his smile through the phone. "You brought your girl with you?"

"I did." I smiled at Rae who was absentmindedly drawing patterns on my arm that were stirring all sorts of feelings inside me.

"She already promised you'd come over for dinner."

I glanced at the clock and realized we'd slept for an entire day. Well, I'd slept. I had no idea what Rae had been up to. Jesus H., this was not the plan.

"Absolutely," I said into the phone. "We'll see you then."

"I can't wait to give your jetlagged self some serious shit for making me wait a whole day to see you," Dad chuckled.

I groaned. "Love you too, Pops."

He was still laughing as he hung up and I dropped my head back against the board.

"How did I sleep an entire day?" I sighed.

Rae giggled, causing warmth to flood my skin, as she climbed on top of me. Her hips settled over mine so deliciously, and suddenly every other thought flew out of my head. All of the exhaustion melted away at the feel of her weight on me. It had been too long since I'd worshipped this woman, and there was nothing else I could focus on.

My gaze caught hers and I knew she was thinking the same thing.

"That wasn't my intention," she breathed, though the flush on her chest said otherwise.

"Dad's place is a five-minute walk from here," I said, my voice low. She bit her lip, and I knew I'd won her. "We have some time to kill, love."

Her hips ground on mine, sending waves of pleasure through me. My hands gripped her ass, holding her still.

"You need something from me, Rae?"

Fire flashed in her eyes as she smirked at me. "If I recall correctly, someone has some groveling to start on."

She punctuated this with a slow sweep of her center over my hardening cock and it ripped a guttural sound from me. When I looked at her again, triumph was shining on her face.

"Whatever you need, I want you to take it," I ordered.

Her eyes shuttered and I saw the moment she gave in to the flames that were passing between us.

Her hands braced on either side of my head as her hips moved in torturously slow movements. Even through our clothes I could feel the heat pouring from her. I loved watching the rise and fall of her chest as she lost control, grinding on me. The sweetest whimpers escaped her mouth, and I let my hands run up and down her sides gently, causing her to gasp and arch into my touch.

"More," she breathed.

I smirked, loving how greedy she was.

"Tell me what you want, Rae," I said. "You know how this works."

She opened her eyes to glare at me before rushing in and locking her lips with mine. This kiss wasn't sweet or gentle. It was demanding. Her teeth nipped my lips as her hands moved to grip my shoulders, pressing our bodies closer.

When she finally pulled back, her pupils were blown and she looked about ready to combust. I was right there with her. It was taking every ounce of self-control I possessed to let her lead this.

She ran her tongue over her bottom lip, tasting me there, and groaned. Her hips hadn't stopped their frenzied pace, and I was about to come in my pants like a fucking teenager.

"I want you to finger fuck me while I ride your lap," she purred.

Holy fuck. My eyes nearly rolled into the back of my head when she lifted herself and shimmied off the little pajama shorts she'd put on at some point during my sleep.

She was soaking wet, and my fingers slid into her easily, earning me a moan that would be seared into my memory forever.

She wasted no time, sinking down onto my hand.

I growled praise into her ear, which spurred her on. I could hardly keep up as she got herself off using my hand and my voice.

When she finally contracted around me, I curled my fingers into that spot that I knew made her see stars and she fell apart. She trembled as she buried her head in the crook of my neck, chanting my name like a prayer. I teased her for a long moment, drawing every tremor from her that I could, before drawing my fingers out and licking them clean.

Goddammit. She tasted like heaven, and my aching cock wept to be inside her. She sat up and grinned at me, her post-orgasm glow blinding me with lust. I gripped her hips and was about to flip her over and take her when she put a hand on my chest, stopping me.

"I think you have some more groveling to do before you've earned the right to fuck me again," she said, her voice ghosting through my ears as my mind scrambled to keep up.

She hopped off my lap and shed her top, wiggling that plush ass as she made her way to the bathroom.

"I'll be in the shower," she called. "Do what you need to before we leave to go to your dad's."

My mouth dropped open in shock. This woman was going to leave me hard and leaking. I hated that she was standing in that shower, knowing what I was about to do, but it also turned me on even more that she was making me work for her. She was punishing me for the hell we'd gone through, and damn if I didn't want her to. I knew that when she eventually let me take her again, it would feel like losing my fucking virginity all over again.

When she emerged from the shower, pink-skinned and grinning like a cat, I was just about done. Her eyes widened as she watched

208

my hand on my cock. I caught her gaze and that was all it took before I exploded, her name on my lips.

When I opened my eyes again, she was smiling even bigger. She wet a washcloth and tossed it to me.

"We leave in ten," she said with a smirk.

I chuckled to myself as I cleaned up. We both were dressed as presentable adults with enough time to make it to Dad's right on schedule. I was anxious to see my dad but knowing that I had this vixen by my side gave me more courage than I thought I could muster.

Chapter Twenty-One

Raelynn

Johnny was the spitting image of his father. Well, what I assumed his father would look like with a bit more weight on his bones and color on his skin.

The cancer had stripped him of that, leaving behind a man who looked as if a strong gust of wind would blow him away.

If I'd been shocked to see him when he answered the door, it was nothing compared to the terror I'd seen on my love's face.

Richard had flung open the door with a huge grin on his face and a hearty welcome, ushering us inside without a second thought. I went in and was immediately swept up in a hug.

"You must be Raelynn." His accent was strong and his voice warm.

He pulled back and took my face in his hands, turning it side to side before nodding once.

"That's settled then. You're definitely too good for my Johnny boy," he said with a wink.

I laughed and glanced over to where said boy was frozen in the doorway.

His jaw was clenched and his cheeks were pale. His gaze was trained on his dad, and it looked like he was trying very hard not to cry. Richard followed my eyes and his smile faltered a bit.

"C'mon in Johnny, you're letting all the air out," he said softly.

I reached out my hand and Johnny took it, glancing at me gratefully. When he looked back at his father, he wore a mask of joviality and mirth.

"How are you, old man?"

His dad laughed but it turned into a wheeze at the end. "Well, as you can probably tell, I've been better."

"Yeah, I can see that." Johnny's words were clipped, though I could tell he was trying to keep his tone light. "You should have called me months ago."

"Well, turns out it was a good damn thing I didn't, wasn't it?" Richard nodded towards me, and I smiled.

"You still should have called," I said with mock severity.

"Everything in its time, lovely."

Johnny sighed and then moved us all further into the house.

It was cozy, if a bit dark. I could tell that men had lived here, and for the past few years a single, aging man. There was a thin layer of dust that coated the shelves, and clear paths through each room that were well-worn. The recliner in the living room was loved, and there were several shelves of books that looked taken care of. A television was hung on the wall, and there were empty microwaveable meal trays stacked on the floor by the chair.

It was fairly tidy but felt lonely.

I tried to imagine Johnny living here and found that I couldn't. He was so full of life, and this place wasn't. Maybe it had been, once upon a time, but this sweet, sick old man was in no condition to take care of a home.

"Can I get you anything to drink, Raelynn?" Richard asked, hovering by the doorway to the kitchen. "Dinner'll be ready in about ten minutes. I haven't had anyone to cook for in a while, so I had to blow the dust out of the oven."

I was only ninety percent sure he was kidding.

"I'm okay," I smiled at him. "I'll have water with dinner, but I'm good for right now."

Richard smiled and shuffled over to the recliner. Johnny and I took seats on the couch, turning so that we could see the still cheery man across the room.

"So, Dad, do you want to jump right into it, or wait until after dinner?"

Richard winced, adjusting so that he could cross his legs. Defensive posturing, Laura would say.

"Can't we just catch up first? I'm dying to hear how you two ended up together." He gave me a hopeful grin, and I squeezed Johnny's arm lightly.

He took the hint and sighed. "Alright, alright. I'll tell you ours and then after dinner you'll tell us yours. Deal?"

The old man laughed loudly and when he looked at his son pure love shone in his eyes.

My brain raced to reconcile the man that Johnny had told me about when he was growing up with the kind stranger sitting across from me, but I couldn't find any similarities.

"Raelynn and I first met about a year ago," Johnny started. He flashed me a glance and I glared at him, trying to telepathically tell him to keep it PG. "We spent the night together, and then she kicked me out the next day."

"You left voluntarily, if I recall," I sniped.

"We'll call it a mutual act of self-preservation," he quipped back. Turning to his dad, he became more animated the longer he talked.

212

I was happy to sit back and observe. It's what I did best, and it helped me to better understand the dynamics at play here.

There was clearly so much love between these two men, but an undercurrent of caution as well. Johnny wasn't as forthcoming as I thought he would be with his dad, keeping to the surface level of our admittedly rocky love story and glossing over some of the major childhood trauma issues I knew we shared. Richard would chime in with colorful commentary, but made sure to keep it light and charming, offering no real insight or perspective into what had been some pretty big stumbling blocks in our relationship.

I blinked when I realized it sounded exactly like a conversation I would have with my mother.

Then I remembered that I hadn't yet told my mother I was engaged. Shit. I knew I'd been forgetting something. In my (weak) defense, it had been a crazy week or so since the engagement.

"Rae?" Johnny's voice broke through my thoughts, and I had the decency to blush.

"I haven't told my mom we're engaged," I blurted out.

"Engaged?" Richard sputtered.

Johnny heaved a long-suffering sigh, as if he couldn't believe the bad stroke of luck that had landed him in this room in this moment.

"Hadn't gotten to that part of the story yet, love," he mock-whispered. "Yeah, Dad, we're actually engaged now."

"Where the hell is the ring? I didn't see one," Richard said, his tone laced with disbelief.

"I haven't had time to get one yet," Johnny chuckled. "Rae sprung this on me pretty out of the blue."

"She proposed to you?"

"I did, actually," I said, tossing my arm dramatically around Johnny and kissing his cheek.

"Good for you," Richard laughed, his surprise finally fading. "About time someone locked down my son. And someone as beautiful and wonderful as you? Ya lucked out, Johnny."

"I did, indeed." He smiled down at me and brushed his lips against mine softly.

The timer went off in the kitchen and Richard started to get up, but Johnny was on his feet faster than we could blink.

"Sit, Dad," he commanded. "I've got it."

The fire in Richard's eyes told me that he hated being taken care of, but the shake in his arms told me he knew he'd have to let it be. As he settled back into his seat, Johnny disappeared into the kitchen.

"He's a good man, my son," Richard said softly, catching my eye.

"I know."

"Nothing like me, in that regard," he sighed, rubbing his hand over his scalp.

I recognized the gesture. Johnny did that all the time, shoving his hair back when he was nervous or frustrated. Richard's fingers skimmed the bare skin of his head, and his hand dropped heavily into his lap. He stared at it for a moment, as if he didn't recognize it.

"I'm glad he found you," he said, his eyes finding mine. "He deserves to be loved, and I can tell from the way you look at him that you love him the way he needs."

"How does he need to be loved?" My own voice was gentle, not wanting to break the stillness that had invaded the room.

"Fiercely," Richard said, his voice hard. "Unashamedly and passionately."

I laughed and his eyes lit up. "Well, I can definitely agree that I love him like that. If not a little bit more. I'm...kind of a lot."

"He needs a lot."

We watched each other for a long moment, and I found my heart breaking for this man I hardly knew.

"I'll never stop reminding him how much he's loved," I promised.

Richard nodded, the motion seeming to drain him.

"Food's ready," Johnny called, breaking the tension that had built in the room.

I smiled as I went over and helped Richard up from his chair. He clung to my arm as we made our way through the kitchen to sit at the small table. Johnny had set out plates and napkins and was waiting.

I met Johnny's eyes and knew he'd heard our entire conversation. He was beaming at me and his eyes were wet.

I knew that my man had been through so much in his life. So many people had promised to love him and had given up on that promise in one way or another. I refused to be one of them.

As I watched Johnny help his dad into his seat, an overwhelming wave of emotion washed through me. I didn't know how long Richard had, but I was going to make sure we soaked up every moment that we could. And when he passed, I would be right by Johnny through it all.

Ring or no ring, Johnny was my forever. I would make sure he never doubted that again.

***

We spent two weeks in Australia with Richard. We stayed in Johnny's old room. I teased him mercilessly about the rugby posters on his wall next to the Paloma Faith ones. We went to all of his favorite places, ate amazing food, saw every part of Sydney that we could. It was a wonderful trip.

I had brought my laptop, so I worked as much as I could while still spending time with the ridiculous pair that was Richard and

Johnny. I went through old photo albums Richard had kept, getting to see Johnny through various stages of pubescence. He'd been a chubby baby, too skinny as a child, gangly as a preteen, and had really come into his looks around seventeen. He'd been in Australia full-time for a few years at that point, and I could see hints of the cocky, self-assured man that I had fallen in love with.

I had been surprised when Richard had first pulled out the albums, and it had shown on my face.

"I know I wasn't winning a world's best dad mug, but I did try my best when I had him," Richard had said softly.

I had given him a tight hug.

"You're human," I'd said. "Johnny is an amazing man, and some of that credit does belong to you."

In between adventures, Johnny and Richard went to the doctor, the estate lawyer, the funeral home. They got everything sorted. We could tell it was getting close to the end. Each excursion we made exhausted Richard more and more. I would catch him watching us, and whenever I did, I saw love and acceptance on his face. He had been holding on to make sure Johnny wouldn't be alone.

After two full weeks with us, I think he had seen everything he needed.

Johnny and I had grown so much closer, which I hadn't known was possible. Him sharing his childhood with me, exploring his old haunts, introducing me to his friends. All of it filled out my picture of the man I had already known that I loved and made that love richer and deeper. We were inseparable, constantly touching each other and sending smitten glances at all hours of the day.

Finally, Richard had pulled me aside one evening as Johnny was cleaning up dinner.

"Promise me you'll take care of him."

His eyes were heavy with grief, and my heart sank.

216

"I promise."

He was gone the next morning.

I'd had a feeling he was going to let go, so I had woken early and gone to check on him. Johnny didn't need to carry the burden of finding both of his parents after they'd passed. I wanted to bear that for him. When I gently woke him up and delivered the news, he'd collapsed into me.

I held him for a long time. We'd known this was coming. Had made all the plans. Richard had passed in his sleep after spending two beautiful weeks with his son. He was happy and at peace. It didn't make it any easier. I cried with him, sharing his grief. I called the paramedics so they could officially declare him, and things went from there.

The funeral was quick. Several dozen people from Richard's company attended, along with friends he'd accumulated over the years. He'd been loved, deeply, and by so many people. I knew it must have helped Johnny to see that.

Johnny would keep the house. We'd figure out what to do with it later. I helped him pack everything, sorting things for donation, trash, and keeping. We couldn't take anything with us back to the States, since Johnny didn't officially live there full-time, so it would stay in the house, waiting for us to return.

All in, we were in Australia three and a half weeks. Our relationship changed so much in that time. Deepened. Strengthened. Johnny leaned on me in a way he had never done with anyone else, and I found a part of myself I hadn't thought existed. The part that would unequivocally put my own needs and fears and wants aside to take care of another person.

As we sat on the plane heading back to Hartworth, Johnny slept and I couldn't stop myself from staring at him.

I loved this man, and I would for the rest of my life.

Chapter Twenty-Two

Raelynn

We slept for two full days after returning to Hartworth. I had insisted that we make a quick stop by my office to check on things before we had hidden ourselves away in my apartment. There was no way I was going to leave Johnny's arms after everything we'd been through the last few weeks, and he seemed to feel the same.

When we weren't sleeping, his was tracing every square inch of my body. There was no agenda behind it. I knew he was still grieving, and we hadn't been together physically since that night in the hotel room, but it felt like he was drawing solace from my skin and who was I to take that away from him?

As we lay tangled together in the afternoon, the light slanted across his face, and it took my breath away. Stupid love. I had never been the sappy type before falling for this man. Now, all I wanted was to lie in that bed and watch the sun trace his cheekbones and lips, before following it with my fingers until he woke up. But that was creepy, right? Before I could think about it much further, his beautiful eyes opened, and a sly grin spread across his face.

"Watching me sleep?" His voice was scratchy, and it went straight to my core.

"That depends, how much would that freak you out?"

"Don't worry about it, love," he said, yawning and stretching before he grabbed me and pulled me close. "If it's creepy then I should've been arrested weeks ago."

"Weeks?" I giggled, running my hand up his arm.

"Well, what else am I supposed to do when I wake up before you? You sleep like a bear in hibernation, and I get bored."

I rolled my eyes and suddenly found myself pinned beneath his hard body.

"Have I ever told you what you rolling those pretty eyes does to me?" His voice was low in my ear.

I bit my lip. He had, but I wanted to hear it again, so I shook my head. A wicked smile flashed on his face and then he was drawing his nose up the side of my throat, making me shiver.

"It makes me want to tie you up and spank your perfect ass until it's red," he growled.

Heat flared beneath my skin, and I couldn't help the whimper that escaped my throat.

"You'd like that, wouldn't you?"

"I really would," I breathed.

He pressed himself into me and I felt his arousal. My hips arched into him, chasing the friction, but he pulled away. Bastard. Taunting, teasing bastard.

"Johnny," I whined, my fingers threading into his hair and tugging to make a point.

He laughed and kissed beneath my ear.

"Pretty girls who roll their eyes don't get to make the rules, Rae."

He took his time tearing apart every cell in my body until I was a shaking mess, babbling incoherently, pleading and begging for him to take me. Johnny was calculated when he wanted to be, and he knew all of my weak spots. Whenever I would beg for more or begin to get impatient, he'd go even slower, until finally I had to just accept

219

that I had no control here. As soon as he felt me soften for him, I was rewarded with his lips on me.

"I guess I've groveled enough?" He smirked at me from between my legs.

My eyes widened as I realized that he'd been punishing me for my sass while simultaneously making up for our time apart. This man was something else.

He backed up and slid his pants down before settling back on top of me. My legs wrapped around him, trying to pull him closer. I needed him closer. He leaned in and took my lips gently. Lovingly.

"For the record, Rae," he whispered, "I will always grovel for you."

As he slid into me, I felt the stars shift into their homes. The planets aligned. The air between us stilled. I had never been so connected to someone. My eyes wanted to roll back into my head, but I couldn't tear them away from the man who possessed me.

When I shattered around him, I knew I'd look at that moment and realize it was the moment I'd finally released any leftover fears of falling in love. I was ready to completely commit to this man. I knew I'd already proposed, but this was deeper than that. I would give anything to stay with this man through every lifetime.

***

We were dozing in the early evening, after having gorged ourselves on tacos, when my phone buzzed on the bedside table.

Johnny groaned and threw an arm over his face dramatically.

I sighed and grabbed it, frowning at the number I didn't recognize.

"Hello?"

"Miss Rogers, this is Sargeant Hitchins, Hartworth PD."

220

My heart stopped beating as my mind went to worst case scenario. The only reason Hitchins would be calling would be if that scumbag Andrew had found Jenny. That was the only path my brain would take.

"Is Jenny okay?" I blurted out.

"She's fine, as far as we're aware, but this is related to her case." His voice was somber. "Would you mind coming into the station? Immediately?"

I glanced at Johnny, who had immediately sat up when he'd heard the panic in my voice.

"Yes, I'll be right there."

I hung up and stared at my blank phone screen.

"What's going on, Rae?"

"I'm not sure, but that was Hitchins with the police. He asked me to go downtown and meet him. Something to do with Jenny."

Johnny watched me for a moment before nodding once and leaping into action. He was dressed and tossing clothes at me before I could blink.

The officer at the front desk was kind, if a little brusque, as they directed us to take the elevator to the third-floor bullpen and ask for Sargeant Hitchins. It took very little time to find his desk. The Hartworth Police Department was small.

"Thank you so much for coming, Miss Rogers," Sargeant Hitchins extended a hand to me and then Johnny. "Mr. Harris, good to see you as well."

"No worries," Johnny said, though his voice betrayed that there might, in fact, be some worries. "Can you tell us why you called us down here?"

Hitchins sighed, a heavy weight descending on his shoulders.

"There's no easy way to say this, so I'll just tell you," he said. "Andrew Coulson broke into your office, and we believe he may have stolen some items."

The blood drained from my body, and I was suddenly overwhelmed with shivers. I cast my mind back to the stop we'd made on our way home, and my vision blackened at the edges as I realized what a stupid mistake I'd made.

"My laptop," I whispered, my voice barely registering.

"What?" Johnny's eyes were sharp as he watched me visibly start to panic.

"I left my laptop in the back office." My voice was stronger with fear. "I know I locked the door, but I didn't use the biometric lock."

"We can confirm that he took your laptop," Hitchins said, his eyes watching my every move. "We have him on the security camera from the coffee shop across the street."

Nausea rolled through me and my breathing shallowed. Johnny wrapped his arm around my shoulders, and I heard him trying to comfort me, but I couldn't stop the panic and guilt that were slamming into me.

"He knows where Jenny is." I knew it. Deep down in my soul, I knew it.

"Was your laptop encrypted?" Hitchins asked.

"Of course it was, but I just know that he found her."

"Do you have access to the address she's at?"

I nodded, knowing that Angels would have records of that. But how could I face Laura after fucking up so badly? I wanted to implode. Sink into myself until there was nothing left of the idiot who had left her laptop with the safety information of dozens of women on it unprotected.

"Angels Are Around is the organization." My brain was numb, shutting down to protect me from the death spiral I was inevitably

222

heading towards. "Dr. Laura Clark will be the contact there. She'll have everything you'll need to know."

Hitchins looked like he wanted to ask more questions, but Johnny was tugging my arm to force me to stand up.

"I need to get her home." His voice was low and urgent. "I'll find Laura's number and have her call you. What are the chances we're able to get the laptop back?"

Hitchins shook his head, his eyes dark. "We haven't been able to track Coulson down as of yet, and it's likely once he has the information he's looking for he'll ditch the laptop so that we won't be able to find him."

Johnny nodded once, his jaw clenching. I looked between the two men, trying to think of something to say that would help. But, in that moment, I wasn't sure I had ever helped anybody. Because it wasn't just Jenny that was compromised because of my mistake. It was every woman I had ever relocated.

The world was simultaneously moving too fast and in slow motion as Johnny navigated us home.

He sat me on the couch and wrapped my blanket around me, making sure I was settled before he pulled my phone from my purse and began making calls.

I heard his voice like it was coming through a tinny speaker a mile away. It was faded, and I couldn't make myself focus long enough to keep up with what he was saying, but I gathered that Laura was his first call. His second was to a twenty-four hour clean up company to go and board up the windows of my office. They'd be back in the morning to start cleaning. His third call was to my brother.

That one managed to break me out of the shock I was in. I whipped my head towards him and glared, but his back was to me.

"Look, mate, I get that you might not like me very much, but I could give two shits about that right now. Rae's in bad shape, and I'm just looking for a little advice on how to help her, and Addy didn't answer," Johnny's voice was sharp. His shoulders were bunched, and his right hand was clenching and unclenching, as if it was itching to punch something.

I didn't hear what Marcus said, but it made Johnny relax a bit. I had to admire how well Johnny knew me. Marcus was the best person after Addy to call who might know how to help me through this. He listened for another minute and then hung up without even a goodbye.

When he turned to me, his eyes were soft.

"Everything's gonna be okay," he said, joining me on the couch and gathering me in his arms.

As soon as I felt his warmth, the ice that had taken over my body melted, and I was sobbing into his shirt. He held me, not saying anything, just letting me feel. When I finally managed to catch my breath, I looked at him with wide, panicked eyes.

"I fucked up so bad, Johnny. Now so many people are in danger."

"Hey now, you did not fuck anything up." His voice was soft, but firm. "You had every right to believe that your business equipment would be safe in your place of business."

"No," I insisted. "I know the kind of people that some of my clients are running from. They're ruthless and will do anything to regain power over the women they believe are their property. I should have been more careful."

Johnny was quiet for a moment, his fingers drifting through my hair in the way he knew comforted me.

Finally, he said, "So, walk me through it. Why weren't you more careful?"

I blinked. I hadn't expected him to agree with me. Then I realized he wasn't necessarily agreeing with me, but trying to force my brain out of the guilt and shame spiral it was on and into reality.

"I needed to back up some data to my server in my back office after our time in Australia," I said slowly. "I went in and plugged my laptop in, but the server was being slow. I figured I'd be back in the next day, so I thought it'd be safe to leave it to load overnight. I've done it before. Then we spent the next two days in bed. I didn't use the biometric lock on the back office, just the handle lock. I deadbolted and alarmed the front, but there's always a risk of someone breaking in. The front of the shop is all glass. I should have taken my laptop home and backed up the data when I went back to work."

Johnny nodded and traced my cheek with his hand gently.

"May I offer some reasonable counterarguments?"

I nodded, though I wasn't sure it would help.

"You'd just come off a three-week grief trip with your emotionally burdensome fiancé," he started. I opened my mouth to counter him, but he stopped me. "I know you'll bear any burden for me, but it took up a lot of your bandwidth, I'm sure. Not to mention the jetlag, on both our parts. You wanted to make sure your clients were taken care of, so you wanted to get the data backed up. Neither of us expected to sleep as much as we did, but we needed it."

He stopped and gathered my face in his hands, forcing me to meet his gaze. He was serious as he searched my eyes, making sure I was fully present with him for what he said next.

"This was not your fault, Rae."

"But –"

"This was not your fault."

"Yes, it –"

"This. Was. Not. Your. Fault."

Of course it was my fault. How could he not see that? I was a screw-up. I did everything wrong. I was selfish and reckless.

Why can't you be more like your brother?

I froze as my mother's voice floated through my head. Where the hell had that come from?

The obvious answer was staring me in the face. I had been blamed for everything growing up, so it made sense that I would blame myself for this.

"Whose fault is it, then?" I whispered harshly.

Johnny was watching the battle raging inside of me with such love and patience in his eyes. How many of these similar demons had he fought and won over his life? Had he blamed himself for his mother's death? Because I would have said the same thing to him about that. It wasn't his fault. The blame lay with the person who made the choice.

"You know whose fault it is."

I took a breath. I never would have wanted Johnny to feel responsible for his mother. As horrible as it sounded, her death was her fault.

Sometimes there was no clear culprit. No one to place the blame on. Sometimes, things just happened.

And other times, a person made a choice.

"Andrew Coulson."

Johnny nodded, drawing me into his chest and resting his chin on my head.

"The man is psychotic," he said gently. "You love so deeply, Rae, that you would take everyone's burdens on yourself. But this wasn't on you. You were doing your job. A job, by the way, hardly anyone knows about and has never caused a break-in in the past, so why would you have expected this? You take every precaution. He chose to break into your office, and he got lucky, that's all."

I sniffled and nodded, believing him more second by second.

It didn't erase the guilt that was searing through me, but it helped lessen it.

"Okay," I finally sighed. "This wasn't my fault."

"Right."

"But I am going to fix it."

Johnny pulled back to look at me, puzzled.

"How exactly do you propose we do that?"

I took a deep breath, knowing he wasn't going to like this answer.

"We go after Andrew Coulson."

Chapter Twenty-Three
Johnny

I was in love with a crazy person.

I already knew that, but she seemed hell-bent on proving it in different ways as much as possible.

"What are you talking about, we go after him?" I asked, disbelief sharpening my tone.

She rose to the challenge in my voice, pushing out of my arms and onto her feet, pacing the living room.

"It won't be easy," she mused. "I have no idea how long it will take him to get into my laptop, but if he was determined enough to break into my office then he'll get in there one way or another. I have the files encrypted as well, but I'm no hacker so if he gets into the laptop, he'll likely be able to get into the files."

"What are you talking about?" I knew what she was talking about, but my brain was still struggling to catch up. Less than a minute ago, she'd been an absolute wreck in my arms, and now she was a wrecking ball out for destruction.

"Jenny went to live with her aunt in Maine," she continued as if I hadn't spoken. "Laura will let Hitchens know that and he'll contact the police there to be on the lookout, but since there's been no real credible threat to her safety there's not much the police can do to protect them."

She paused and looked at me as the plan started coming together in her mind. Her face was so easy to read, I could see every thought as it flashed through her brain at warp speed.

"We have to find him first," she said, resolution in her voice. "Get him to confess and record it."

"Recording another person without their consent is illegal."

She flashed me a look that wondered how I knew that off the top of my head, but didn't press it. Good. I wouldn't have wanted to tell her it was from binge-watching crappy true crime documentaries when I couldn't sleep.

"Then we coordinate with the police," she said, as if this was something she did every day. "They do wire taps and shit like that, right? They'll know how we can get his recorded confession and have it be admissible in court."

She was fired up, and it reminded me of the feral woman that I'd fallen in love with. She hadn't lost that side of her, exactly, but with me she was softer. I think, for the first time in her life, she knew she could be. We'd talked about it once and she'd told me that she had never felt safer than when she was with me. I had puffed up like a peacock at that. But, I'll admit, I had missed this side of her. The no fear, no rules matter, no holds barred vixen who played the game of life with brilliant strategy.

Instead of wallowing in what she felt was her mistake, she was taking action.

I loved her so damn much.

That's also why I would never let her do something this outrageously stupid alone.

"Fine," I acquiesced. "We'll visit Hitchins in the morning, then Laura, and then figure out how to make this crazy plan of yours work in a way where no one gets hurt."

"Someone might get hurt," she muttered darkly.

"Rae, I love you, but I'm not down for conjugal visits, so no murder."

She grumbled a bit but smiled up at me when I got up and took her in my arms.

"You're insane, you know that right?" I asked.

"Only as insane as you are."

I grinned before taking her lips with mine.

I was in love with a crazy person. But she was right that her crazy matched mine.

***

"I must say, this is highly unusual." Hitchins ran a hand down his perpetually exhausted face and then glowered at us from beneath those bushy brows.

"I understand that, sir," Raelynn said, her tone respectful but sharp. "However, I also understand that your hands are pretty much tied without actionable evidence of harm. I can provide that for you."

"You're talking about a cross-jurisdictional sting operation. Across state lines. That's a massive, not to mention expensive undertaking." He raised an eyebrow, and a glimmer of a smirk crossed his face.

"I'm aware," Rae's words were clipped. She hated being talked down to, and Hitchins was dangerously close.

I was leaning against the empty desk across from his in the bullpen, watching the interaction. Rae didn't need me to jump in and help, Lord knew, but as I watched Hitchins talking with her, I began to realize where he was going with this.

"If only there were some other course of action that would be a lot cleaner in court than a messy, undercover op that may or may not produce anything," Hitchins mused.

I could feel the barely controlled anger rolling from my fiancée and couldn't help but jump in to push her buttons some more.

"You mean, like the fact that he already has an outstanding warrant?" I asked.

Hitchins glanced at me, his eyes dancing, as Rae spun around. Her eyes were considerably less mirthful as she glared at me. Then they widened as she realized I was right.

She whirled back around to Hitchins.

"He has a warrant out for breaking into my office?"

Hitchins nodded, leaning back in his chair and resting his hands on his stomach. His gaze flicked between the two of us.

"Then why hasn't he been arrested yet?" Rae demanded.

"We haven't been able to find him." The light drained from the cop's face and anger simmered in him. "Can't arrest someone you can't find."

"So...if someone were to find him," Rae said slowly, "how would they go about reporting him to the police?"

Hitchins' mustache twitched in amusement. I wondered how often it was that he got a five-foot nothing firecracker sitting at his desk asking to play detective.

"Warrants are public, so anyone might have access to viewing them," he mused. "And they're public nationwide, just so that if a perp decides to make a run for it, we can make the public aware. It wouldn't be out of the realm of possibility for someone to recognize young Mr. Coulson from his warrant photo and call in a sighting to whatever police department they happened to be in the jurisdiction of at the time."

I watched Raelynn as she processed this information. Whenever she thought hard about something, she had this habit of chewing on her bottom lip and scrunching her eyebrows together, which was the face she was making now. My heart swelled a bit with that stupid, warm, love that I felt growing somehow stronger every day. Her face cleared and she smiled slyly at the Sargeant.

"I really hope you catch him, Sargeant Hitchins," she said, standing and offering him her hand.

He followed suit with an amused smile as they shook.

"Call me directly if you need anything, Miss Rogers."

Rae turned to me and her smile widened as she looped our arms together.

"You've got a new crazy idea, don't you?" I sighed as we walked out of the station.

"If it makes you feel any better, I think this one keeps me a bit safer than the sting operation would have."

"Oddly enough, it doesn't."

"Oh." She pursed her lips, thinking. "Well, not much I can do about that. You down for another adventure?"

I couldn't help the grin that split my cheeks.

Every single moment with this woman was an adventure. I would follow her anywhere, do anything she asked, and never regret a single, solitary second of it.

Instead of saying that, I shrugged noncommittally and said, "Yeah, I guess."

She giggled and bumped my shoulder, so I spun her around as we walked and caught her when she inevitably lost her balance.

She gazed up at me with those big brown eyes, so trusting and open.

I pulled her up, all the playfulness leaving me.

"Real talk for a second," I said, cupping her cheek with my hand. "I can't lose you, Rae. So whatever plan you've got cooking, I am always going to be a part of it. To have your reckless back, if nothing else."

She was quiet as she studied me. Then, she rose on her toes and pressed her lips softly to mine.

"I wouldn't want anyone else to be on my team."

She flashed me a grin before taking off down the sidewalk towards the car, leaving me staring after her.

I couldn't help the tightness that wrapped around my chest, making it hard to breathe for a moment. God, I hoped we got through all of this in one piece. I needed to marry this woman before she decided how we were going to end up dying together.

Chapter Twenty-Four

Raelynn

Addy tossed a pair of jeans to me from where she sat on my bed. She was sorting through the massive pile of laundry that had just come out of the dryer, helping me pack for yet another trip.

She was pouting, and for good reason. I had hardly seen her in what felt like months, between the time I'd been spending with Johnny, and then Australia. Now we were going to Maine.

"I don't like this, Lynnie," she grumbled, fishing out a sweater and passing it to me.

"It'll be totally safe, I promise."

"You're going to confront a psycho who broke into your office!"

"Not confront," I corrected. "Lightly stalk and then report to the police. If all goes to plan, he'll never even know it was me who reported him."

She was quiet for a moment, watching me closely.

"Why is this so important to you? You can always just get a new laptop."

My hands stopped folding, and I froze.

I guess now was as good a time as any for this conversation. Addy was in a good place, the best she'd been in a long time, and I knew she was worried for me and confused about how I had ended up in this situation at all.

I went and sat down with her, holding her gaze.

"I've been keeping something from you," I started. Her brow furrowed, but she didn't say anything, waiting for me to get out what I needed to.

"A little bit after your attack, I started working with a non-profit called Angels Are Around. Dr. Laura is one of the founders, and that's how I heard about it. They provide relocation and safety resources for victims of domestic abuse."

Addy blanched and her lips pressed together, but her eyes were steady as she held mine.

"This was why I didn't initially tell you about it," I said softly. "I didn't want to bring up anything that you didn't need to confront. But this was my way of making a difference after what happened. I felt – feel – so guilty about not stopping you from seeing Derek in the first place. Working with Angels gave me an opportunity to help other women where I couldn't help you."

"What exactly do you do?" Addy asked after a long pause.

"I help with relocation. Because of my job, I have a lot of helpful connections that can give these women a second chance away from their abusers."

Addy was quietly watching me, and then tears were tracing down her cheeks. I wrapped her in a hug immediately.

"This was why I didn't want to tell you. I didn't want you to have to go through what happened ever again, even just the memories."

"That's not why I'm crying, dummy," she sniffled, pulling back so that she could look at me. "I'm crying because I know how much guilt you've carried when you didn't need to. But if it led to this... Lynnie, what you're doing is amazing. I am so unbelievably proud of you."

Now I was crying, and I hated crying.

Addy laughed as I angrily wiped the tears off my face.

"You're an incredible human being," she insisted.

"Stop it, you evil woman," I grumbled as a fresh set of tears escaped.

"So, this guy that broke into your office, how is he connected to Angels Are Around?"

"He was the boyfriend of a girl that I helped relocate," I said quietly. "He had followed her to my office for one of our planning sessions, and there was an altercation between him, Johnny, and I."

"Johnny's involved in this?"

"Not really, he just happened to be there," I sighed. "It actually caused a huge rift between us. I didn't hear from him for days. That was when I disappeared."

Her glare spoke volumes. She hated when I disappeared for days at a time because it usually meant I was in a terrible mental health spiral.

"So, why did he break into your office?" she asked, choosing not to comment on those dark days.

"We got Jenny out, relocated her to Maine. I can only assume that once he'd realized she was truly gone, he snapped. He must have put together that her visiting a travel agent wasn't random, so he broke in and got lucky. I'd left my laptop there to upload data overnight when we got back from Australia."

"So, he could know where Jenny is and go after her." Addy's voice was soft as she put the rest of the story together.

"It's my fault she's in danger," I said. "I have to fix this."

Addy reached out and clasped our hands together, giving me comfort and strength from the simple touch.

"It's not your fault, but I know I can't be the only person that's told you that," she smirked. "And you feel like you have to fix it because you're a ridiculously caring human being."

"You must think I'm crazy."

"No."

I raised an eyebrow at her, and she smiled.

"I know you're crazy. But I've known that for years."

I grinned at her and the tension melted. I had missed my best friend.

"Johnny's going with you?"

I nodded, flopping back onto the pile of clothes.

"I'm so tired of traveling."

She settled next to me and giggled. "Now there's something I never thought I'd hear you say."

"Fly to Australia one day, you'll get it."

"At least you'll have company," she said.

I turned to face her, a smile on my face.

"The second I get back, we're doing an Addy and Rae Day, got it?"

"Introvert or extrovert style?"

"We'll see how I'm feeling," I said with a laugh. "But regardless, one full day. No men, no parents. Just you and me."

"Deal."

Addy sat up and poked me until I groaned and stood to continue packing. We easily fell into a rhythm that we'd cultivated over years of friendship, and I was suddenly hit with how extraordinarily lucky I was.

Regardless of whatever had happened in my life, I knew I had Addy. I owed her some serious best friend time when we got back.

***

Brendan and I had only met in person a few times, but every time it was like reuniting with a long-lost cousin.

We were sitting in a coffee shop that was known for its strong WiFi and stronger dark roast. I'd dragged Brendan here on his day off with the promise of as much coffee as he requested, because I needed him. Aside from knowing all the ins and outs of airline travel, he was also a wizard with a keyboard. I was hoping he'd be able to hack into my computer remotely and figure out exactly what Coulson knew. If we could get that information, we'd know what we were heading into when we got to Maine.

Brendan was on his second cup, his fingers flying over his laptop. Every so often, his eyes would dart up and appraise Johnny, who was sitting next to me with his arm slung across the back of my chair.

"So, Johnny," Brendan said, his gaze back on his screen. "Do you travel much?"

Johnny's laugh was warm and friendly.

"For work, often, and for pleasure too."

Brendan hummed and clacked away. "Seems like you're a good match for dear ole Raelynn here."

"That's just the tip of the iceberg, my friend," Johnny said happily, his hand moving to rest on my shoulder.

"How did you end up involved in this whole mess?" Brendan waved one hand at the computer while the other continued to type.

"Well, it started out wrong place wrong time," Johnny shrugged. "But then I fell in love with this madwoman and knew I'd end up following her wherever she went."

Brendan smiled at us briefly. "That's some forever type shit, right there."

"Well, she is my fiancée, so I'd hope so."

Brendan lifted an eyebrow as he glanced at my left hand.

238

"We haven't exactly had time to go ring shopping," I laughed. "It's been a whirlwind since I popped the question."

Brendan laughed and we joined, the mood lightening as we did. Then, his computer fan buzzed heavily before a wide smile flashed across his face.

"I've got remote access," he announced, his eyes narrowing as he flicked his fingers across his mousepad.

"You're amazing," I gushed, standing up to peek over his shoulder.

He was looking at several different things all at once, but none of them looked like my computer screen. I had no idea how he knew what he was looking at, but I trusted him. Especially when he blew out a long breath and looked at me with wide eyes.

"Bad news, babe. He found Jenny's address."

All the color drained from my face. I had already known that, deep down, but I had hoped I was wrong.

"Can you tell when?"

"He was able to access the file this morning."

"That's not too long ago," I breathed. "We could still beat him to Maine."

"Especially with my help," Brendan preened, his focus back on his computer as he typed at the speed of light. A minute later, he beamed at me. "There. Two tickets on the soonest flight to Maine. Rental car and hotel are booked, and you should have confirmations going to your email right about now."

My phone dinged a second and a half later, and so did Johnny's. I threw my arms around Brendan, giving him a sloppy kiss on the cheek.

Johnny looked impressed, if a little peeved at my display of affection, and offered Brendan a strong handshake.

"You're a good man, Bren," my fiancé said in that tone that made everyone feel like his closest friend in the world.

"Just take care of her, okay?" Brendan said, a brief moment of seriousness clouding his otherwise playful personality.

"I am perfectly capable of taking care of myself," I huffed.

"You are a magnet for trouble, and you know it." Brendan rolled his eyes.

I suddenly understood why it bugged Johnny so much when I did it.

"You guys need to leave now if you want to make your flight."

We said a quick goodbye and left money for another coffee before taking off to the car.

***

I had always known I would never end up with someone who didn't like flying, but as we sat on yet another plane, I found myself marveling at the fact that I'd somehow ended up with the only man in the world who seemed to enjoy time on an airplane. Johnny was stretched out, sipping his ginger ale and snacking on the tiniest bag of pretzels known to man, completely at ease.

I was over the travel at this point. I just wanted a solid few months at home in Hartworth to start really building a life with Johnny.

I stared out the window into the dark sky.

I had never been able to imagine a future with anybody before. I held myself to a probably ridiculously high standard, and I had expected anybody I'd dated to meet that standard and then some. Nobody had, and after awhile it had been easier to have no expectations for men rather than high ones.

240

Then Johnny came along. With his stupid charisma and face and genuine interest in me. He'd chipped away at my walls until there was a crack, and then had come back with a full-on wrecking ball.

In an instant, the future I'd seen of me traveling the world alone, bringing back gifts for nieces and nephews, never settling down, was replaced with quiet mornings wrapped in Johnny's arms and late-night Chinese food in front of the TV. The trips to Fiji and Sao Paolo weren't by myself, but with this infuriatingly handsome Australian by my side. Making jokes, trying new food, dancing in the streets. Visiting my family wouldn't seem like such a chore when I had Johnny there to remind me that I wasn't invisible. That I was loved for exactly who I was.

I had been fine with a future of facing the world alone. But now that I had Johnny, I couldn't wait to see what the future would hold.

We just had to get through this next adventure. I knew I had promised everybody I would be safe, but I couldn't shake the nagging feeling that at some point on this trip things would get hairy. I wasn't one to run away from a fight, so I could only hope that this didn't scare Johnny off for good. Our future was going to be different than I'd ever let myself dream, and I wanted to make sure we both got to experience it. Together.

Chapter Twenty -Five
Johnny

Small-town Maine was stunning, plain and simple. I'd made a mental note to bring Rae back here every year for as long as she'd let me, because everything about this place was picture perfect.

This trip so far had been smooth sailing, I'm sure in large part to whatever meddling Brendan had done to make this all happen so quickly. Our rental car was nondescript but comfortable, and the hotel was small and cozy. Surprisingly romantic.

Rae hadn't wanted to wait to get to work, but I convinced her that we needed at least a few hours of sleep before diving into full stakeout mode.

I had so many doubts about this plan. How in the world were we supposed to identify this Andrew guy without exposing ourselves to him? He could be wearing a disguise. We had no idea what kind of car he was driving. Jenny lived in a nice neighborhood that was all houses, so how were we supposed to stakeout her place without seeming suspicious and getting the cops called on us instead?

I didn't want to derail Raelynn's momentum, but I couldn't help but think we hadn't fully fleshed this out.

We were sitting in a café across the street from the entrance to Jenny's neighborhood. It was a beautiful day, the first hints of fall in the air. Leaves were just beginning to turn, and the sun was pleasant but not overbearing. We were sitting on the patio, both of us barely picking at our food as we took turns surveilling the turn across the street.

We'd been there for an hour and hadn't seen anything suspicious.

I sighed and Rae shot a glare at me.

"What's the problem now?" she asked, stabbing an olive in her salad and popping it into her mouth.

"It's not a problem," I said, trying to soothe her nerves. "I'm just wondering if we need a better plan?"

Her glare lessened as her cheeks turned a delicious shade of pink.

"This does seem pretty useless, doesn't it?" she sighed. "I don't know what else to do. I don't want to tell Jenny unless we absolutely have to. I'm worried she'll hate me."

I watched her silently for a moment. She watched me back, the way she always had. It was one of the first things that had amazed me about this woman. She was fearless when it came to confrontation. Because even something as simple as holding someone's gaze was a confrontation. She faced the world, throwing herself into things head-on with reckless abandon. Yet, she sat in front of me confessing a fear that I knew sat so deeply within her there was nothing I could do to wipe it away, no matter how hard I tried.

She cared immensely what other people thought of her. It broke my heart to think that she was worried that the woman she had helped escape could ever hate her. Especially when she'd gone to such incredible lengths to keep her safe.

I reached out and took her hand. "If Jenny knows what might be coming, she'll be ten times safer than if she didn't."

Rae dropped her eyes and chewed her lip. "I know you're right," she finally sighed. "And we do need a better plan."

"So, Plan Master, what do you suggest we do?" I grinned, squeezing her hand to let her know I was right there with her.

"Let's go find Jenny, I guess," she said.

As I pulled out cash to pay for our meals, Raelynn stood and walked towards the exit, throwing me a smile over her shoulder when I hurried to catch up. Since we were stalkerishly close to Jenny's house, it took all of three minutes in the car to get there.

Rae was fidgety as we stood on the porch waiting for someone to answer the door. I had never seen her like this before. I'd seen her loving, tender, angry, possessive, obsessed, sleepy, silly...but never nervous. I tried to keep my own nerves in check. She needed me to be calm and sensible right now.

Finally, after what seemed like a decade, a svelte older woman answered the door. She was stunning. Her gray hair was almost down to her waist, her eyes were sharp, and she was dressed how I'd always imagined refined mob wives would.

Her gaze narrowed as she took us in, and the door closed a bit tighter between us.

"Can I help you?"

"We're here to see Jenny," Rae's voice was small.

With a look like she'd eaten a sour lemon and seen a ghost all at once, she went to slam the door on us. Rae was quicker than me, and stuck her hand out to stop her.

"Please, we're not here to hurt her," she started. "I'm Raelynn. We spoke on the phone a few weeks ago?"

Some of the tension eased, but not all.

"I remember you," the woman snipped. "What are you doing here?"

"Is Jenny here?" Rae insisted.

"She's at work."

"Can you please tell us where she works. We're worried Andrew might have found her."

I glanced at Rae, amazed at how well she was keeping herself together.

Jenny's aunt paled. She closed the door quickly and before either of us could process what had just happened, she was launching herself outside. She'd grabbed her purse and a coat and was tearing down the stairs.

When she realized we weren't following her, she whipped around and glared. "Well, come on then."

Jenny didn't work too far away, it turned out. A cute little boutique on the main strip that sold clothes and trinkets. Since it was a Wednesday, it was pretty quiet.

Jenny saw us approaching through the window. Initially, her eyes lit up when she saw her aunt, and then confusion flashed when she saw Raelynn and me.

Because I was watching Jenny, I saw the moment she lost all the color in her face. Because I was watching Jenny, I saw that she wasn't looking at our group when it happened.

I followed her gaze but wasn't fast enough.

Time seemed to slow down as I watched Andrew Coulson appear from the shadows of an awning next to the boutique.

He reached out, anger etched in every line of his face, and then his hands were wrapping around Raelynn's arm, dragging her to him.

Every rational thought left my brain. I froze.

Rae's startled scream shattered any ounce of self-control I had once possessed.

"Call nine-one-one," I snarled in the general direction of Jenny's aunt.

The inferno thundering through my blood heightened my senses. My eyes narrowed in on every spot that his touch was fouling Raelynn's skin as she thrashed in his arms.

I saw red. I lunged towards them, hoping I might catch him by surprise.

My girl was putting up a good fight, but she wasn't a fighter. The ghost of her mean right hook echoed on my cheek, but she couldn't get any purchase on him.

Coulson looked pissed and scared, and finally had enough as he hooked his arm around Rae's throat, trapping her against him.

That stopped me in my tracks.

One wrong move and he could end her life.

Rae stilled, her chest heaving. Her gaze found mine and she was panicking.

I took a step closer to them and Coulson growled.

"Stay back, or I'll kill her."

"Why?" I couldn't stop the question from falling out.

"She ruined my life!"

I was quiet for a moment. I didn't want to spook him and risk Rae, but I had no idea how to talk this maniac down.

My heart was pounding, and I could barely hear over the adrenaline coursing through me. Fear bit the back of my tongue. I prayed to any god that would listen to send the cops soon.

Taking another step, I lifted my hands in front of me, trying to show him I wasn't a threat.

I was, but I didn't want him to think so.

"How did Raelynn ruin your life?" I asked, somehow managing to keep my voice level through the anger and terror that were ripping me apart.

"She sent Jenny away." Fury flashed across his face, and he squeezed the arm around Rae's neck tighter.

246

She gasped and clawed at his arm, but he apparently didn't feel it.

I was taking slow, measured steps towards him, trying to back him against the wall. For each step I took, he stepped backwards, dragging my fiancée with him.

"I know you're not gonna want to hear this man, but Jenny left on her own," I said.

He snarled, but didn't say anything, his eyes trained on me.

Fuck.

Where were the goddamned police?

A bell jingled and Coulson's head whipped around.

Before I could react, Raelynn flung her weight to the side, stepping as she did. It opened a gap big enough for her hand to fly back into his groin, and when he doubled over from the shock and pain, her elbow slammed up and into his nose.

She broke away from him and bolted towards me.

"Get him," she shrieked as she flew past.

That was all the permission I needed to unleash the hellfire that had been singeing my blood since she was grabbed.

I launched myself forward, tackling him sloppily. I was slightly bigger than him, but he was solid muscle. He landed a quick punch to my gut, nearly knocking me off.

I grabbed his flailing arms and tried to pin them, but he brought his knee up and caught me in the side.

The immediate pain that flared through my chest told me he'd probably cracked a rib.

I didn't let go.

I knew that if I let go, there were at least three people that were in immediate danger, not to mention anyone else that might have stopped when the shouting began.

He managed to break a wrist free from my grip, and I lost track of it as I wrangled his other arm and his swinging feet.

"Johnny, look out!"

Rae's voice broke through the red haze that had been blinding me, and then the searing pain cleared it all away.

Son of a bitch had a knife.

Which was currently sticking out of my thigh.

A visceral growl rippled through my chest as I glared down at the man beneath me.

His eyes were shining like he'd won, and I relished watching the light leave them when he realized all he'd done was piss me off.

Fueled by rage and protectiveness, and, I'll admit, more than a bit of spite, I grabbed his shoulders, lifted his bulky frame, and slammed him back onto the concrete.

His head smacked with a satisfying crack, and he stopped fighting back.

I pinned his arms down and stayed hovering over him, just in case he woke up, as I barked instructions to Raelynn.

"I need something to tie him up with. And something for this fucking knife in my leg."

Less than thirty seconds later, Jenny and her aunt were handing me duct tape.

I flipped his unconscious body over and bound him. He wasn't dead. I'd checked.

Secretly, I was pissed. Scum like him didn't deserve to breathe. Logically, I was glad I hadn't just killed a man.

Once his ankles and wrists were secured, I rolled off him and dragged myself over to lean against the wall of the boutique.

People were gathering around now, and in the distance I heard sirens. About fucking time. Though, in reality, the whole fight had lasted maybe four minutes.

I didn't care about any of that, though, because the second I was off Coulson, Raelynn had run to me. She collapsed next to me and her hands fluttered over my body, as if she didn't know how to help.

Jenny shoved some towels into her hand.

I took a deep breath and caught Rae's panicked eyes.

"Hey, pretty girl," I smiled at her.

Her eyes narrowed. God, I loved her.

"Don't you pretty girl me, asshole," she huffed. "You could have been killed!"

"Well, now we're even," I quipped back.

My leg throbbed and a low groan escaped.

"What can I do?" Her voice was laced with concern.

"Don't pull the knife out," I said quickly. That was always everyone's first thought, and it was a bad one. The flash of guilt on Raelynn's face told me that's exactly what she'd been about to do. "Take the towels and place them around the wound and put a bit of pressure on to try and keep the bleeding to a minimum."

"I hate blood," Raelynn groaned. But she didn't hesitate in getting her hands covered in mine as she pressed on my leg.

Finally, three cop cars and an ambulance skidded to a stop in the street.

Raelynn and I shared a long look before we were bombarded with paramedics and police. I knew that Rae saw everything I couldn't say in that look. How grateful I was for her. How scared I'd been. How happy I was that she was safe.

She had to stay to explain everything to the police, but I caught her eyes one more time as I was loaded into an ambulance.

So much love and passion filled her gaze. Then, she shot me a saucy wink right as the doors closed, leaving me laughing and wondering how soon I could make that insane woman my wife.

Chapter Twenty-Six

Raelynn

I hated hospitals. Surprising nobody, I'm sure. Aside from prison, they were the biggest embodiment of restricted freedoms. Only, in hospitals, more often than not the people hadn't done anything to deserve being there. Sometimes, their genetics turned against them. Sometimes, it was the cruel randomness of fate. And sometimes, it was an angry guy with a knife.

My stomach was in knots as I was led to Johnny's room. He'd been processed and admitted fairly quickly – it was a small hospital, and they didn't get many knife wound emergencies, apparently. The nurses hadn't been able to really tell me anything about his condition, but since I was his fiancée they'd sent me up to visit. I was hoping to see the doctor while I was there as well.

When I rounded the corner and saw his name written in scrawling, loopy handwriting on a whiteboard, my feet stopped.

My nerves flared, and I spun my ring around my finger. I was scared to see him, I realized. Even though he had seemed fine enough when they'd taken him away, he'd still been stabbed.

Because of me.

I took a deep breath and blew it out angrily. Now was not the time to wallow in self-blame again. That's how we'd ended up in this whole mess to begin with.

Nothing was going to calm me more than just being with him, so I steeled myself and opened the door softly.

Johnny was sitting up, his head resting on the pillows and his eyes staring blankly at the ceiling. As soon as he heard the door, his head snapped up and he met my gaze. A slow, simmering smile laced with relief spread across his stupidly handsome face.

"You're okay," he breathed.

I laughed in disbelief. This man.

"I should be the one saying that," I said as I went to stand next to the bed on his uninjured side.

He was having none of the distance that I'd been trying to keep and reached out to grab my hips and plant me on the bed with him. His arms wrapped around me, bringing me into his chest.

I laid there for a moment, relishing the steady sound of his heart beating through the thin gown. My eyes closed and a few tears fell. I hadn't even realized I needed cry, but the relief at being in his arms washed all of the stress and worry away.

I sat up and traced my fingers down his cheek, studying him. He had good color, and his eyes were bright. That shit-eating grin was still there. He was okay.

"So, what's the verdict?" I asked, glancing at his leg.

"Numbnuts missed anything important," Johnny sighed. He flexed his foot and winced. "Still hurts like hell, but I'll make a full recovery. Doc said it probably wouldn't even scar too badly."

"Shame," I murmured, leaning in and ghosting my lips against his. "I'm a big fan of scars."

He laughed softly. "Of course you are."

Then, he claimed my mouth in a searing kiss. Every pent-up emotion both of us had was poured into our connection. I could feel his fear, his anger, his satisfaction that we were okay. I knew that he could feel my guilt, and my relief that this whole thing was finally over.

We were interrupted by a polite cough from the doorway. The doctor had come in to check the wound. He reiterated how lucky Johnny had been and commended him for his bravery.

"The police are downstairs getting checked in," the doctor told us. "They'll be up in a moment. Just thought I'd give you a heads up."

"Thank you, Doctor," I beamed. He blushed a little and coughed again before giving a single nod and fleeing the room.

"Your power over the opposite sex is something that should be studied in labs," Johnny laughed, reaching down to lace our fingers together.

His eyebrows pinched together, and he held up our hands, turning them to inspect mine. A smile of utter bliss flashed across his face when he saw my ring.

I rolled my eyes but couldn't help but smile back.

"Don't go thinking that this means you don't owe me a ring," I warned.

"Well, what's this one doing on my fiancée's finger then?"

"I wanted the admitting nurse to believe me when I told her we were engaged," I explained. "People are more likely to do that when they see the ring as confirmation. Since *someone* hasn't bothered to get me a proper engagement ring yet, I had to improvise."

Johnny laughed heartily and brought my hand to his lips to kiss my fingers.

"I will get you a ring, Rae. I promise."

"Good. I deserve one."

252

"You deserve everything," he said seriously. "And I will give you everything that I possibly can."

"Another promise?" I tried to keep my eyes from watering, but the man was so damn sincere.

"A vow," he winked.

The police interrupted us this time. They talked to Johnny for a long time, getting every detail of his version of events. He held my hand the entire time, his finger lightly tracing back and forth across my ring. I couldn't keep my smile from leaking through, even though I was trying to be serious as we explained how all of this ended up happening.

I made sure to give them Sargeant Hitchins' card so that they could call him if they needed any more details, and they left us with a thank you and a goodnight.

After they'd gone, I curled up next to Johnny and rested my head on his chest, enjoying the evenness of his breaths. His grip was tight on me.

"I couldn't see anything when he grabbed you," he finally whispered, breaking the stillness.

"All I could see was you," I admitted.

"What do you mean?"

"I fought him as hard as I could, but the fucker was strong."

"Right? Stupid twit," Johnny laughed softly. I loved that we could have moments of levity, even when we were baring our souls to each other. He knew exactly what I needed to be comfortable sharing my feelings, and I was hit again with a profound gratefulness that I had him in my life.

"When he got his arm around my throat, I saw your face. I couldn't stop staring at you. I thought that if I was going to die, then I wanted you to be the last thing I saw. Then I couldn't stop picturing the life we could have had. I went full worst-case scenario," I admitted.

He rubbed soft circles on my back.

"I almost gave up, but I knew that you'd kill me if I did that. The second I felt his head turn, I saw my chance."

"How did you know how to do that, by the way?" Johnny asked. "I didn't think you had any kind of self-defense training?"

"After Addy's attack she got really into mixed martial arts and self-defense," I said. "She insisted I go to the first few classes with her. I think mostly because at that point she was terrified to go anywhere alone, but she also wanted me to know a bit for myself. Turns out she was right. I'll never hear the end of it from her about it, I'm sure."

We fell into silence as we both sat with our own thoughts.

"I don't know what I would do if I lost you," I said into the silence.

"I'm not going anywhere, love."

"Promise?"

He kissed the top of my head and whispered, "Promise."

***

They kept Johnny for one more day in the hospital in Maine to watch for infection. I stayed with him the entire time. We watched crappy hospital TV, gorged on soft serve ice cream from the cafeteria, and talked about everything and nothing. We laughed and we cried a bit and we made plans to visit everywhere we had ever heard of. Anything to pass the time.

Jenny and Annie came to visit. Jenny was beyond grateful that we'd been there, and she was insistent that she didn't blame me in the slightest, even after I'd told her how Andrew had found her in the first place. She had given me the tightest hug and her phone number. She wanted to keep in touch with me. I had turned into such a big softy since falling in love, that I had spent a good twenty minutes crying after they'd left.

When they finally discharged Johnny, he was itching to get home. That was another lengthy journey away, but we took our time, savoring every second we spent together.

When Johnny was in the bathroom after we'd landed, I had called Addy to let her know we were back. We'd texted a bit over the last few days, so she knew what happened. I needed her help getting my apartment ready.

I was going to ask Johnny to move in with me permanently. He was there all the time anyway, and this way he could have a permanent address to list in the States. It was time to jump all in. My heart already had, so it was about time the rest of me caught up. I had to laugh when I thought of how out of order we'd done this whole relationship.

Johnny was quiet on the car ride home. The meds the doctor had given him made him sleepy, and he was dozing with his hand in mine as I drove. It felt right. For all the times Johnny had driven me home when I couldn't, reversing the roles was a natural fit. Which was what I think I had always needed. Someone who could take care of me whether I wanted them too or not, but who also would let me take care of them.

I glanced over at the sleeping man in my passenger seat and was hit with a wave of disbelief. My life had changed so much in the last few months. Johnny had been a tornado of fire, burning down all my defenses and helping me to rebuild from the ashes. He'd shown me that he wasn't afraid to love me through all of my insecurities and doubts and reckless abandon. He'd woven me into the fabric of his life so easily, even though I'd resisted at every possible turn, because he had fallen in love with a broken girl after a one-night stand.

I had never experienced a love like this, and I was happy that I had finally gotten over myself and let it happen. I was more sure of the love between Johnny and I than I had been about anything in my life. Ever.

I sighed when I realized what that meant.

It was time to tell my family.

Chapter Twenty-Seven

Raelynn

I was obsessively straightening the tablecloth for probably the thirteenth time when Johnny's hands landed on mine. He caged my body between his arms, his chest pressed into my back as he nuzzled into my neck. I took a deep breath as I felt his warmth seep into my skin, and it helped calm my nerves.

We were hosting a dinner party for my family. Well, hosting was a bit of a stretch, considering we were at Marcus' house because our apartment was too small. And Marcus' wife had cooked all the food. We had brought wine, though. Very expensive wine that I knew my mother loved. And we'd helped set up everything and decorate.

Tonight, I was introducing Johnny to the rest of my family. Formally. He and Marcus had already met and been talking, apparently, when the occasion called for it. I hadn't known they'd had each other's contact information but leave it to Johnny to have everything he would need to take care of me.

I wasn't nervous about my siblings, necessarily. They would all calm down after a few jokes at my expense. I was more concerned about my mother. Dad would give probably a few grunts and glares, and then eventually warm up, but I was worried Mom would be at her worst.

I knew this was her biggest dream for me. She'd been praying and wishing and making ritual sacrifices to any god she could in the hopes that I would one day find someone and settle down. But now that I had, I was worried she was going to hate Johnny.

Our relationship hadn't exactly been conventional, and Johnny could be...a lot. Of course, he could charm the pants off the Pope, but he was also fiercely protective of me, and not the biggest fan of my mother. He knew how I'd been treated in my life, and he refused to pardon that behavior.

I leaned into his touch and smiled.

"You're going to be nice, right?" I asked.

"When have I ever not been nice?" He pretended to be offended.

"When it comes to someone not treating me the way you think I deserve, you can be downright nasty."

"I'll second that," Marcus said as he came in from the kitchen carrying a veggie tray.

"I have never been nasty to you a second of my life, mate," Johnny laughed.

"I think I distinctly remember being hung up on, on various occasions."

"Yeah, well that's just rude. Not nasty," Johnny said with a wave of his hand. "Parents love me."

"I'm sure they will," I said, turning to face him and smoothing my hands down his chest. "As long as you're nice."

He leaned down and nipped at my ear. "What do I get if I'm nice today?" he purred, sending goosebumps breaking out on my arms.

"Not in my dining room, please," Marcus groaned.

I grinned, loving that I had new and fun ways to torture my eldest brother.

Marcus was saved from my sass by the doorbell ringing and my siblings and their partners descending on us. There were hugs and greetings, but everyone was focused solely on Johnny.

He took it like a champ, answering questions and introducing himself over and over. Throughout the whole thing, he kept me pinned to his side, as if to tell my family that they weren't allowed to ignore me just because he was there.

If I hadn't always been a melty pile of goo around the man before that, it would have rendered me permanently liquid.

Johnny knew how small and invisible I felt in my family, so he refused to let that be the case today. And my siblings seemed to catch on. Soon, they were sending questions to both of us instead of just Johnny. They wanted to know everything about our relationship. It felt nice. Normal. For once, I didn't feel like the outcast in my own family.

The chatter in the room quieted when Mom and Dad arrived.

Dad eyed Johnny for a moment before sticking his hand out. I saw the approval in his eyes when he was greeted with a firm handshake and a "Nice to finally meet you, sir," from Johnny. Then he came and gave me a big hug that nearly made me cry.

Mom was next. She gave me a hug, but her focus was the tall man who was still standing resolutely at my side.

"Mom, this is Johnny," I said. "You met once before, but I wanted to officially introduce him."

"An official introduction is a big deal for our Raelynn," my mom said, her words warm but her tone sharp. "You must be something special."

"It's your daughter that's special, ma'am," Johnny said, wrapping his arm around my shoulders and squeezing me. "I love her with all of my heart, and I'm glad to finally get to meet her family."

Mom's face flushed, and that's when I knew Johnny had her. He was damn charming, and my mother was a sucker for compliments about her children. I knew that she saw us as reflections of her, and I had always been the part of the mirror that showed her the worst parts.

"How long have you two been together? Since that night at the restaurant?" Dad asked.

Surprise flitted through me. I hadn't been sure he would have remembered that. He wasn't the best at paying attention.

"Oh, no sir," Johnny laughed. "It took me a good few weeks after that to convince Rae to give me a chance."

"Whatever could have compelled you to spend so much effort on chasing Raelynn?" Mom asked.

I winced. There it was.

I felt Johnny stiffen beside me, and his arm pulled me impossibly closer.

I glanced at his face, sure I'd see anger there, but instead it was plastered with a jovial smile.

"I've loved Raelynn since the first moment I laid eyes on her," he said softly. When he looked at me, adoration poured from him and I couldn't look away. "I would have chased her to the ends of the earth and back just for a brief second of her attention. I cannot believe that I got so lucky that she would choose to be with me forever."

The room stilled as he spoke and went dead silent on that last word. I had been so caught up in making lovey googly eyes at him that it didn't register in my brain until a few seconds later.

"Johnny," I whispered, a warning.

We hadn't said anything about us being engaged, even to Marcus. I'd wanted to get the initial introductions out of the way first.

260

"I think it's time, Rae," he said, a smug, rakish grin on his stupid face.

He dropped to one knee and took my hand in his. I tried not to flutter over him when I saw him wince a bit. He was still recovering from being stabbed on my behalf, though he was significantly better. Apparently better enough to kneel in front of me and my entire family, looking like a goddamn rom-com movie star.

"I keep my promises," Johnny said, pulling a wooden, spiky thing from his pocket and handing it to me. "I told you I'd steal a star for you."

I rolled my eyes and quickly untangled the puzzle, looking at him with a triumphant smirk.

"Pity it's not an actual star," I said, keeping my tone dry.

"You sure about that, love?"

I unlocked the final piece of the puzzle and as it slid apart a dazzling sparkle caught my eye. My breath caught in my throat as I pulled out a beautiful ring.

I looked at Johnny, who was grinning that grin that had melted my heart from the jump. He took the ring from me and held it up. An offering.

"Will you?"

I couldn't help the tears that spilled over my cheeks as I gazed at this perfect man before me. He'd promised me a ring, now I had it. He'd promised me that he'd win my family over, he'd done it. He'd promised me forever. I just had to accept it.

"Yes, of course I will, you idiot," I sniffled.

His grin was blinding, and suddenly I was lifted from the ground and wrapped in his arms as he kissed me senseless.

Then we were surrounded. My brothers were clapping Johnny on the back, and all the women were gushing over my ring.

I glanced at my (now official) fiancé, and he winked.

I was the center of attention. My family was seeing me. It was everything I had wanted my entire life.

All of that meant almost nothing to me, though. Because I had Johnny.

Johnny had always seen me. I had always been the center of his attention. He had always insisted that I was special, and beautiful, and worth loving.

It had taken me a long time to accept it, but he hadn't given up. I knew that with him by my side, we would live an amazing, adventurous, and reckless life together.

Epilogue

Raelynn

"I will murder you in your sleep, you little Australian weasel."

Addy's threat wasn't unwarranted. Johnny had just hit her with a triple Draw Four stack when Addy had been about to win the round of Uno we were playing. Those two were merciless when it came to game strategy. They were cutthroat and ruthless. I hadn't thought I would ever meet someone as competitive as Addy, but there Johnny was giving her a run for her money.

Game nights had become a regular thing at our apartment since Johnny had moved in. He and Addy were close, which I loved. Johnny had been very deliberate about cultivating a friendship with Addy outside of just "my fiancée's best friend". It was nice, having two people in my life who knew me, all of me, and chose to love me every day. Even when they were going at each other over a silly card game.

"You wouldn't make it past Rae, and you know it," Johnny teased, sitting back in his chair with a self-satisfied smirk.

"I know I basically helped save her life, but she would never win in a good old-fashioned fist fight," Addy laughed.

"Are you ever going to stop saying you saved my life?" I rolled my eyes, earning me a heated look from Johnny. Apparently, it was a turn-on, even when it wasn't directed at him. I had made a mental note of that and used it as a weapon more often than not. I loved teasing that man.

"Nope," Addy and Johnny said simultaneously.

They glanced at each other and laughed.

The games continued, and we all got more tipsy as the night went on. We played a few more rounds of Uno, a couple of board games, and finished with an exceptionally terrible round of charades. Finally, Addy was calling herself a cab and Johnny was walking her to it, telling her to text us when she got home.

I began cleaning up the random cards and game pieces that were scattered on the table. I put the empty wine glasses in the sink and wiped down the counter. I heard Johnny come back inside and lock up. When I turned around, he was leaning in the doorway watching me with hooded eyes.

"Addy told me to tell you to sleep with one eye open," he said, watching me closely as I took several slow steps towards him.

"I'll take that under advisement," I laughed.

I stood in front of him and slid my hands up his chest, marveling at the way he shivered beneath my touch. I slowly wrapped my arms around him and pulled him down for a kiss.

In an instant, he shifted the energy from slow and sweet to hungry and frenzied. He backed me up against the counter, hoisting my legs up to settle around his waist as his tongue dove into my mouth, claiming every part of me. I didn't think I would ever get tired of the way this man knew exactly how to wring every bit of pleasure out of my body and still leave me wanting more.

I giggled when he nipped down my neck, leaving little red marks that I prayed wouldn't be there in the morning.

264

"I can't wait to devour you tonight," he murmured into my skin.

His fingers traced down my arms, slowly pulling the straps of my shirt with them. His lips followed the exposed skin, sending tingles throughout my body as I arched into his touch.

"Don't wait then, fiancé," I said, tangling my fingers in the hair at the nape of his neck and pulling him back to me for another fierce kiss.

He groaned and grabbed me, racing to the bedroom where he threw me onto the bed with a grin.

"When will I get to call you my wife?"

He began unbuttoning his shirt, making sure my eyes were on him the entire time.

I shuffled up the bed and watched.

A lifetime ago, it seemed, our story had started in this very bed. I never would have imagined this man calling me wife, at that point. Now, I couldn't wait for the day.

"You were the one who promised my mother an actual wedding," I reminded him, my gaze following his hands as he slipped his pants off.

"I was caught up in the moment," he sighed, climbing on top of me and peppering my chest with kisses.

"Yes, but you always keep your promises," I said breathlessly.

His eyes found mine and they were so full of love that I wanted to combust right there.

"I do, indeed."

I didn't need a huge wedding or some piece of paper to know that I was going to spend forever with this man. As he made good on his promise to devour me, I realized that a part of me had known that from that first night. Another part of me realized that as long as I had Johnny, I would always feel like the luckiest person in the entire world.

The End

The Bell Tower Series

Want to spend more time in Hartworth and fall even more in love? The Bell Tower Series are all standalone novels that can be read in any order and without having to have read the others. Although, we see several side characters recurring throughout the series, and get to see the evolution of everyone's favorite brewery, The Bell Tower!

Slowly & Surely, which follows Greg and Justine in a slow burn, second chance, enemies to friends to enemies to lovers romance. This book dives into how opposites really do attract!

Truly & Deeply, the story that started it all (not chronologically), follows Addy and Bell. As Addy works through the aftermath of her attack, she struggles to accept that someone could love her. Bell is persistent, patient, and pining for Addy. This book explores what it means to move forward, and the overwhelming acceptance that love brings.

Afterword

Now that we've come to the end of the third Bell Tower book, I have so many emotions. I want to laugh and cry and sleep for a thousand days. I never thought I would write romance novels. Growing up, the stories that I wrote were all coming-of-age, more YA type novels (which makes sense because that's what I was reading at the time). Then, I discovered adult contemporary romance as a genre and fell headfirst into it.

Lo and behold, it inspired me to start seriously writing again, and led to three stories that resonate with different aspects of who I am as a person. I can only hope that young women see themselves in Addy, Justine, and Raelynn as well, and that for anyone who wonders (like I do) whether they're worthy or capable of romantic love…we are.

Speaking to Utterly & Madly specifically, I actually had the hardest time writing this book! I was blocked on so many occasions, and for the life of me couldn't figure out why. I didn't like the story or the characters that I started with. After many revisions and changes, however, I love this book in the series the most. Of the three, it holds a spot very near and dear to my heart, and I can only hope that my readers love Raelynn and Johnny as much as I do.

I know that throughout this series the characters dealt a lot with the concept and topic of domestic violence. In the United States, more than one in three women and more than one in four men have experienced intimate partner violence in their lifetimes, resulting in nearly 1,300 deaths and two million injuries each year in the US. Intimate partner violence in the US accounts for fifteen percent of all violent crime. Intimate partner violence is one of the leading causes of pregnant women in the United States. I say all of this so that you know that it's not something I write about lightly, but rather something that is incredibly important to talk about.

If you, or someone you know is experiencing domestic violence, there are resources available to help.

National Domestic Violence Hotline
    Call 800-799-7233
    Text BEGIN to 88788
    Visit https://www.thehotline.org
    .

Acknowledgments

As I come to the end of the third and final book in The Bell Tower Series, I can't help but think about how amazingly lucky I am to have so many incredible supporters in my life. I've wanted to be an author since I was a kid. When people asked me what I wanted to be when I grew up, the first thing I can remember saying was "author". Now, I've written three whole books!

To everybody that has bought every different version of these books that I've put out as I've learned and grown as an indie author, I cannot thank you enough.

To my family – my mom and dad, my sister, my aunts and cousins, my grandma – knowing that I have your love and support is so grounding and uplifting all at once.

To my friends who have been my fan club from the beginning, I love you all so much.

To everyone who has read my books who doesn't know me personally, I hope that these stories find a special place in your heart and your bookshelves. I love each and every one of you more than you will ever know.

About the Author

Rebecca has been a storyteller as long as she can remember. She loves bringing people's stories to life and giving voice to things that might not get talked about that often. With a background in acting, she loves diving into new worlds and new characters. She believes in fairy tale endings and happily ever afters. She is happily chasing adventure wherever the wind takes her with her cat, Evie.